ALINA MARTYN

From My Past

Contents

Trigger Warnings

This story, while a complete work of fiction, does contain some graphic scenes of domestic abuse, physical abuse, verbal abuse, and talks of sexual abuse. There are mentions of human trafficking as well, however, just the rescue scene is included in this book.
Read at your own risk and understanding.
Your mental health matters.

Dedication

To those who like Mafia Romances because they love the bad boy with a heart of gold, the dangerous hit man that will burn the world for his girl, the stoic loner who is cold and demanding, but becomes a big ole teddy bear around her.

Yeah, I like them for those reasons too.

Chapter One

Talia

Before...
I sat down on a gross, dirty, weathered lawn chair and wondered how the hell I got here.

There was throwback music playing, the kind that everyone knew every lyric to even if they didn't want to. Bodies were grinding and thrusting against each other as the music blared and everyone was in their own world. Arguments were happening on either side of me, along with heated declarations of love - or lust - and cocky guys, bragging about this, that or the other thing.

I was able to break apart from the drinking games and find a moment for myself away from others while I tried to recharge my own social batteries. I'm already pretty tipsy, but the thing about me is that I might put on a tough, confident exterior, but inside I'm a ball of anxiety and want. I *want* to make everyone happy while still proving myself and succeeding as much as I can. I *want* to prove myself and show everyone that I'm a badass to my core.

That's why I'm here. At a party that I wasn't even formally invited to. I overheard some of the other guys in my class talking about how big of a 'rager' it was going to be. I figured that they wouldn't notice one more girl sneaking in and after I heard them say the Sigma Epsilon Delta house, I decided to go. Worse case scenario; they tell me no at the door and I leave.

Best case; I get some free booze and maybe I could make a friend that wasn't nose deep into a textbook at all times like myself and everyone else I know.

"Talia! What are you doing here?" A singsong, twinkling voice called from behind me. I turned to see the beautiful Morgan Hull approaching. She was one of the most popular girls at Pryde with her lithe, toned body from hours of yoga and running, her sleek waves of fiery red hair and her pale blue eyes. I watched the guys around her as she walked up to me, out of five guys she passed four of them watched her walk, watching her short mini skirt barely keep her ass covered.

"Morgan!" I said with an equally high, fake on my end, voice. She came up and hugged me in an overly friendly way for someone who wasn't a fan of me. It was a struggle to not roll my eyes at her. This girl had been the bane of my existence in high school and when I found out she had decided to come to Pryde, I was pissed.

"What are you doing here? I never thought I'd see you out of the computer lab. Thank god, Talia Jones finally decided to grace us with her presence." She laughed at her sarcasm and took a swig from her own red cup. I didn't even try to hide an eyeroll.

"I just needed a night out. Midterms were hard."

"Oh, you poor thing. My midterms were a cake walk. Are you sure you're studying enough?" Morgan had this unique way of speaking that was almost always an insult, but her tone was genuine. It was a talent. One that pisses me off to no end. Thank fuck I hadn't seen her almost the entire time I've been here at Pryde. My buildings for classes were nowhere near hers were apparently.

"I'm doing just fine. Thanks." I needed another drink quickly, but she had cornered me before I could find another one. If this bitch was going to continue to be such a cunt, I am going to need much more and much harder liquor.

"Oh, honey," Said so condescendingly that it made me want to slap her. Morgan patted my dark hair. "You didn't answer my question. What are you doing here?"

I moved out of her reach before she could touch me again. When I spoke, there was ice in my tone to match my poorly concealed anger. "I heard there was a party and people could come, so I came. What are *you* doing here?"

"I have a standing invitation here." Morgan said confidently with a flick of her hair over her shoulder.

"Good for you."

"You know, if you looked a bit more like you did in high school you could get the guys to pay a bit more attention to you."

That was one of the reasons I changed my looks so much and finally let myself look on the outside like I felt on the inside. I look out into the sea of people to see just how different I am. Not only in looks, but personality as well. I don't know what I was thinking trying to drink and party with these sorority girls who all look like copies of each other.

Once upon a time, I looked like them too. Long blonde hair, perfect "natural" makeup, flawless skin. Mine was natural and unintentional, borderline unwanted. Theirs is perfectly crafted and painted on.

Looking down at the empty red solo cup in my hand, I notice my chipped black nail polish and the carefully designed snake tattoo that spiraled up around my forearm, weaving in between flowers. I love this tattoo; I love the design, I love the meaning. It was the first one I ever got and it made me feel like I stood out. I was no longer the perfect barbie doll that everyone saw of me and made their assumptions. A snake in the roses. Maybe I should have put on the 'perfect' girl costume, just for the night to make it easier on myself. A short skirt that showed my long legs and a tight tank top that left nothing to the imagination. The hardest part would have been taking my eyebrow, nose and tongue piercings out and covering all the tattoos. But why would I have done that? Changed myself to fit into the masses after I had worked so hard to do the opposite.

"I'm good."

"Your loss. But having one of these guys take you and fuck you senseless, ah, it's so worth it." Morgan shivered and said with a moan, like she was putting on a show for the guys standing around us to get their attention. Which of course, it worked when two tall guys wearing polos and khakis turned and looked her up and down.

"Again, I'm good."

"What, are you a virgin?" Morgan said, slightly too loud for my liking.

"Fuck off, Morgan." I turned on the heel of my biker boots and left her standing in the mass of admirers.

"Oh honey, don't be scared! It's okay if you're a virgin, you don't need to be embarrassed."

Instead of looking back and going off on her, I just kept walking. She wasn't worth it and I did not want to be around the group of people that had heard her. Why did I come here? I could have gotten drunk by myself and passed out happily in my own bed.

I knew why. The longing to let myself go, let all the worries and fears lose for just a few hours was much too tempting to pass up. I've been working on my midterm project in computer graphics. I'm only a sophomore at Pryde University in Boston, but I'm working to get my degree in engineering. That's right, engineering.

I want to build engines and create technology to advance travel. I hope that one day, I'll be designing the next airplane, taking passengers safely, faster and more luxuriously from one destination to another than is possible now. I may not look like it, but I'm a complete grease monkey. I love pulling apart things and figuring out what makes them tick. Watches, computers, engines, you name it.

Pushing my way past all the other partiers, I made my way inside the fraternity house to find better alcohol. With the fucking hell that just happened, I needed to get drunk faster.

The inside of the frat house was exactly what you would expect it to look like; full of empty alcohol bottles, pizza boxes, and packed to the brim with people. The dark wood paneling of the interior of the house made everything darker, more masculine somehow but with all these people crowding around, the house seemed smaller and darker than it was. Not that I would know what it looked like without all the people. I've never been here, and I assume that I'll never be here again. I squeezed through the bodies and found the kitchen which seemed to be the only room with the overhead lights on.

"Finally." I whispered as I picked up a handle of vodka that was opened on the kitchen counter and poured a generous helping in my cup.

"Kieron! My man, glad you could make it!" I heard behind me. The man in question had bright red natural hair, like Prince Harry but brighter. Actually, he kind of looked like Prince Harry if I thought about it. Orangey red hair with a strong jaw and a smile that lit up his whole face. But what really drew my attention was the man who had walked in.

He was gorgeous and something inside me reached out for him. I needed to talk to him, needed to know him, if only for a moment.

The nerves in my stomach were quieted by the straight vodka, but I took another sip as I studied the mystery man. He was giant, in every sense of the word. His height, his muscles, his hands. When he reached up his hand to clasp the first one's hand in greeting, I was able to see just how muscled his arms were as his biceps flexed. The material of his navy t-shirt held on for dear life.

Dear lord, this man was delicious in a way that I haven't seen before.

"Trenton, hey." His voice. Fuck, his voice. I felt my heart clench and I felt a fire light inside.

"I'm so glad you could make it. There is a keg outside, liquor on the counter and mixers in the fridge." Trenton told him and was pointing out all the places he was telling Kieron about.

"Thanks man."

I wonder where he worked or what he did that kept him so busy. I don't think I've seen him around campus, I definitely would have remembered seeing him, even if it was just a second.

I took another drink of my vodka and let the heat bring me back into myself. It went down smoothly, but then the last dregs caught in my throat and made me start to cough. I tried to keep the coughs quiet, not drawing attention to myself. But I couldn't catch a full breath and the coughs became louder and more aggressive no matter how much I tried to dampen them.

How fucking embarrassing.

"Are you okay?" I could feel two large hands on me; one hit my back hard and one spanned my hip to keep me upright. "Get her some water!" He barked.

After a few more hard hits on my back, I felt like I could breathe again.

"Thank you," I put my hand on my throat letting the air soothe my now sore throat. And all too soon the warm hands that had saved me, left my body. I wanted to move back into them, but I didn't know where they went. I reached for the bottle of water that had appeared in front of me and gulped it down.

"Hey, slowly now. Don't want you to choke again." A shiver ran through my body at his words.

"I'm okay. Thank you." I was able to finally turn and see who my savior was and I locked eyes with the short haired, tattooed God in a navy shirt with the darkest eyes I've ever seen. I'm totally sure that my mouth was open and eyes were glazed over.

"You already said that. I'm Kieron." The most beautiful smile I've ever seen graced his face. His eyes had a sparkle to them as he stuck his hand out for me to shake.

"Talia." I said as I took his hand and shook it tightly. I felt a shift inside as our hands came together. It felt...right.

"Nice to meet you."

"Nice to meet you too." I smiled at him and let go of his hand. Reluctantly.

"Can I get you another drink? You seem to have choked on your last one." Kieron moved closer to the counter and grabbed another two cups.

"That would be great."

"Kieron! Man, what are you doing?" Trenton walked over to him before stopping suddenly and made a show of looking me up and down. "And where have you been all my life?" He rested his body against the counter and crossed both his arms and his ankles.

"Hiding, obviously." I smirked at him and mimicked his posture.

"Ouch. Burn," Trenton covered his chest with his hand and acted as if he had been shot. "Okay, I like you."

"I'm so honored."

"I'm Trenton." He leaned over and offered his hand for me to take, which I did with a smile. His personality and charisma were infectious.

"Talia."

"Nice to meet you, doll." He took my hand and brought it close to him and kissed my knuckles. I couldn't help but giggle and looked over to Kieron who was barely containing his own smile at his friends' antics.

"Finally, someone who can match your nonsense level, Trent."

"I know! And if you're not careful enough I will take her from you. Damn you for seeing her first, but I will honor the dibs." Trenton said with a gallant wave of his hands and pushed me ever so slightly in Kieron's direction before running off into the sea of drunk people. My heart started to race slightly at what Trenton implied.

It was hard to tell in the dimmed light of the kitchen if he was as affected by me as I was by him, but I could swear I see a hint of a blush cross his cheeks. There is no way this fine specimen of a man saw me and called dibs in the way that I'm thinking. No way.

"You called dibs?" I hoped with everything inside me that I sounded confident and like I was teasing him but even I could hear the breathlessness in my voice. The wonder and awe.

He chuckled and moved his hand up to nervously scratch at the back of his neck while putting his other hand in his pocket.

"I did. I hope you're not offended, but some of these guys are not all winners. I didn't want to take the chance that one of them gets to you first. It didn't help matters that you're a knockout and I had my eye on you since the moment I walked in here."

"Really?" Call it whatever you want, but I had a hard time ever accepting that a man wanted something more from me than just my temporary company. I had a hard time accepting that they might actually want *me* instead of always trying to trick me in some way.

"Yes, really." Kieron said quickly.

"That's very sweet of you."

"'And you're a knockout too, Kieron.'" He teased in a high-pitched girls voice and it made me laugh.

"I'm so sorry for my ignorance. And you're a knockout too, Kieron." I said, bringing my hand to my stomach to help the ache from laughing.

"I love your laugh. I could listen to it all night." He said with such conviction that I had no choice but to agree.

"Thank you," I whispered as he stepped in closer to my personal space. I could feel his heat and smell his scent, he was so close. I stopped breathing. He smelled crisp and clean with a hint of something spicy but warm, like cinnamon.

"So, what about that drink?" He whispered and I swear I could lose myself in his voice. It was deep and strong, with a hint of some kind of accent that I couldn't place yet. One quick glance up to his face showed me that he knew what he was doing.

"Let's do it." I answered with as much sass and confidence as I could muster. "I'll take a vodka and orange juice, please."

"You got it." His dark eyes held mine for a moment longer before he vanished from my personal space and I felt like I could breathe again. I sat back to the side and watched him work, pouring and mixing, making sure it was chilled before handing me a cup and taking the other for himself.

He didn't say anything as he took my hand, his large, tanned one engulfing mine, and pulled me back in the direction of the backyard. I prayed to every god I knew that Morgan wouldn't show and embarrass me or try to seduce this god-like man away from me. Even though, it was highly possible that that exact scenario would happen in my nightmares, I dreaded that it had even the possibility to be a reality for me.

I stumbled slightly over nothing and caught myself before it could really become embarrassing, but Kieron's grip on my hand tightened slightly, like he was making sure that nothing would happen to me if I did fall.

"I'm good."

"Be careful."

"Yes sir." I said in a mocking tone, but when Kieron looked back at me, I saw a fire in his eyes of pure lust. So, he liked being called that, he liked being in control.

Noted.

"Over here." He pulled me closer and led me to a spot in the back that was fairly isolated. Or at least others hadn't found it quite yet. It was by the wooden fence, but partially hidden by a shrub. Someone had gone through the trouble of making it a little sitting area with a self-made looking bench and some cushions and a small string of lights along the fence.

"Wow, I didn't see this earlier."

"It's a hidden secret. I made this back when I was a brother." He explained and gestured for me to sit first.

It wasn't the most comfortable thing in the world, but in that moment, I didn't care.

"When you were a brother, does that mean you aren't anymore? Isn't there some 'once a brother, always a brother' bullshit line like that?" I said bluntly, taking a drink. It was perfectly made, strong but the juice covered the bitterness of the vodka.

"Like you said, it's a bullshit line." He took a long drink himself and looked anywhere but at me.

"Fuck, I'm sorry. Sometimes when I'm drinking, I can be too…"

"Direct?"

"I was going to say bitchy, but I like direct better so let's go with that." I laughed and took another drink. I didn't need to say that most people found me bitchy no matter what. But that was the price I paid for trying to break free of people's assumptions of me.

"I like it. There are too many fake people in the world. Say what you mean and mean what you say, is what I live by. That's actually one small reason of the many reasons I'm not a brother anymore." Kieron leaned back against the fence, kicking his feet out to relax. He looked so…rocker with a soft side. His tight black, ripped jeans showcased his strong thighs that looked like they were products of hours at the gym. He had on a black belt that met his Heather navy shirt that was fitted so nicely to his torso. I tried my best not to stare so obviously at him, but I wanted to really see him.

"I agree. People like to hide behind niceties and small talk, but no one really wants to show their true colors. God, I hate the politics game in almost everything. If you don't like me, stay away or talk shit to my face, don't pretend to be my friend and then talk shit behind my back. I always kept to myself after being burned one to many times. It's one of the reasons

I sucked so hard at high school. I didn't want to play the popularity game." The entire time I was talking, venting, ranting, Kieron just stared at me like I was a breath of fresh air.

"That's so interesting to me. Most girls I meet, or rather met, at these kinds of parties were all about climbing the social ladder."

"Well, I'm not most girls."

"I can tell." He said with a smirk, his eyes shining in the twinkle lights. He looked at me as if he wanted to devour me whole. Take me someplace private and have his way with me. But underneath that overly cocky, well perfected-womanizer look, was genuine interest and awe. Something I wasn't used to from men who looked like him.

"You mean that in a good way, I hope." I said, looking down into my cup instead of making myself look into his eyes.

"The best." He whispered. I could feel him shift his body so that he was closer to me in a shy position; there wasn't any space between our legs as he shifted closer to me, our thighs touching. Kieron turned into me and smiled; a sweet, shy smile and we both took another drink.

The guys that I have met in the past, they act genuine with me. They act like they care and want to get to know me, but there is always a feeling. I *know* they aren't being genuine but are only acting. They are fully aware that they are going to hit it and quit it, but they play as if they truly want to make a connection. I usually just ignore that when I actually want to hook up, but with Kieron…this connection feels solid. He doesn't seem to be trying to simply get into bed with me. At least not yet.

"So where do you work? I heard you tell that guy that you were at work before this?" I take a drink, effectively breaking the bubble of tension and chemistry that had been building.

"Yeah, I graduated last year but Trent still keeps in touch. He's a junior and he was my surrogate little brother while I was here. I work for my dad." He said. His fingers were tracing the rim of his cup absentmindedly.

"Does he own his own business?" I ask.

"You could say that. I'm working my way through the lower-level positions right now. Grunt work and some really nasty situations." His head hangs a bit as he looks anywhere but me "Some things I'm really not proud of."

"That sounds ominous." I chuckle weakly.

He looks at me with surprise, like he let his guard down unintentionally.

"It's frustrating. Because I want to be able to work for my father, but I don't want to run the business like he did. People see me and they know my family and assume that I have to be a certain way, the way they are, but maybe that's not what I want. Why should I do something just to make others happy and myself miserable?"

The look on his face was like everything I had ever felt and still feel. The judgement from others, the assumption, the pressure to be a certain way. I get how he felt completely. Assumptions, that was the problem. With men, with women, with everyone. They took one look at you and judged you making it a million times harder to get anything done.

I took another drink from my cup and let the liquid burn down my throat. He moved away from me just slightly, leaning over so his forearms rested on his knees and one of his hands went to rub at the back of his head. He looked so…defeated almost. As if he was fighting a losing battle but giving it his all.

"I get it." I whispered and put my hand on his shoulder.

"Do you?"

"I do, believe it or not. I'm in school to be an engineer, I want to build engines and design planes. I used to look like all those sorority girls out there and every single time I would go to apply to join clubs in high school or even interview at jobs to beef up my college application, I got laughed at. They would actually laugh at me." I lean back and cross my arms over my chest, closing in on myself even more. "Or made crude comments. Or condescending ones. They didn't think I looked like I knew what I was doing so I proved them wrong. I made myself into the roughed up, confident and serious version of myself to make sure that no one ever fucked with me and my dreams again. I let myself be *who* and *how* I wanted. I'm not usually in an outfit like this." I said gesturing to my outfit and face that I had spent an hour painstakingly painting on.

"What do you normally dress like?" Kieron said after a moment of appreciating my legs wrapped in fishnets and my crop top that exposed a sliver of skin at my waist.

"I'm usually in baggy clothes and no makeup. I work on engines as much as I can so most of my clothing has grease stains on it. I get looks from the girly-girls of pity and just completely ignored from the guys. But, I'm a better engineer and designer than all those motherfuckers I'm in classes with and that's what matters."

"I'm sure you are. Don't you feel like you shouldn't have changed anything?" Kieron asked me, no judgement coming from him. Just genuine curiosity.

"Like Elle Woods in Legally Blonde?" I rolled my eyes and took another drink. My cup was getting low and I was feeling it. Kieron laughed loudly, his joy being infectious and making me smile back.

"That wasn't exactly what I was thinking, but sure."

"The difference is that Elle was trying to hide her true self in order to do something for someone else. I am letting my true self free in order to accomplish my dream. I've never been the cheerleader or sorority type. I'm just me."

"Something tells me there is nothing 'just' about you." He said and nudged his shoulder with mine.

* * *

Our lips never left each other's, even as Kieron pushed me back through my apartment with the lights off. My hands ran all over, touching any part of him I could.

"If you don't stop that, we'll never make it to the bedroom." He groaned as my fingers raked down his back under his shirt. I loved feeling the broad expanse of his back, all muscled and firm under my fingers.

"Is that a bad thing?" I whispered breathlessly as his mouth devoured mine again. He kissed me like my kiss would be the only thing to save him; deep, passionate and wholly consuming.

I wanted more.

"Come here." He leaned down and grabbed my thighs, hoisting me up into the air and I wrapped my legs around his waist so he could carry me.

Fuck, I loved it.

We'd both subtly stopped drinking after our conversation in the backyard, I wanted to be sober for this because something inside told me this would only, could only be a one-night thing, even if I didn't want it to be. And I want to remember it.

His lips move from my mouth to my neck as he pressed wet, hot, open-mouth kisses against my skin; under my ear, down the column of my neck, the junction of my neck and shoulder. When he got to the base of my neck, he kissed me once and then bit down. I moaned loudly and hoarsely; I loved it.

"You like that, huh?" He whispered, giving a peck to the spot he had bitten.

"I do."

"Good." He said with a smile and continued walking to my bedroom. The whole time he was walking, I kissed him in any place I could reach. His cheeks, his lips, his chin, his neck, his ears, anywhere. But like I said before, he was a big man and I could only stretch so far. I ran my fingers through his short hair, marveling at how silky and soft they were while still looking so styled.

His steps quickened; his boots made his steps sound even louder in the hardwood hallway before he found the door he needed and kicked it open. I was still latched to his front, hugging and rubbing all over him. I felt like I was on fire and only Kieron would be able to stop it.

"Fuck, baby." He whispered hoarsely, and I felt his fingers bite into me harder.

"Please."

Kieron threw me on the bed and I bounced slightly. He turned and flipped the light switch, and once the lights were on, I was immediately grateful.

The expression on his face would be feeding my fantasies forever.

His eyes were even darker as he drank me in. I could feel his gaze on me like he was touching me as he just stared at me before him. His mouth was slightly open and I watched his tongue peek out and wet his lower lip slowly before he bit down. So hot.

"So… are you just going to stand there?" I said as I sat up on my elbows to get a better look at him.

Kieron broke out into a smile that showed just how much he liked my sass. And how much I was going to pay for it. He reached up behind his head and pulled the collar of his shirt up and over his head to reveal his broad chest.

And, oh my god.

He was delicious. I knew he would be ripped and he was. I couldn't help but stare. My thighs clenched together in anticipation as I tried to find some friction to ease the ache between them.

"Trust me, baby, I'm going to do so much more than just 'stand here'. But first, I want to watch you shatter on my fingers. I will see every single inch of you as I make you cum and then I'll take you. How does that sound?" He said, his accent thickening as he leaned over me on the bed, our chests touching.

His scent wrapped around me. It was so much stronger without his shirt on and with how close he was. My eyes closed slightly as I arched into him to get more contact.

"I need you to say the words, Talia."

"Yes. Please. I want that." I breathed out. I wanted him to touch me, *now*, and he wasn't.

"Are you sure?" He taunted, one of his hands went down to my legs and slowly grazed in between my legs from ankle all the way up to my inner thigh. I was still completely clothed and desperately wanted to be naked so I could feel him. Every single part of him.

His fingers blazed between the space of the fishnets. It was slow, this torture. One moment his calloused, hot fingers were touching my bare skin, the next I was covered by the net.

"Please." I had no issues begging for what I wanted. Especially when I saw just how much it turned him on. "Please… Sir." I tried.

Kieron's eyes rolled back into his head and he let out a soft groan.

"I like that."

"I noticed." I smirked.

"Minx." He said with a smile of his own as his hands finally went under my skirt and pulled my fishnets down. More like ripped them off me, throwing them to the side. Oh well, one less layer.

I reached for the hem of my crop top and pulled it quickly off to expose my lacy bralette that was just see-through enough to entice.

"Oh god. Shit, Talia." He whispered and quickly took my nipple into his mouth through the lace. A jolt went through my body and I felt my thong get wet. I didn't know I liked that rough texture on my nipples until he did it and now, I can't think of anything sexier.

"Again." I whispered, my eyes were closed and I arched into his mouth.

"Again, what?" He said and bit down on my breast, just enough to bring a sting.

"Sir. Again, sir."

"That's my good girl." He smiled and sucked again, harder. My heartbeat quickened and I felt butterflies at being called that. *Good girl.* His good girl.

Kieron moved down my body, leaving wet, open kisses and down my torso until he was met with the waistband of my skirt which he quickly made work of pulling the button open and sliding it down my hips.

All that was between us was a thin lacy thong and his jeans.

I need that to change quickly, so I reached down in between our bodies and unbuttoned his jeans and pushed them down using my feet.

"Needy, aren't you?"

I could feel his hard cock press against me while he was teasing me but I wanted to see it now. Based on the feeling, Kieron was well-endowed, proportional to his height for sure. My mouth started to water.

"You want me?" He asked, standing back from me and the bed. He put his hands on his hips, and my eyes went to his cock. It was straining against the grey material of his briefs.

"Yes, I want you. I want you, sir. Please." I whimpered, reaching out for him.

"Such a good girl for asking what you want. Lay back." He ordered, a low demanding tone in his voice.

It was embarrassing how quickly I complied and laid flat on my back. I was so turned on that every movement, every slight sound made me flinch in anticipation for when Kieron would actually touch me where I wanted.

Just when I was about to stand up and rip his briefs off myself, I felt his hands on both legs just above my thighs and he slowly pushed them apart. He leaned down and pressed small, sweet kisses up my thighs until he got to my mound that was still covered in lace.

Both hands moved slowly up my thighs, up my hips and he dipped both index fingers under the lace. I thought he would move my thong down my legs, but instead, he ripped and within seconds the lace was pulled from my body.

"Oh god…" I moaned.

"My name's Kieron, baby. I just want to make sure you're moaning the right name while I make you come harder than you ever have." He said with bravado and then his face disappeared from my sight.

The moment that his tongue touched my slit, I cried out. He had been teasing me so much that I knew it wouldn't take much to push me over the edge. And between his tongue flicking and twirling around my clit and his hands holding me so tightly like he couldn't get enough, I was losing my self-control. My moans and cries were getting louder and louder, and I was starting to get embarrassed but I knew I couldn't *stop* making noises when he was playing my body perfectly.

Kieron sucked hard between my clit and my lower lips, that made cover my mouth with both hands to keep from screaming. I didn't want him to stop. He had to do that again and again.

And then he was gone from between my legs and he was hovering over me. His lips were shiny as he ripped my hands from my mouth. When he spoke, he sounded angry.

"Don't you dare keep those sounds from me, I fucking earned them. Let me have them." He growled.

"But what about the neighbors?" I gasped.

"Do you think I care about them? I want to hear every single sound that I cause come from your beautiful lips. Be as loud as you want, I love it." His mouth went to my ear as he whispered the last words and nipped my ear lobe and he rolled his body against mine. I could feel everything; his weight, his hardness and his need. He rolled against me again, his cock rubbing my clit in the best way. My eyes rolled back at the friction and I groaned loudly.

"That's a good girl." With those words, he slid two fingers deep inside me. My eyes rolled back into my head as I felt him twist and cross his fingers inside, before crooking them both in a hook motion and massaging my front walls while his thumb was circling my clit.

"Do you like that?" Kieron said, biting down on the same spot at the base of my neck.

I nodded, and he moved his fingers faster.

"Tell me how much you like it, baby."

"I like it, oh god, I like it so much. Don't stop. Don't stop." I mumble. He tsks but adds another finger. It's a stretch, my body resisting the addition, but soon the pinch of the stretch turns into undeniable pleasure. I grab his biceps quickly, needing something to hold on to. I was so turned on from his teasing and our tension before that I already felt my orgasm coming on quickly. It surprised me because it usually took me a long time to get to this level, but with Kieron it was mere minutes.

"You're doing so good, taking my fingers to nicely. I've got to stretch you out a bit in order to take my cock." He murmured, his praise sending me closer to the edge. I could hear my wetness with every press of his fingers.

"Do you hear that? Hear what I'm doing to you? So fucking sexy." Kieron whispered in my ear.

And I snapped.

My orgasm hit like a freight train and I screamed. My back arched, my eyes screwed shut, and I screamed his name.

I crashed back down on the mattress, breathing heavily. The bed shifted and I opened my eyes to see Kieron bringing his fingers to his mouth and making a show of licking them clean.

I sat up, pushing him up with me, and pulled his briefs down before he could say no to cause me more beautiful torture. And what a sight he is to see. He was thick and veiny, so hard that it looked painful and I couldn't wait to feel him inside me.

"Lay down." I push him lightly down on the pillows and it was his turn to moan and have his eyes roll. I didn't wait for him to respond before I knelt down and pulled the tip of his cock into my mouth. The sound that came from him was strangled and dirty, it caused me to burn hotter.

I wasn't a fan of the taste of men usually, but Kieron was different. I could suck his cock all day and thank him for it. I brought my hand to the lower part of his shaft and moved my hand in tandem with my mouth to reach all of him. I bobbed up and down quickly for a few minutes before one of his hands fisted in my hair and tried to lightly pull me off him. But I wasn't done yet and ignored him.

"Talia, baby, wait, wait," He groaned, pushing my shoulders slightly. "If you keep doing that, this will be over much faster than I want it to."

I released him with a pop and offered him a smile as I licked my lips slowly. Kieron's eyes tracked every movement as he stroked his cock *very* lightly. So lightly that I don't even know if he knew he was doing it.

"Fuck, come here." He grabbed my hand and yanked my body closer to him. Our chests met, my breasts smashing against his pecs. My core pressed against his, creating more heat. I wrapped my legs around his waist as I sat on his lap and wrapped my arms around his shoulders.

"Are you sure?" He whispered "Because once I feel you completely, I will not be able to stop. And you won't want me to."

A shiver ran down my spine and I grinded my core against his, resulting in a groan from both of us.

"Does that answer your question?" I said breathlessly, grinding against him again.

"It does." He said confidently and flipped me over so smoothly, tossing me around like I weighed nothing. Before I could formulate a comeback, he entered me in one thrust. I was so wet there was no resistance at all.

"Yes," he hissed as he pushed in as far as he could and I screamed. He hit my cervix and pulled out slowly, my walls clenching around him.

"Fuck Talia, you're so tight."

"Please, please, fuck me." I groaned. Don't get me wrong, I like the slow and steady but what I wanted, *needed,* was it hard and rough.

"As you wish." He cupped the back of my thigh and pushed it up to my chest so he could thrust in deeper. I cried out at the deeper angle, thinking there was absolutely no way he could fill me anymore. "That's it."

Kieron pulled out and started to thrust in a slow rhythm, enough to make my toes start to curl and have me claw at his back.

"Faster, Kieron, faster." I moaned, thrusting up against him to try to force him to move quicker. When he caught on to what I was doing, he released my leg and held me down with both hands on my hips.

"Patience."

"I don't have any."

"Clearly." He smiled and I swear, my heart fluttered at his expression. He was looking at me with such lightness but with such sincerity. "But let me take care of you."

He kissed me with such bruising force that my mind went blank.

I let go then, let myself just feel and relax. Let myself fully be in the moment.

"That's it, sweet girl. Just let me take care of you." He muttered in my ear and I closed my eyes but wrapped my arms tightly around his neck.

His movements did speed up, only slightly enough to drive me crazy and kissing me with such fervor. It was like he was trying to map and memorize every part of my body with his mouth, his hands and his cock. And I was doing the same. I couldn't get enough.

The sounds coming from my mouth when he wasn't plundering my mouth with his tongue were loud, breathy and desperate. I should have been embarrassed but he said he liked it, and he seemed to be spurred on by every sound, so I didn't censor it.

The more noise I made, the more talkative he got. Kieron would whisper sweet nothings about how perfect I was, how beautiful I was. But then, it turned absolutely filthy and his movements sped up.

"Fuck me, you're going to kill me. You're trying to strangle me, aren't you? You're doing so good, goddamn it." He grunted and he sat up bringing my hips up higher with him. I all but shrieked at the sudden change in angle and I saw Kieron smile briefly before he started to piston his hips into mine.

"That's it. Yes, yes. Talia, come on, come for me." He said, his words broken with his effort and one of his hands came to my little nub and he started to rub in circles quickly.

"Yes! Yes!" I started to shatter. Kieron leant down and kissed me soundly with an open mouth kiss. We were breathing each other's air, intimate and hot and I had no choice but to let go and surrender. Stars danced beneath my eyelids and I swear, I left my body.

"Goddamn you feel so good. So fucking beautiful. It's like you're squeezing me and I can't-I can't…Talia." He groaned and his hips went even faster than he was before, but his rhythm started to falter. His eyes screwed shut and he shoved his face in my neck, biting down while he groaned and I felt his warmth fill me up while my walls were still convulsing.

We both stayed still for a moment, breathing heavily and holding each other tightly. Our skin was cooling from our sweat and we both knew that if we moved, our bubble would break.

"I wish I'd met you sooner." He whispered into my neck, his words tickling my neck and I hugged him tighter.

"Me too."

Chapter Two

Talia

resent...
Beep, beep, beep. Beep, beep, beep.
My arm flew to my alarm clock to make the noise from hell stop. I'm never drinking again. Ever. My mouth was so dry, if I didn't know any better, I would have thought that I licked sandpaper. *What time is it?*

I peeked open one eye and looked around. I could see the room darkening curtains that I had purchased were wide open.

Or never shut, I don't remember much of getting into bed last night.

The violently red numbers on the alarm clock said 7:30 and I cursed every god I knew for this hangover. Although, it was my fault for getting blackout drunk on a Thursday. Or if I was being even more specific, it was Luca's fault for everything.

I turned over in my, *our*, bed and threw my arm over my eyes to block out some of the sun.

I look over to his side slowly, fearfully, and it's immaculate. Like he never even laid his head down on his pillow.

Fuck, that wasn't good. He tends to be fairly passive aggressive when I choose to drink and his passive aggression usually turns into aggression. Always with me apologizing in the end. Apologizing and icing something.

I can't believe I'd dreamt of that party again. I always did when I drank or was scared. And now, it caused me to wake up turned on. Turned on and wishful. I longed for it to be happening now; back in bed with Kieron, back before morning came and he was gone.

Kieron was the first person I really felt like I clicked with. The first person, only person, who I felt got me. Even in such a short time of knowing him, but it wasn't meant to be. We spent the night together and then I never saw him again. I had forced myself to keep moving forward, move on and forget him. I met Luca a few months later and it seemed like everything would work out.

And it did…for a few years. Now, I'm not so sure.

I force myself out of bed and swing my legs over the side and stretch my arms over my head. I needed to get ready for work even if I was nursing a tequila hangover. My long blonde hair fell over my shoulders and I pushed it out of my face.

I hate my hair this long. I hate this color. But Luca had talked me into it a year or so into our relationship. Then, demanded it. Now, I wasn't allowed to change it, unless I wanted to hurt for going against him.

I look in the mirror and I can see the appeal. It's easier, less costly. But I don't feel like myself. Not like I did back then.

"Luca?" I call out meekly, walking out of the small bedroom into the hallways of our apartment. The walls are covered in little mementos of our lives both together and alone.

I love looking at photos, memories, every day to remind myself how far I have come in life, how I was happy once. Back when we were decorating and actually happy, the one stipulation from Luca was that none of my pictures that I display have anything to with other men.

At first, I was offended and annoyed but so in love with this handsome foreigner that wanted to be with me, actually make a life with me, that I relented. His sweet talking after blowing up in my face about it didn't help either. After he explained, I understood and followed his rules. Not only in decor for our apartment, but for our life.

Little did I know that this controlling, manipulative behavior was only the beginning. It got so much worse after the incident.

As I passed the end of the small, darkened hallway, I stopped and looked at the last picture on the wall. One taken of me at the party, standing by myself but only half of myself was visible. The photo had to be cropped to ensure that Luca didn't find the rest of the picture and punish me for having a photo of another man. Especially a man that had such an impact on me, like Kieron did. I was wearing fishnet tights and my cropped black band shirt, confident and wild. Free.

It was one of the only photos I have of myself in college and I love it. I love what it represents and the memory associated with it. I had pull him aside before we went back to my place and begged for a picture. With a broad smile, Kieron had agreed, asking his friend to snap one on both our phones.

The photo itself was blurry but I took in every detail. My cheeks were flushed, an obvious indicator that I was tipsy. But what really got me, every single time I look at it, is the smile on my face. It's pure. I looked like I felt I belonged, finally. A feeling that I hadn't felt in forever at that point. My eyes latch onto the fingers gripping my hip tightly in the photo and I thank my lucky stars that Kieron was wearing rings on his fingers. His thick middle and index fingers were adorned with heavy silver bands.

When Luca saw this picture, he was convinced that I was posing with a girl just based on the rings. And I have never corrected him, nor will I ever. I cut the photo before he ever saw the whole thing. If he knew who the owner of that hand was really, he would freak out.

And I would be in pain.

Back when we first got together, Luca's freakouts weren't so bad. But over the course of the two years we have been together, it's gotten really bad. And after the incident with my sister… I owed him, and he knew it. I never thought I would have to get good at doing makeup in order to hide bruises from the outside world.

"Luca?" I called out again, my voice cracking slightly with the nerves. It wasn't a good sign that he hadn't come to bed after I had. It meant he was fuming in his rage and I would be hurting soon.

"In here, amore." My boyfriend-turned-jailor said in an overtly false calm tone from the kitchen where he sat at the beaten-up kitchen table I'd found at a garage sale. He was staring down at his white porcelain espresso cup, softly tracing the rim. Over and over again.

Luca looks every bit the Italian dreamboat he presented himself to be. He wasn't very tall, but he made up for his height in muscle mass. If there was one thing that you could always count on, it would be that Luca would rise with the sun and spend hours at the gym, pumping iron.

Today was no different. He sat in the wooden chair, equally as beaten up as the table, a glass of water in front of him next to his coffee cup.

"How are you feeling, darling?" I stopped dead in my tracks. His thickly accented words sent a shiver down my spine as I felt like I was being electrocuted by him. Dread filled my body with the question he posed. To anyone else it would be an innocent question from a doting boyfriend to his girlfriend. But to us…to us it meant something far more sinister.

It meant that what was going to happen was going to happen and I was powerless to change it.

"Please," I whispered.

"You are awfully shy now. Not last night when you drank your weight in tequila and ignored your duties? Don't you remember that your body is mine to do what I please?" He said calmly, too calmly. He still wasn't making eye contact with me but when he said I'd ignored his needs, I knew. His eyes snap to mine and I could see the anger at being rejected flare to life. It was one of his rules; that I'm always welcoming and open with my body, but I have to be wasted to even stomach kissing him anymore.

"I'm sorry." I whisper, letting the blonde tresses fall around my face for some kind of barrier.

"It's too late!" He roared, the chair scraping against the floor and the cups of liquid were thrown because of the force of him shoving the chair.

I wish I could say I wasn't scared anymore, but even after all this time; I was still cowering. I was doing whatever it took to get by without pain, without punishment, that had become a near daily constant.

"Please, Luca, let's talk. I didn't…I didn't do it on purpose." I said, lying through my teeth, with a much calmer tone than I was feeling inside. Putting my hands up in front of me and slowly walking backward. It was one similar to what a lion tamer might do when trying to keep the beast back while the tamer got to safety.

"It's too late for that, darling. You broke the rules, rejected me, kept me from what was mine and all while destroying your body. You're lucky I am so disgusted by you and the state you were in otherwise I would have just *taken* what I wanted." His chest expanded and deflated so quickly, a sure sign that he's extremely angry. My heart beat even faster, my fight-or-flight response kicking up a notch. Looking around me, I tried to find somewhere to hide.

"You know that it helps me sleep…" My eyes clocked the open bathroom door right next to our small living room and I started inching towards it as inconspicuously as possible.

"You're so gross. God, why do I even keep you around? I spent so long trying to train you to be an acceptable girlfriend and you still cannot do anything right." His words dripped venom, designed to attack me but I'd stopped caring what he said to me a long time ago. All I cared about was finding a way out.

"Why do you? If you don't want me then why can't I just leave? You'll never have to see me ever again." I cried, tears were starting to build as they lined my eyes and my head started to pound harder from my hangover and now this.

"Because, you're still mine. Until I don't want you anymore. Until you're destroyed for any other. Until you pay me back for what I did for your sister." He said slowly with a smile that promised so much pain. "Or, I could take the file on what I have about your sister to the police. She'll only get 25 to life in prison."

"No!"

"It's your choice. Your poor dumb sister. Thinking she could get away with murder in cold blood. Stupid, stupid girl. But I guess that stupidity runs in the family. At least she's pretty. Unlike you." He said with a snarl, his cup falling from the table as he stands, pushing up from the chair so quickly it knocked over.

"She did what she needed to do!" I yell at him and take another step, inching backward.

"But she did it so sloppy. So sloppy that you had to call on me. Isn't that right?" He said with a smile that sent chills down my spine. His lips were pulled up over his teeth and he looked like he truly was a wild animal I had to inch away from.

"Isn't that right?!" He yelled in my face, causing me to cower. His hand came down hard on the wall next to him. Luca always, *always* expected an answer.

"Yes." I whisper, the tears in my eyes fall over and track down my cheeks. I'm so tired. So tired of this.

"You're going to be with me forever. You owe me and you owe my family and you fucking know it."

Tears fell steadily against my cheeks and a sob left my chest. I did know it. I was stuck between this hell for my lifetime; being a doll, a maid, a slave, in exchange for protecting my sister. She was beaten within an inch of her life seven months ago by her boyfriend who was not a good guy in any regard. Why she started dating him, I'll never know. But he was a bad guy and so I didn't know about it until I walked in on him beating her. He was throwing punch after punch and she wasn't breathing.

I lost it. My sister, who is my everything, was laying unconscious in a pool of blood with a guy straddling her waist and beating her. She was going to die and I knew it, so I grabbed the closest thing and I hit him over the head with it. He stumbled but it got him away and off of my sister so I ran. When he turned his fighting to me, I saw in his eyes there was no stopping him, no reasoning, and no way he was going to let me or my sister go…I did what I had to do to stay alive.

There was a fire poker by the small fireplace in her apartment and I grabbed it. When he advanced on me, I swung as hard as I could and the poker…the poker struck him in the temple, through his face and he fell. I'll never forget the moment I realized I'd killed him. The moment I saw the light leave his eyes and fall.

I couldn't dwell on it when it happened, I'd run to my sister and gotten help.

I called the one person who I thought would be there for me, the one person I knew could make this go away. Luca hadn't straight out told me that he was in the Mafia, but I wasn't stupid.

So, I'd made the call. Begging him to come help my sister, to protect her. And he did. But it had come at a price.

It was a secret I'd kept closer to my chest more than any other, that it was actually me who had killed him. I killed her boyfriend, called Luca to help clean up and he assumed she'd killed him... with a bit of convincing and acting from me.

I made a deal with the devil. More importantly, I made a deal with the Italian Mafia by way of their Prince. I didn't know exactly that was the position he held when we met, I just thought that his father owned the Italian Stallion, the most popular Italian restaurant in Charleston. I was unpleasantly surprised when I found out and discovered exactly how fucked I was.

Now, Luca charged towards me in anger and I bolted backwards like a gazelle running from the lion. I dart towards the bathroom, turning my back on him in favor of being able to run faster.

But just as I reached out for the doorframe, I felt a hand on my ankle and my body slide backwards violently.

Chapter Three

A hand wraps around my ankle tightly and yanked my body backward. My knees hit the floor hard. I broke my fall with my hands so that my face didn't hit the hardwood floor.

"Get back here!" He yells and pulled me backward again as I tried to hold onto anything. I just needed something to grab onto so I could pull away from him. Adrenaline coursing through my veins.

"Please! Leave me alone!" I cry out, hoping my screams would alert someone but in the back of my head I knew no one would come. No one ever has.

My hands clawed at the floor, trying to get any inch of space from him. I wasn't a tiny girl, but I was definitely smaller than Luca.

"You're going to make this worse, but keep fighting me. I like it." He laughs, his words full of promise for more than just beating me, and it was terrifying.

"Please! Please! Help!" I scream, one last hope that he would leave me but knowing it was futile.

"Shut the fuck up!" And his fist came down on my face. Pain bloomed under my cheekbone, white hot searing pain radiating up my face to my brain as my head snapped to the side from the force of his blow.

"Shut. The. Fuck. Up!" Each of his words was met with a strong punch to the face. He alternated sides so I knew I wouldn't look like myself when I looked in the mirror next. Tears and sobs heaved through my swollen eyes and busted lips as the pain was excruciating. I couldn't think, I couldn't move. He'd never hit my face quite this much at one time before. It was always a slap or one well-placed hit so that his handy work could be hidden.

But not this time.

He didn't care. And that, that was terrifying.

"You don't seem to understand the weight of what I have on you. Of what would happen to your darling Auggie if I pulled my protection. Unless you want your sisters prison sentence on your hands, I'd suggest you start fucking acting better." He snarls, I could feel him shifting closer to me, but his face was still blurry as I watched his face coming in close to mine and I flinched.

"You got off easy this morning, amore. Next time I won't be so nice." And, he was gone. I didn't dare move, in case he came back. I was in too much pain, my head and face felt like they were on fire and bloodied, to do anything but lay there and cry. I heard the front door slam shut and I sob.

* * *

"Hi, Mark. I'm not going to be able to come in today," I told my manager through the phone. I stood in the bathroom, the door firmly locked and blocked with as much stuff as I could find in the bathroom, and I tried to clean myself up. The cuts weren't too deep, but they would take time to heal. The bruising however, that would take weeks. Hissing, I dab the cotton ball with alcohol over a particularly deep one on my cheekbone.

"Are you okay?" Mark asks. I honestly and truly tried to find a job in the aerospace industry, but after talking with Luca about some of the places I was interviewing at, he convinced me that was the wrong direction for me at that time. I didn't want to give up my dream, but what could I do?

"Yes, I'm fine, I just don't feel so well and I don't want to get anyone else sick." I tried to make my voice hoarse and keep the tears out of it as well.

"Okay, so just let me know tomorrow if you are feeling better. I'll have someone else cover your shift."

"I, uh, I don't think I'll be in tomorrow."

"Oh, okay."

"I have a fever. With medicine. So, I think it will be a few days." I looked at my face, taking inventory of the damage and I knew that I would be hurting and covering bruises for days.

"I'm sorry, Talia. Feel better." Mark said, his voice so full of sympathy that I almost felt bad for lying to him. But with one look at my face, I knew it would bring far too many questions, too much attention about my relationship than I could have right now.

"I will, thank you." I hung up and sat down with my back against the wall and brought my knees up in front of me so I could rest my head on my knees.

I was stuck. Forever stuck.

* * *

"Get your fat ass ready, we're going out." Luca yells at me through the door as his fist pounds against the wood, shocking me awake. My face had gone from sore to burning, sore and painful as I had cried myself to sleep against the tiled floor of the bathroom. Based on how sore my body is from laying against the hard floor, I'd been asleep for a long time.

"Answer me!" His fist rains down on the door again and I jump away.

"Yes, I hear you. How long do I have to get ready? Where are we going?" I asked, my voice squeaking.

"We're going to a bar. Make sure you're dressed to the nines, you better look hot. You have an hour." He barked and then I heard the heavy steps of him leaving before I let out a deep breath.

The first thing I needed to do was shower, then I would have to focus on covering up the damage to my face.

I'd do what I'd have to do for my sister to ensure her safety and freedom, even if it was for a crime she didn't actually commit.

* * *

I'd dragged myself into the shower and done everything that I knew was expected of me. I shaved, exfoliated, moisturized, and made sure to bathe myself in the very specific perfume Luca wanted me to wear at all times when out in public.

He wanted to control my every aspect of being. What I wore, where I worked, what I ate, when I slept, what I drank, who I met with, and every little thing in between. At first, it was so subtle, I didn't notice it happening. A comment here, a suggestion there, always added with a smile and a kiss. Then it turned more obvious. He would order my meals and drinks for me, would talk for and over me, went over my head for important decisions we should have made together. These were always met with an argument between us, nasty words being said as I made myself and my wants known. That's when the hitting started, a slap, a rough shove, a bruising grip on my arm. But I always thought that it was an emotion that he couldn't control, he was so apologetic after. Luca would shower me with love and gifts, apologizing as much as he could. Then my sister was beaten and he had something to hold over my head to keep me there, regardless of what he did. It was like the last piece he needed to ensure that he could do whatever he wanted and I wouldn't leave. The love, the romance, the apologies; they all vanished. Left only with the bad.

Luca was the Italian Mafia Prince and if I valued my life or the life of my sister and family, I had to play my role. So, I do. I'm trapped with no one to help me. And even if I did have someone to help, I wouldn't pull them in and give Luca and his family one more person to hurt.

I spent an insane amount of time and makeup to cover the bruising which had deepened to a dark purple and would be so much worse tomorrow, and my eye was definitely swollen, almost shut. I did my best to cover it, but there wasn't anything I could do to hide the swelling. I had curled my long blonde hair to perfection and put on a tight, little black dress. One that Luca had deemed 'slutty' but still was long enough to provide me some coverage.

I set my bronzer brush down and stepped back to admire my work. As terrible, awful and used as I felt on the inside, my outer appearance was passable as someone who was happy and taken care of.

"Are you ready yet?" Luca's voice was harsh and short as he hit the door, signaling the end of my hour time limit.

"Yes." I croaked.

"Good, get out here."

I took a deep breath and smoothed my hair back, off my shoulders. I hoped that there wasn't anything wrong with my appearance, I don't think I could take any more hits.

I opened the bathroom door and slowly stepped out for inspection. Luca had changed into his going-out uniform; his too-tight skinny jeans and a white v-neck t-shirt that he layered with thick necklaces. The overall look was very popular and polished, but on him, it screamed false. Like he was trying too hard to be something he wasn't.

Like a good person.

"About time." He muttered and pulled my wrist so that my whole body fell towards him.

"Is this the best you could do?" He snapped, gesturing to my makeup. Instead of talking back and telling him to fuck right off like I wanted to, I just nodded.

"I guess it will have to work."

"Where are we going?" I said with a soft voice.

"To meet some of my college buddies who are interested in joining the restaurant." He said and I stumbled in my heels as he shoved me towards the front door. I didn't need a purse or a phone, Luca wouldn't let me order anything I would want anyway.

"I didn't think you handled recruitment."

"I don't, but these guys are my friends. Don't be such a nosy bitch." He snarled, leading me towards the car. I let him move me around because at least, I was going to get out of the apartment for more than just work.

We sat in silence while Luca sped through the apartment complex and then got onto the highway.

"Now, listen here, amore. You will not talk to anyone except myself and Trenton. You will not go anywhere except the table we sit at and the bathroom if needed but only after telling me. You will not get drunk and you will not get sloppy. You will keep your mouth shut about our business and if people ask about your face, you tell them you fell. Do you understand?"

I nodded silently and clasped my hands tighter on my lap.

"Say it!" He said sharply, like every other word he has said to me recently.

"I understand."

"Good." He said as he pulled a cigarette out from the package with his teeth and threw the package towards me to catch. He looked and shuffled around the middle console for his lighter. When he found the yellow Bic lighter, he flicked it on and sucked in a deep breath making the tip turn cherry red as it caught fire.

"Do you have to do that while I'm in here?" I ask, choosing to fight this battle. See, my fight wasn't gone but I'd been fighting long enough to get smart about it. Choosing when and what to push him on.

"Does it bother you?" Luca blew his smoke in my face, the grey cloud swirling through the enclosed space and I waved my hands quickly to try and dissipate it before it reached my lungs.

"You know I have asthma and smoke makes it flare up."

"You know I hate when you open your mouth to talk."

"It's not good for my breathing."

"I don't care." He replied with the cigarette hanging out of the corner of his mouth as he turned the car into the bar's parking lot.

Thank god we were here, I could feel my chest starting to get tight. We pulled up to a well-known Italian mafia-owned bar right in the middle of downtown. I wondered why we weren't meeting at the restaurant that Luca's father owned but I wasn't about to ask.

"Out. And remember how to act."

I didn't say anything and just got out of the car. I wanted to slam the door, scream like hell and punch him all in the face, but I couldn't. I wouldn't. My sister was my best friend, she was only a few years younger than me but she knew exactly what she wanted to be and told people to fuck off when needed. She was my hero and I never knew about that asshole Ian who had been beating her, until I walked in that day. I knew that he had caused a rift between us, forced a wedge there, but she was still my little sister.

I would protect her until I couldn't anymore. If I told Luca that I had killed Ian, my threats would be worse, and I'd never get out from underneath him. He would be able to use Auggie against me and I don't want to know how they could hurt her in order to make me his puppet. Not to mention, he would pull his protection on her. However, if he continues to believe that Auggie killed him, she would still be under the Italians' protection. If only so that Luca could continue to hold it over my head.

It seems backwards, but when he's hurting me, I can rest easy knowing that she is safe.

"Today, amore!" Luca yells from across the packed parking lot, his voice was falsely light. A sure sign that his 'good boyfriend' persona was back in place.

I moved quickly then, weary of his fake mood but also wanting to soak it up while it lasted. The bar, Momentum, was one that most businessmen and women frequented, it catered to their tastes. Low lighting, top shelf liquor that was actually purchased and savored, comfy seating and low volume of background music. It was also a place that was very heavily associated with the Italian mafia. I'd come to find that out once Luca decided I wasn't any kind of threat to bother hiding anything about his family. In fact, the first few days after the incident, he seemed to find great pleasure in telling me just how deep of shit I was in.

"Remember your place." He said harshly under his breath as his fingertips bit into my hip. He steered me through the entrance, a sleek black metallic door with a tinted window that was so dark it was almost opaque. He nodded to the bouncer who was staring people down as they walked in. The bouncer nodded back to Luca, obviously recognizing the Princeling and completely ignored me.

"I will." I said softly, plastering on a fake smile that made my cheeks hurt and cuts burn.

"This could be a very big recruitment commission for me. Don't fuck it up."

"I understand."

"You better. Now sit down and shut up." Luca pushed me towards an empty table towards the back, away from wandering eyes but close enough where we could see the front door so he could watch for the man he was meeting.

I slid into the booth as Luca sat on the other side of the table and took out his phone to properly ignore me.

Being that I wasn't allowed to bring anything with me, I people watched. There were so many people at the bar tonight, it was truly packed. In the far corner of the room there were some, very obviously packing, older gentlemen deep in conversation that was getting more heated by the second. Across from them were a couple; a too-young woman laying on the lap of a man easily three times her age. From the looks of it, the man was loving it but the girl's eyes were straying every few seconds to check out the hot bartender.

The hum of chatter was calming, I could just be one in the crowd. I didn't have to worry about expectations or punishments. I didn't have to fear for my life or my sister's. I could just close my eyes and pretend I was just fading into the masses.

"Open your eyes." Luca hissed. "He's here."

I hadn't realized my eyes had closed but at his words they snapped open. Maybe he had done more damage than I realized. Do I need to worry about a concussion?

I sit up straighter and push my blond locks over my shoulders to appear more put together. At least I hoped I look more put together than I feel.

"Trent! Good to see you. Thanks for coming." Luca's heavily accented voice cried out as he approached a man and their hands met in the middle for an enthusiastic handshake.

"Thank you for meeting with me. I appreciate you taking time to answer my questions." The taller man said. I still had yet to see him, but his voice sounded very vaguely familiar. I could see a tuft of bright red hair but before I could see any more of the mystery man, Luca stepped in front of me. He stood in such a way that I was being hidden from everything and everyone by his body.

"Of course. And I'm so sorry but, I had to bring my girlfriend along. She fell down the stairs. I worry about her brain and making sure she doesn't have a concussion. So, I had to bring her." He said with a roll of his shoulders as if to show that it was my fault this happened. With that, he turned and revealed me to the man. A shock of electricity went through my body.

Trent was the man from that frat party all those years ago, before my life went to shit. Trent, short for Trenton, was the same man who introduced me to Kieron. He didn't look like he remembered me, but really why would he? And I looked so completely different now than I did back then.

I smiled shyly and raised one shoulder in a very small shrug, being the perfectly demure little girlfriend Luca wanted me to play.

"Oh my god, are you okay?" Trent asked with alarm. He rushed to me and tried to look for the extent of the damage, but I flinched backwards.

"She's fine. Aren't you?" Luca said, menacingly from behind his back. My eyes quickly darted over to Luca's and I saw the threat in them. I had a part to play and if I didn't, I would pay for it.

"I am. Thank you." I said softly and smiled as much as my cheeks would allow.

Trent's expression changed then, his eyes narrowed and his lips flattened.

"Okay. Let us know if you need something. I think I have pain killers in my car." He said and slid in next to me. I could have moaned from the relief that would have come from pain relievers, but I knew that Luca wouldn't allow that.

"Thank you." I wrap my arms around my waist and hunch my shoulders over a bit to try and hide myself, maybe take their attention off of me a bit.

Trent turns to me and I can feel his eyes burn into my face as he takes in every detail of my face. His eyes locked onto mine and I could see a dawning happen. "What's your name?"

"Talia."

"Talia…" He whispered, his eyes flashing with recognition for a split second before he turned back to Luca.

"So, Trent," Luca said loudly, pulling Trent's attention back to him. "What makes you want to join our ranks?"

Luca was much more political and sounded stiffer than I had heard him in a while. He leaned back in his chair and crossed his arms over his chest. Knowing who he is now, it does seem intimidating, but before, I would have said that he was just peacocking. It took a lot of strength to not roll my eyes at his inflated ego.

The two men started to chat, and I let myself dissociate. The pain from the beating and noise level of the music wasn't helping me. Before I knew it, my eyes were closing, and my head was resting back against the wall.

Chapter Four

Talia

I am in deep shit.

I'm woken up by a sharp poke to the throat, making me cough and wheeze, and then a tight squeeze of my neck.

"Shut up." Luca whispers. I didn't mean to fall asleep at the bar in the meeting with Trent and Luca. I'm becoming more concerned that when he hit me earlier, he caused some real injury like Trent thought.

Luca decided to send me home after he woke me up, the look in his eye was scary and I know that I'm in trouble.

"You go back to the apartment if you're going to keep embarrassing me like this. I gave you very specific instructions and you failed. Leave." His voice is low and threatening while he refuses to look at me. Anxiously, I slid out from the booth and headed away from them before he said anything else. I didn't want to see if there were any requirements for me or anything he demanded I do before I got out of there.

I didn't wait to say goodbye to Trent, I didn't say goodbye to Luca, I simply left. Luca had the car and I didn't have any money or ID on me so I had to walk. At least I was alone. I had walked the streets in my strappy heels for about ten minutes before I heard a car pull up next to me. The passenger side window rolled down as they approached me.

Immediately I was on edge. I tried to think back in my memory about any self-defense I remembered but all I could remember was how to throw a punch correctly. At least I had that. I threw a pretty good punch, but that was when I had at least ten pounds more muscle on me. If I hit anyone now, I'm sure it would feel like a butterfly landing on their arm.

"Are you Talia?" The man, who couldn't be more than 30 years old, leaned over the side to ask.

"Who wants to know?"

"Trent sent me. He's a friend and said you might need a ride home. He also asked me to keep it hush-hush." The man answered and I relaxed.

"What's your name?" I asked.

"Bryan. I'm a friend from college and we work together. He texted me a little bit ago and asked me to come get you, that it was very urgent." He said, pulling his phone out and the blue light illuminating in front of me. He held it out of the car so I could see the text thread. It did seem that a 'Trenton' asked Bryan to drive along Helena Street looking for a girl named Talia with my description.

"'Absolutely no harm to come to her', huh?" I read from the last text Bryan received from Trent.

"Yeah, I was hoping you could shine a light on why Trent demanded me to come get you. This is definitely a first." Bryan said, gesturing with his head to the passenger side.

I took the gamble to trust Bryan, but honestly, I didn't think too much about it. I was already in hell.

I slid into the black vehicle into the equally dark matching interior and shivered at the heater that was blowing deliciously warm air on me. It might be summertime, but after walking in the dark for 10 minutes, I appreciate the heat.

"So, Talia, want to tell me how your face got busted up?"

"So, Bryan, want to mind your own goddamn business?" As soon as the words leave my mouth I flinch. I wait for the hit, the slap, the verbal threat. But none came. Instead, a deep chuckle came from the driver side.

"Touché." He said and started to drive. "Where am I going?"

"1400 South Beach. It's an older apartment."

"Gotcha."

We both stay quiet, tension in the car is incredibly awkward. I pull the visor down to see the mirror and inspect my face. I was sure that I had put on enough makeup to hide the bruising, I hope at least that no one else could see the extent of the damage.

"Yes, I'm able to see it." Bryan said softly.

"I fell down the stairs." I said, robotically, monotone.

"Okay, if you say so."

From his tone, I could tell that he honestly didn't believe me, but he was accepting my lie.

"So, how do you know Trenton?" He asked, thankfully changing the subject.

"I knew him way back in college. But I hadn't seen him in years and honestly, I didn't even really know Trent. I knew Kieron and back then, they were friends. I don't even know if Trenton put it together that we knew each other."

"Interesting. Kieron is a good guy. We still talk often." Bryan said and turned the blinker on to turn onto my street.

"That's cool. I hope he's well. I haven't heard from either of them in five years. A lot has changed since then."

"I bet." He said and pulled up in front of my building. I desperately didn't want to get out of the car. Once I got out, I would have to sit there and wait for my abuser to get home.

Just sit there and wait. The anticipation of what I was in for was almost as bad as the punishment itself sometimes.

It had been a nice moment, feeling like someone cared about me. But I knew it had to end.

"Thank you for the ride, please thank Trent for me as well. I don't have any way to get in contact with him and I don't think I could even if I did." I opened the door and took a deep breath, gathering my courage to get out.

"Wait, Talia." Bryan said before I stepped out and I turned to look at him. "If you need anything, anything at all, call either of these numbers." He pulled what looked like a business card out and handed it to me. "That's my number and Trent's number. I know you're in a… situation… right now where you're scared, but you're not alone. Not anymore." He said with a sad smile.

I leaned over and took the card and looked at it reverently, like a lifeline. Which I suppose it was. Then I looked up to him and smiled as best I could while I held it close to my chest.

"Thank you." I whispered.

"Please, *please*, take care of yourself. Take some painkillers. Rest." He said to me, his eyes and tone urgent. I nodded slightly, knowing I couldn't take painkillers because Luca wouldn't let them in the house. He wanted me to feel the pain. Always had.

I climbed out of the car and walked up to the door. Expecting Bryan to drive away as soon as I stepped out, I looked back and was surprised to see him still waiting. I punched in the code to the door and when it opened, I turned back to Bryan. He waved through the open passenger window but still didn't drive off.

I waved back, surprised, and shocked that he was still watching and waiting for me to get in safely. I walked into the lobby of my building and closed the gated door. Once the door was latched, he waved one more time and drove off.

I climbed up the stairs to the second floor and walked to our apartment. Thankfully, I had hidden a key in the fire extinguisher right across from our front door, otherwise I'd be sitting out here all-night waiting for Luca to get home.

* * *

After I wiped off the seemingly endless layers of foundation and cover up from my deeply purpled, swollen face, I pulled on my favorite sleep shirt. It was an extremely oversized, white t-shirt that I'd saved from five years ago. I didn't wear it often, only when I really needed comfort, and tonight was definitely one of those nights. His smell had long since been washed away, but it was enough.

Kieron had left the next morning in such a rush that it wasn't until later in the day that I found his undershirt under my desk, hidden from view.

I kept it. It wasn't like I could call him and give it back to him anyway. Even when I started dating Luca, I just pushed it to the back of my closet. Always there, but out of sight.

I let my blonde hair flow freely down my back as I went to the large window in the living room. It was dark out so I needed to close the blinds, but I couldn't help but think that as I looked out into the vast night sky, that this life had to get better. I had to hope that my life wouldn't always be like this. I wouldn't always have to sit and wait in fear for being an individual. I wouldn't always have to pay for doing what I had to do to protect my sister. I would be able to be with someone that I truly loved and felt loved by.

My true partner was out there somewhere. Either staring at the moon and stars like I was or waiting for the sun to come up. But they were out there somewhere and all I had to do was find them. Hopefully, before Luca kills me.

With that thought, I pull the blinds shut and sit on the couch waiting for Luca to do what he was going to do for me 'embarrassing' him by falling asleep.

Chapter Five

Kieron

"What up, Trenton?" I put the cell phone on my shoulder to hold it to my ear. I was working on my Harley Davidson bike, my pride, and joy that I'd built from nothing. I blew the strands that had fallen free from the bun that held my wild long hair so that it was away from my face while I was trying to work with the small pieces necessary to fix the drive chain.

I was thankful that my garage was air-conditioned because, holy fuck, it was hot as Satan's asshole. I set my phone to the side and put it on speaker as I pulled the white t-shirt over my head to wipe the sweat off my brow. Stray curls were sticking to my neck.

"What was the name of that girl that you could not get out of your head a few years ago? The one that totally screwed you up?" My best friend was never one for small talk. His voice was different this time from his normal aloofness though, it was urgent and pushy. I pushed a hair behind my ear to keep it out of my face as I leaned back over my bike engine. My hands were already covered in grease, as per usual.

"Talia. And you know it." I chuckled towards the phone.

Talia had been one of the most unique, most genuine people I had ever met. She was true to herself and went after what she wanted, regardless of other people and their fucking assumptions and judgements. I could tell that even in the few hours that we shared. She had been tipsy, but stone-cold sober when we had sex, showing me just how amazing she was inside and out.

I had thought about that night and her many, many times over the years that have passed. She was the one that got away, for sure. No one has ever come close to making the same impression as Talia. I sighed deeply with regret.

Trenton knew that too; he had picked me up after too many drunken nights that I had tried to drink myself silly to not go out searching for her. She had so many dreams that she had worked so hard for and I sure as shit wasn't going to hold her back from them. Besides, my job, the grunt work at that time wouldn't have allowed me to have a girlfriend. Not to mention, I literally wasn't allowed to have a girlfriend or any attachments.

When we met, I had been working my way into the Irish Mafia here in Boston, the same group my father and grandfather had been Skipper, or the Leader of, for generations. All my life I had been groomed to take over once I was old enough and that meant sacrifices, it meant being shown the ugliness of the world and becoming part of it.

"I found her. And it's bad." Trenton said through the phone, those six words shocking me through and through. I stood upright quickly and braced both hands against the workbench right behind me. It felt like all the air got sucked out of the room.

"You what?" I choked on my breath, dropping the nut I was holding. "Shit."

"I found her. She's passed out at this bar I'm meeting Luca at right now. She's here in town still and man, she's in trouble."

My world stopped. Everything zoned into the last words he said. I picked up the phone in my hand, anger and fear causing me to grip it tighter than it could withstand.

"How do you know it's her? What do you mean that she's in trouble?"

"Well to start with, she looks like she hasn't aged a day. The short black hair and piercings are gone though. But she still looks just as smoking hot as she did back then. Plus, you've described her enough times for me to recognize her anywhere. Then to hit the nail on the head, she told me her name was Talia. That's not exactly a common name." He explained.

My heart started to beat faster.

"And what do you mean she is in trouble, Trent?" I walked over to the other side of the garage, tossing the precision tool on it and grabbing a rag to roughly wipe my hands off. In the second drawer of the shelving unit is where I kept spare t-shirts, I pulled one out and slipped it over my head. Like I said, I'm usually covered in grease, so I learned to keep spares.

"This guy she's with, he's bad news, man. He's high up, way high up, in the Italian mafia and from the looks of it, he's beating her. Badly. I came to the bathroom to call you when I figured it out."

I stopped, frozen in my tracks.

"What?" I growled.

"She's here at the meeting, you know the one your father wanted me to sit in on." Trent explained.

"We will talk more about the meeting later, but I need to know more about Talia now. Why do you think he was hitting her?"

"Other than the fact that her face is bruised and so fucking swollen and they told me that she 'fell down the stairs' like I am an idiot who didn't know about bruising from fist fights, she passed out sitting next to me in the booth after clearly being told exactly what to say, how to act. Fuck, she wouldn't even take a painkiller after I offered her some. Then when she fell asleep, he looked livid. I couldn't imagine being mad at the woman I'm with especially after what they claimed was an accident that had caused that much damage. I don't think I would be out at a bar if my girl was that injured."

"Where do I find him?" I said through clenched teeth as my hand gripped the cell phone tightly. I grabbed my leather jacket off the back of a chair and made my way to my Mustang. It was a vintage GT with black exterior, black interior, and purred like a damn kitten.

"I'm still at the meeting with him so calm down. But from how I just watched him wake her up, he's going to send her home and then take care of her later. So, if you're going to do anything, I'd go to their house. I'm watching her leave the bar by herself from the little hallway across the room, I'll have Bryan go pick her up and take her home."

"Where do they live?" I turned the keys and started the ignition, hearing the engine purr to life.

"I don't know. But man, I have to go, she is leaving and I'm sure he is starting to think something is up if I don't get back there soon. Give it a bit and text Bryan so you can get the info from him."

"Thanks, man."

"Of course. I know how much she meant to you and I am never okay with someone putting hands on a woman. She needs help and we can help her." With that, Trent hung up and I stared at my phone as the dial tone played. I needed to get her address. Knowing that Bryan was with her, I rested a bit easier.

I rested my head against the steering wheel. Fuck waiting for a bit.

I pulled my phone out and messaged Bryan quickly. He was used to my short, clipped messages from the orders I give at work.

Now, all I have to do is wait for his response.

* * *

I sat in my car letting the engine idle outside Talia's apartment building. I'm happy that Bryan was so forthcoming with everything that happened, but I wish it had been me. I needed to see her. Bryan had suggested that I not go in, guns blazing and rescue her. He told me how scared she was, but I couldn't just sit there, doing absolutely nothing.

Not now that I knew where she was. It was like the dam that I had built up broke, I had spent so long staying away from her that now I couldn't.

So, I sat here. Outside her apartment building like a tatted up, mentally unstable guardian angel who was still infatuated with a girl that I only had one night with, five years ago. The building was an older one; brick exterior with wide windows that had iron grids on them. It wasn't a very tall building and since Bryan told me that her apartment number was 202, I'd wager that they were on the second floor.

Who said she even still remembered me? I was the one who had left the morning after.

Who's to say that I wasn't going to make things worse for her if I did rush in? Was this Luca asshole packing, would he hurt her further if he saw me coming?

There were too many unknown variables for me to just run in. I was taught to think things through rationally before making decisions, it was one of the main things my father taught me before he let me be Vice, his Second-in-Command.

I punched the steering wheel; it was too frustrating. Too overwhelming. Too out of my control.

The light flicked on in a window and it gave me a pretty good view into the apartment. I made mental notes about how the apartment was laid out based on what I could see, where the front door was and entrances/exits from the complex. I had no idea if it was their apartment or not, but I had hope.

Leaning forward over the steering wheel, I watched as a person approached the window and my breath caught.

It was her.

Talia.

The girl who turned my world upside down.

Trenton was right, she was beaten up. She had long blonde hair and was in short black shorts that hugged all her curves and a baggy t-shirt that she had tucked into one side to show her shorts. Her face was a mixture of purples and blues, one of her eyes was almost shut. God. What did he do to her? I tightened my grip on the white steering wheel to the point where my knuckles were turning white. Even with the injuries, it was still without a doubt her.

I sat, every bit of my attention on the woman in the window, watching as she put her forehead against the window and her shoulders sagged. She was surviving.

I watched as she took a deep breath and stood up straight, pushing her shoulders back like she had just made a decision. She grabbed the curtains and pulled them shut.

With the view of Talia gone, I sat back in my seat and let a deep breath out. My heart was hurting as much as my head. The girl that I knew was locked in there somewhere and I had to save her. I pulled the elastic out of my hair and let the curls fall.

I need to get her out.

And I would.

* * *

I sat there. And sat there. It had long since passed midnight, but I just couldn't bear to leave her knowing that her abuser was coming back to hurt her more.

My phone started to buzz in the seat next to me. Trenton's name popped up and I answered it in record time.

"You're outside her apartment, aren't you?" His voice was loud and relaxed. I could hear the sounds of the bar in the background.

"You're outside smoking, aren't you?"

"This isn't about my bad habits, it's about yours." He laughed boisterously.

"Yes, I'm outside her apartment. I haven't seen the asshole yet, but I can't just leave her here."

"But what are you going to do man? Stay there outside her door continuously, never showing your face? Luca just left and so he should be pulling up soon. What are you going to do? You need to think this through so that you don't get yourself killed."

I rested my head against the steering wheel again. He was right. I did need to think this through, I needed a better plan.

"I can't just leave her." I said softly into the phone. Trent let out a deep breath which was no doubt filled with smoke, after a few drinks he always started chain smoking.

"I know. But honestly, what can you do at this point, Kieron? Storm in after five years and save the day?" He said with a chuckle, but I was seriously thinking about it and my silence must have been enough of an answer for him. "Oh my god, that is what you were wanting to do, isn't it? Kieron, fuck. Do not do that. You always have had a hero complex."

"I just can't let him hurt her more. I saw what he did to her face." I said, my voice broken. My heart and my head were at war between what I should do. Maybe it wasn't just my head and my heart, it was what I wanted to do and what I should do.

"You can't do anything right now." White headlamps turned onto the street and swerved slightly. Just fucking great, a drunk driver. The car turned into the parking lot by Talia's building and my hackles went up.

"I have to go." I say to Trenton before I end the call quickly.

The car swerves and the driver pulls into a parking spot very poorly. The whole car is at an angle and both tires are over the line. The driver got out, revealing himself in the darkened light of the lamp above.

When the man got out of the car, I could see his dark hair color and slicked back hair style, his hair shined in the light above. I don't know how much more gel that man could have put in his hair before the goop would start sliding off his head. He tried to lean down to lock the car, but his keys slipped through his fingers. It was Luca. The next in line, spoiled brat of the Italian Gang. God, I fucking hate this guy. I've never met him in person, but being in rival gangs we knew of each other.

He kept one of his hands on the car to keep himself steady, and on that hand, I could see his bruised knuckles.

Anger took over me and I started to get out of my car. The only thought in my mind was shutting this asshole down and making sure he never did anything like that to anyone again.

The car door slams behind me. The warm breeze wraps around me. My feet pound on the pavement as I make my way to the stranger that I'm certain is an abusing piece of shit.

"Hey, can you help me? I can't find my keys." He slurred, his body was leaning heavily against the frame of the car and his head was barely supporting itself as he looked at me with glassy eyes.

I could feel my muscles tensing, preparing for a fight, under my black leather jacket. I hated everything about him; his thick eyebrows, his tan skin, his barely understandable accent. I took in the man who had somehow won over the girl of my dreams and instead of cherishing her, he is beating her. The bruising on his knuckles, that had a different skin color around them like someone had tried to cover up the damage, proved it.

I took a deep breath and looked up at the sky to gather my thoughts and stop myself from putting my hands on this excuse of a man. My father would be furious if I killed the son of the Italian Don. It's asking for war, war that we aren't prepared for.

"Please, I could really use the help." He said as he dropped to the ground to look for his keys.

"Should have thought of that before you got so drunk." I tried my best to keep my anger out of my voice, but even to me, my voice sounded low and threatening.

"What the fuck is your problem?" He slurred, looking up at me, a stranger to him that towered over him. I was surprised at the amount of bravado this guy had, not being intimidated by a stranger in the dark. Stupid fucking idiot.

I bent over and picked up the ring of silver keys that were just barely under the car, shrouded in darkness.

"You need these?" I said, holding them with one finger through the metal ring.

"Yes! Grazi." He tried to lean forward to grab them but I pulled them out of his reach. His face fell when he realized what I was doing. With how he smelled, I doubted that he would remember much from this night.

"What's your name?" I asked darkly.

"What's it to you?"

"I just need to check something."

"I don't know you. I think you should give me my keys and fuck right off."

"These keys?" I shook them in front of his face, the keys clanging together. "I'll give them to you. For two answers."

"Don't you know who I am? You are messing with the wrong guy."

"Why don't you tell me?" I said with snark.

"Give me my goddamn keys." He leaned up and tried to rip them from my hands. It wasn't hard to sidestep his drunken misstep.

"What is your name?" I demanded.

"You are going to regret this. I promise you."

"Let me guess," I put both my hands in my pockets, my fingers still clenched around the keys in my hand. "You're Luca Garzino. The son of the head of the Italian gang here in Boston. Am I right?"

I could tell that if Luca had been sober, he would have kept his emotions and thoughts on lockdown while in a stranger's presence. But luckily for me, he was completely wasted and like an open book.

He truly didn't think that I knew who he was. And I could tell that he recognized me, but in his drunken stupor he couldn't place who I was.

"Now tell me, what happened to your knuckles?"

His head lobbed down to look at his hands as if he didn't know what I was talking about. But then when he saw the bruising, I saw his fingers curl and he made fists with both his hands.

"Just some asshole who wouldn't listen. It's my business, not yours."

I wanted nothing more in that moment than to kick his drunken face in, make him stop breathing. But I couldn't. I couldn't do anything.

I stood up and tossed his keys at his feet.

"Now, see. That wasn't so hard." Using all my inner strength, I turned my back on him. With every step I took, it felt like I was walking away from Talia again. The sheer knowledge that she was inside, that I could protect her, could make her life easier, was stifling. But I had to play this right.

* * *

I peeled my car into my garage and the roar of the engine in the confined space helped calm me down. Trent's car was parked on the street in front of my house so I know that I'm going to be taking care of his drunk ass.

Turning the engine off, I climbed out of my car and listened to the pops and creaks of the engine cooling. I loved this car. It'd been with me through most of my life and I made sure to take care of it so it can continue running like a dream for as long as possible.

I leaned my hands on the hood and took a deep breath. That didn't go how I wanted it to. I don't know exactly what I was expecting to happen, but that wasn't it.

"Fucker, what did you do?" Trent said from the doorway into the house from the garage. I looked over to my friend, thankful that he was there and also annoyed that I couldn't wallow in peace.

"Nothing, I didn't do anything. I asked his name, and asked how his knuckles got busted. And I left." I walked past my red-headed friend and into the house, going straight for the fridge to grab a beer. I needed alcohol, lots of alcohol.

"Wow. That's actually kind of impressive." Trenton laughed and stood by the sink as I downed the beer from the bottle.

"Fuck off." He must have seen how much I was torn apart over this because the smile melted right off his face.

"What can I do?"

I shook my head and let it hang. "I don't know yet. I need to think." I opened the fridge and got another beer bottle.

One hand went to my head to run my fingers through my hair and my fingers got snagged in the bun my hair is pulled up in. I slammed the bottle down on the counter and pulled my hair out of the bun again. My curls fell loose around me and the tension headache that was starting to form relaxed.

"Did you see her?" Trenton asked, he stood with his arms crossed over his chest as he leaned against the counter.

I nodded, taking a drag of the beer.

"How do you feel?"

"Like I should have never let her go. And like I wanted to murder the son of the bitch that put his hands on her, but if I am going to do this, I need to do it clean. Probably call in the Clan and Kellan."

"Are you sure that is a good idea?"

"I just want to get her out. However I can, and I'm going to." I vowed.

Chapter Six

Talia

A scuffling from the front door woke me up from my nap on the couch. A quick glance at the clock showed that it was after midnight and Luca still wasn't home yet, but the scuffling meant that he was here and more than likely drunk.

Maybe the meeting went well after he sent me home. Dear god, I hope it went well. Otherwise, I was going to be blamed. I might still be blamed.

I stood up quickly as the door swung open and slammed against the wall.

"Stupid fucking idiot thinking he can intimidate me like that...lucky I didn't shoot him in his face...too much attention...lucky." Luca was mumbling under his breath, stumbling and tripping over his own feet as he tried to close the door. I hid behind the corner before he saw me, maybe if he didn't see me, he would leave me alone.

"Oh, amore!" He called out through the entryway. His voice light and high like a demented hide-and-go-seek game we were going to play. I raised up on my tiptoes and ran as fast as I could without making any noise.

"You better be here! I don't know how you got home, I don't really care, but you better be here waiting." He called out again, I heard a *thunk* and a dragging. I didn't answer, and climbed into the bed, pulling the covers up over my ears to wait for him to reach me. I hated nights like this more so than others because when he drank, I had absolutely no idea who or what I was going to get. Sometimes, he left me alone like he forgot I was even there. Other times, all he wanted to do was torture me. He'd hit me, he'd force me to sleep in the shower, he'd make me do things to him sexually.

"Wake up!" He said, stumbling into the bedroom and turning the light on. The room was flooded with light and the abrupt change made me squint to see. Luca looked awful; his hands were covered in what looked to be dirt and his knees were as well, his usually slicked back hair was all out of place and his cheeks were bright red with anger.

"Sometimes, I think I should just let you go. But then I think about how we used to be, back before I had to come up in the family business and I think maybe we can be that again." He slurred as he left dirty handprints on the wall as he walked towards the bed.

"How did the meeting go?" I sat up and pulled the covers up and over my chest. Maybe if I got him talking, he'd leave me be.

"Good, good. Fine. Trent will be a fine addition. Although, he did seem a bit too concerned with you." Luca approached me and it was like everything turned to slow motion as his hand came to my face and gripped my chin. Hard.

"What did you do?" His rank, stale alcohol breath fanned across my face.

"What do you mean?"

"Why did he care for you so much? What did you do? Did you tell him?"

"No! I didn't, I barely talked to him." I said as clearly as I could with my cheeks pushed together and my jaw in a stronghold.

"You better hope that is true. I will not have you go around and attempt to ruin my reputation with people. Get your shit together or you'll pay for it." He sneered and slapped my cheek once, the sound ringing out in the silent room. My cheek was already throbbing with the bruising from earlier and the slap pushed it even more.

"I didn't." I cried, holding onto my cheek and my eyes filled with tears.

"Stop your crying. Your tears are wasted here and very unwanted." He rushed into my space and smacked the spot by my head.

Luca breathed into my face and I wanted to move away from him but was too scared that the next time that his hand came down it would be on my skin again. The rancid smell of his breath was enough to make me cringe, but I refused to move in case he wanted to hit me again. All I could do was make sure that I did what he wanted.

I tried to hold back my tears and make sure that none of them fell.

"I'm going to shower and when I get back, you need to be out of my bed." He hissed in my face before ripping himself away from me and walking towards the bathroom.

Once the door was fully closed, I let myself cry for a few seconds. The tears ran down my face while I silently sobbed and left the room.

When I got to the living room, I felt slightly relieved because if he wanted me away, at least I wouldn't have to do anything with him. That would be worse. I'd gladly take sleeping in the bathtub or on the floor before having to do anything with him.

At moments like these, I couldn't help but think about Kieron and what he would think about me now. Instead of being the confident, sexual, ambitious girl, I was someone who was following every order and command to try and hide as best I could in plain sight. I hoped everyday to become invisible and free.

He wouldn't give me the time of day.

I laid my head down on the couch cushions and if I'm being honest, it felt more comfortable than the bed I shared with Luca.

I could hear the shower turn off so I could feel my body tense with the noise. If he was getting out of the shower, that meant that he could come for me.

I sat (or laid) on pins and needles; waiting for Luca to yell at me, to come running to get me, to smack me, to rape me.

But nothing happened.

The light under the bedroom door shut off and I felt like I could breathe again. I let my eyes flutter closed, still not fully letting myself relax.

I didn't think I could relax ever again while I was under his roof.

* * *

The next morning, I woke up to the sun streaming through the curtains. Thank fuck that Luca hadn't tried anything last night, I know I wouldn't be able to do anything against him but it made it so I didn't have to try to fight.

I wanted to work today so I got up and tried my best to sneak into the bedroom where my uniform was and then slid past him. He was completely passed out, spread full eagle on the bed, face down and snoring softly.

I was so thankful for my job because it got me out of the house. I was able to leave my personal hell for a short period of time.

In the shower, all I could think about was how stuck I was.

How far I'd fallen.

I didn't want to just survive, I wanted to *live*. To feel passion and to make mistakes without fear of some punishment hanging over me.

* * *

"Hello, how can I help you?" I said from behind the desk, I was filling out some report so I wasn't looking up. The bell rang, letting me know that someone was in the store.

"I'd like to talk to the woman in charge, if that's okay." A deep, familiar voice said, his tone commanding the empty room. I almost didn't want to look up because I didn't want to see the man that had haunted my dreams for the last five years to see me like this. My breath caught in my chest and I couldn't breathe. He was here. What were the odds that the man that got away from me would come walking back into my life.

"That would be me." I said with a smile and I looked up to see the most welcome, most handsome view I had seen in years. Kieron walked into my store; black leather jacket and just as handsome as the last day I'd seen him. He looked older, but in a good way. He was taller than my memory, and was sporting so many more muscles. He looked like a linebacker. Kieron had many more tattoos than I remember and they suited him, I could see a peak of a flower and a vine creeping up his neck. His hair was long and luscious, pulled back into a low bun. I didn't think that I was attracted to the man-bun, but he could pull it off beautifully. Through all the changes, his kind eyes hadn't changed whatsoever.

I shrunk back into myself, well aware that I didn't look the same as the last time he'd seen me. I did my best to slowly move my hand to my nametag to pull it off without drawing too much attention.

"Can I help you?" I asked him, turning back to the reports and trying to hide my face slightly.

"Yes, I would like to get a speaker upgrade for my car." He said, walking closer to the desk where I sat. I jumped up, thankful for the distraction. The sooner I could get him what he wanted, the sooner he could leave.

"Right this way, I can show you the different kinds of speaker systems we have and you can make an informed decision." I guided him over to the section of speakers and turned to leave.

"Wait, if you have a moment, could you help me?" Kieron said. Thankfully, he hadn't recognized me yet. What was the harm?

"What kind of car do you drive?" I asked.

"A 1969 Mustang that I restored a few years back. It's my baby." He said with a smile, both hands in his leather pockets.

"Beautiful. How old is the stereo?"

"Only a few years, but I tend to listen to my music louder than normal so they are already starting to fuzz."

"Ah, I see. You probably need the one that has extra bass protection to prolong the life of the speaker. Our Heliokuzo brand over here," I said, pointing to the top tier speaker, "would be the best."

"I do think that feature would be the best for me. I tend to like heavy metal or classic rock."

"Let me get this wrapped up for you." I said, picking up one of the boxes for the speaker and walking back to the register to ring him up. I dreaded our time coming to a close. Having him here was like a breath of fresh air. A stark reminder of my past and how he had left me.

"So, what is your name?" Kieron walked over to the register and pulled his wallet out of his back pocket.

"Um," I start to answer, but really, I'm almost embarrassed. He left me in the early morning after we had spent the night together. He'd made toast and coffee, leaving it on the side table for me and left.

"I'm Kieron. You look familiar. Very familiar. Do we know each other?"

"I think we met back in college once. Cash or card?"

"Card." He said and handed over his credit card. "When?"

"When what?"

"When would we have met? What year?"

"Um,"

"Don't lie to me, baby."

With the use of a pet name, I melt. But I still don't know if I should say anything, I still don't know if I should bring attention to the embarrassing morning after a wonderful, breathtaking night we shared.

"About five years ago."

"You're Talia. My Talia." He said without any hesitation and a smile.

"My name is Talia. And you're Kieron."

"You remember me."

"Yes, I do. Clearly, you did not." I said with some sass and I crossed my arms over my chest. He stood there with his mouth slightly agape so I got to work. I ran his card and wrapped up the speaker. The receipt printed and I wrapped it around his credit card, holding it out for him to take. I knew my facial expression was hard and not at all friendly, but it hit me hard that that evening that I hold dear to my heart, a memory I cherish, was nothing more to him than a quick fuck.

"I think I went about this the wrong way." He said, taking the receipt and card from my outstretched hand.

"What do you mean? Is the speaker not what you need?" I asked, putting on a falsely positive customer service voice.

"No, Talia, the speaker is fine. I meant, I should have just come in here and said, 'Hi Talia, how are you?' I knew exactly who you were, I knew I'd find you here. Trenton told me he had seen you and I couldn't hold myself back anymore."

"Yeah, okay." I said with a huff and a small eye roll.

"No really." He said, he moved around the partition, and I stepped back. He noticed my flinch and immediately stopped. "I'm sorry. I wasn't - I wouldn't - hurt you. I didn't mean to scare you."

I nod, believing him. It was just an instinct at this point though, to flinch when a man comes at me quickly.

"It's okay."

His expression changes and his eyes zero in on my face. I did my best to cover my bruises again, but obviously the layers and layers of concealer and foundation weren't enough.

"I'm fine." I said with a shrug and let my arms fall. I stepped back into the spot in front of the register and really didn't know what to do now. I didn't know what he wanted from me; I didn't know how to proceed from here.

"Talia," His hands balled into fists and I could tell that he was struggling to keep his breathing under control. "What happened?"

"I fell."

"Yeah, right."

"No, really."

"Don't lie to me." He said through clenched teeth.

"I'm fine. Back off." I stand up straighter and try to be more intimidating than this 6'3", leather jacket wearing, entitled man who thought because he rocked my world *once* that he could just come back and demand answers about my life. I haven't seen this asshole in years, *years*, and he has the gall to ask me intimate things.

Kieron must have seen the fire in my eyes because he does indeed back off.

"I'm sorry." He said and put his hands up in front of him. "I just keep fucking this up." He said quietly under his breath, interlocking his fingers behind his neck as he looks up like he's in pain.

"Talia," He said with a smile. "It is so good to see you. How are you?" Kieron held his hand out for me to shake.

An olive branch extended and I smile at his cute gesture.

"Kieron. I can't believe it; it's been a long time." I smile softly and shake his hand.

"How have you been? Can I take you out for a coffee to catch up?" Kieron looked down at the floor and I could have kissed the shy look off his face.

"I can't leave work right now, but maybe some other time."

"Can I get your number? Trent told me where you work, but nothing else really."

Giving Kieron my number immediately would break one of Luca's rules, and most definitely be signing on for more pain… but I don't know how he would know, I was trying to convince myself because I wanted to give Kieron my number. I really wanted to.

"I, uh… Sure."

"Here," He handed me his phone. Our fingers brushed over each other as the phone passed between us and that spark from five years ago was alive and well.

I smiled and plugged my number into his phone before I could change my mind. He took it back and quickly texted my number.

"Are you normally busy around this time?" He asked, putting his cell phone in his pocket. I tried not to gulp as his phone disappeared, cementing that I broke a rule.

"You're the only one that has come in in the last two hours so you tell me." I said with a weak laugh. It was just after two in the afternoon so the people that had come in over the lunch rush were long since back at their jobs.

Kieron's head dropped with a low chuckle and I watched as a curl tumbled from behind his ear. He looked so hot and happy. He was so attractive back in college, but now he'd grown into his looks. There was still a hint of concern and anger hidden in his eyes but to my delight, I could tell none of the anger was directed at me.

"Okay. I'll be right back." He said, striding towards the glass front door without looking back.

I didn't know what he was planning, I didn't know if he actually was going to come back. As soon as the bell rang above the door signaling that he had left, my anxiety started to build.

What had I done? I gave a man my phone number and now, Luca would… could….

I backed up behind the desk until my back hit the wall and I slid down until my ass was on the ground. What had I done? What is he going to do to me? Fuck, fuck my life. Goddamn it.

My heart was beating crazily fast and I couldn't breathe.

The air was being sucked out of the room. Clawing at the collar of my shirt, I tried to pull it away to get more air in. The room started to spin.

"Talia?" A voice called out; I hadn't even heard the bell ring to let me know that someone was inside the store.

I couldn't pull myself out of this panic attack. There wasn't a way for me to. Oxygen wasn't getting into my lungs and I was definitely gasping deeply.

"Talia, Talia, baby. Breathe." I could barely see anything. My vision was darkening so quickly. I could feel two large hands on me; one rubbing comforting, soft circles on my back and the other holding my head to a warm, firm chest.

"Breathe. In, Out." The voice demanded and I followed their orders. I breathed in and out slowly. "Again." And I did.

"Good job. Good girl." The praise slipped from his lips so easily. "What happened? I was gone for only a few minutes."

My world stopped spinning and I was finally able to focus on my savior. Kieron held onto me, and his hand never stopped moving on my back. His chest was straining against the white shirt under his leather jacket and was soft against my forehead. He smelled strong and clean like grease and leather.

Oh god, if Luca were to walk in right now, he would murder me on the spot for being in the arms of another man. I scurried away from Kieron as fast as I could, pushing him away and standing up. I tried to keep my panic under control and not surrender to it again, but my anxiety was so high that I couldn't do anything, I had absolutely no idea what to do.

"Talia," Kieron stood up and slowly, with his hands up like he was calming a wild animal, started to walk towards me. "I'm going to be honest. Okay?"

I nod.

"I know what is going on…at home."

My heart dropped out of my chest. Complete and total horror filled every single space in my body.

"What?" I whispered.

"The bruises on your face are not from a fall. I used to get in fights all the time, so did Trenton. We know how bruising from a fist looks. He called me when he saw you at the bar and he saw how Luca talked about you. Then I went and met Luca for myself. And I knew."

"Why do you care? You walked out on me five years ago, don't you remember that?" I interject.

"We can talk about that at another time." He said, walking closer to me. "Please, calm down. I'm not going to hurt you, I promise."

Chapter Seven

Kieron

The terror and confusion laced with betrayal on her face made my heart break.

I know she had a very valid point that I needed to explain about leaving her that morning five years ago, but at this moment, all I cared about was making sure she was safe. I looked around the small electronics shop and started looking for surveillance that wasn't part of the store. If Luca was as good as he thought he was and kept a good eye on his "property" then I would bet that he had some kind of bug in here.

I pulled my phone out of my pocket and started to type a message to Talia in my notes asking about any bugs or additional cameras. She read it and shook her head.

I typed; *Can I see your phone? I just want to check to make sure he didn't tap it as well.*

Her eyes bugged out a bit, as if she had never thought about it and then her breathing picked up again. She was going to have another panic attack right before my eyes.

"It's okay, I promise." I reassured her, taking one of her hands in mine. After getting to hold her close again, I knew I was going to crave it. She smelled intoxicating; like sunshine and lilacs in the summertime, and even with all the bruising and swelling she was easily one of the most beautiful women I've ever seen. "Can you tell me why you're panicking?"

"He will know. He knows. He knows." She started to whisper, the panic overtaking her again.

This asshole was going to fucking die and he was going to die by *my* goddamn hand for doing this to her.

"He knows what?"

"Your number, tapping, he knows, he knows, he knows." She whispered, over and over, gripping my leather jacket like a safety net.

It dawned on me then what had happened. I texted her so she would have my number. Something innocent and small so that she would feel a bit safer, he was going to punish her for it.

Over my dead body.

I came into this store with a plan and I knew that once I made contact with her, I would take whatever hell came our way so long as she was safe and happy.

"Look at me, Talia." My voice deepened because I needed her to know I was serious. "I will not let him harm you again."

"You don't understand!" She cried, her eyes filling with tears. "You can't help me."

"The fuck I can't." I said stubbornly. "I am the Second of the Irish Mafia, Boston chapter. You're going to come with me."

"I can't."

"You can."

"Please, Kieron. So much as happened, you don't know everything and I doubt you would want to help me if you did. This is my penance." She said, her sobs layered in her words. What she confessed surprised me, but didn't deter me at all. I turned from her and walked a few spaces away, trying to think.

She didn't know what power I held. She wasn't aware that I already knew what had happened.

"I can protect her too." I said softly, my hand going to my hair to smooth back some flyaway pieces. The utter surprise on her face was amazing and was almost enough to make me laugh.

"How did you-"

"You don't know what being the Second of the Clan means. I have people everywhere and know almost everything. I've been keeping an eye on you for a long time. Always in a roundabout, anonymous way that kept you and your location out of my knowledge. There were many nights I had to drink myself stupid to make sure I didn't find my sentinel, the solider I had put on your guard and beat him within an inch of his life to tell me where you were."

There were too many of those nights.

"Why?" She whispered, her voice broken and disbelieving. I couldn't say I blamed her after how I'd just left that morning. No note, nothing but coffee and toast on her bedside table to let her know how I felt.

"I'm…not a good man, Talia. I've done things, terrible things because I had to put the Clan and my men first. I do what I need to do to ensure that our chapter continues on. That our connections and our businesses stay afloat and thriving. Back when we met, I was… in training. I wasn't allowed any relations or distractions. All my focus had to be on proving myself to the Skipper so that I could join the ranks, so I could prove myself to the Clan that I could be a good Second regardless of lineage. Do you remember how back then I told you about the family business and how I was expected to follow?"

She nodded.

"Just because my family has always been in the mafia didn't mean that it was given to me. I had to go through initiation and trials. When we met… I had to give up my life to prove my allegiance. After meeting you, I realized this had to be my path and I could do what needed to be done. In making that decision, I had to give you up. I thought I'd bring you down, bring nothing but trouble to your life, so I left. I did what I could from a distance, but you found trouble all on your own, didn't you, baby?"

Talia looked at me stunned, her eyes wide and blown out like she was slowly sorting through and retaining all the new information.

"I didn't know." She said finally.

"I know. How could you have?" I smiled down at her and hoped that she understood what I'm trying to say.

"Why now, Kieron? Why come into my life now and turn everything upside down? If you know what happened then I'm sure you can guess what is being held over my head. I can't take on the Italian mafia by myself, especially with my baby sister in the balance." Talia's tone turned violent and strong, a flash of the woman I remember sitting by at the college party so long ago.

"Because your life finally entwined with mine. Because I found out what was happening and even though your life hadn't been threatened to where the sentinel I had put on you might have stepped in, you have been getting hurt. And believe me, baby, I will be kicking his ass every way from Sunday for this fucking 'oversight'. The minute you stepped out with so much as a mark, I should have been informed. Because I can't stay away from you anymore." I confessed, my chest feeling tight from the vulnerable position I'm putting myself in, but I knew she never would trust me if I didn't tell her the truth.

"Even if you don't feel anything for me, even if it was just a one-off thing for you five years ago and you barely remember me, I will not sit by and watch you get hurt." I take her hand and interlace our fingers.

"I came in here not confessing everything at first because I was scared you wouldn't remember me, so I acted like a right fucking idiot. Then I thought, if I gave you my number you might feel a little safer knowing you could contact me if you needed. But I see now just how far that fucker has gone and I refuse to let him harm you anymore, in any way. So, get over it, get your shit and let's go."

* * *

"I have her, Trent. Go ahead and get going on the next part." I demanded into the phone before ending the call and wrapping Talia under my arm. I was trying to keep an eye on our surroundings because based on my recon, this son of a bitch didn't let Talia breathe a breath of free air. I wouldn't put it past him to have someone watching her every move.

"This isn't a good idea." She whispered, clutching her purse to her chest and gripping onto my waist. I could feel her warm, dainty hand against my abs and I loved it.

"Trust me. I know I haven't earned it quite yet, but I will. Is there anything at the apartment you absolutely can't live without? I can get you new clothes and stuff like that. But I'm talking sentimental items that can't be replaced."

"No, I had to get rid of all that stuff a while back. There are just pictures left." She said softly and my heart broke for her.

"Let's get you back to my apartment. You'll be safe there." I pulled her closer into my body and pressed a quick, chaste kiss to the crown of her head. The blonde was a different look than I remembered, but she was still stunning. I could tell she didn't like it though with how much she fidgeted and tugged at it.

"Where do you live?" I heard her ask quietly as I steered her in the direction of my Mustang. Her eyes lit up when she saw my car and I felt pride in my chest that she seemed to love my baby as much as I did. "Wow." She breathed and ran her hand over the hood of the car.

"I know." I winked and opened the door, sliding into the driver's seat.

"She's beautiful."

"Thank you, I've spent many nights and shed much blood, sweat and tears fixing her up." I answered honestly.

"Thank you, for your sacrifice." She said with sass and a smile. Talia, my Talia, was coming back to the surface. I would make sure she was able to be herself again; free from her cage and abuse and let her fly freely.

The old phrase *'if you love something let it go, if it loves you back it will come back'* flitted through my head and I knew that I'd give her anything she needed and if she wanted, I'd let her be truly free.

Chapter Eight

Talia

Dear god, this car is beautiful. The roar of the engine was deep and powerful and enough to completely turn me on.

"So, where do you live?" I prompt him since he skillfully sidestepped my first attempt and finding out.

"I live in a beachfront home permanently, but I crash at the Clan headquarters so much I may as well claim that as my permanent residence." He said. Kieron looked like a model out of a damn magazine with his black leather jacket, light brown hair pulled back into a bun with tendrils flying in the wind from the open window, and a panty-dropping smirk.

"A beachfront home. Fancy."

"It was always my dream to live by the ocean. To go to sleep hearing the sound of the waves crashing on the sand and the utter peace that the ocean brings. So, once I started to really make money and climb the ranks, I bought a house. My dream house. I don't stay there much because of work, but I have it. I thought staying there would be the best and safest choice."

"The ocean is your happy place, huh? Does that mean you surf? You look more like a biker than a surfer, although it would explain the hair."

"I love my hair. And you can't tell me that you don't find it sexy. Everyone does." He smirked at me again and I couldn't help but get lost in the way his dimple showed when he did that. His eyes were sparkling with happiness and I felt myself smile back as much as I could through the bruises.

"Yes, the ocean is where I want to be. It's part of the reason why I never moved very far from home. The other being the obvious family business assumption. Surfing is one of my hobbies, but I never seem to have any time anymore."

"I've never been."

"Ever?"

"Nope." I said, popping the p.

"Wow, Talia. You have to go. At least once. It's peaceful and makes you feel powerful. Like having an engine between your thighs and going over 100 miles an hour. You feel free. Completely and totally free."

"Is the beach house where we are going?" I asked. Just because he had a beach house didn't mean he wanted to sully the place with me.

"Eventually. I need to take you to my father first." He said. He was trying to look confident and nonchalant, but I could see the nerves under his expression. Kieron, for some reason, was nervous about it. Me meeting his dad.

Granted, I couldn't blame him, he seemed to be skipping a few relationship steps.

Not that I thought we were in a relationship.

That's embarrassing. I could feel my cheeks start to heat up.

"Why?" I asked.

"Because I more than likely started a war by taking you away from here. And I need alliances. My dad, Trent and I have already discussed and have a plan, however, he wants to meet you."

"Should I be scared?"

"I mean, not to make you more anxious, but you are going to be meeting the Skipper of one of the most powerful, prominent, and influential Mafia clans in the in the region. You and I have a history, but don't forget that I'm dangerous. And my father even more so. It would be in our best interest to have him on our side."

"Oh god," I whispered, the nerves and anxiety growing in my stomach. I started wringing my hand together to try and dispel some of the nerves and then his large, warm hand enveloped both of mine.

"It will be okay. I am doing this to protect you and my father knows that. So don't worry too much."

I held onto his hand and was too worried to wonder if he minded. His hands felt so comforting and strong in mine and I held onto it like a lifeline.

"Are you in any pain? Do you need some pain meds? I'm sorry, I should have asked sooner." Kieron looked to me with concern in his eyes and I felt my heart soar.

"Can I?" I asked him softly.

"Can you? Have pain medicine?"

"Yes. Is that okay?"

"Of course, it is. Here," He said incredulously and let go of my hand to rifle through the glovebox and pulled out a small bottle of pills. I held it up and slowly opened the bottle. I hadn't been able to freely take any medication for anything. I took two pills out and dry swallowed them.

"Where you…Is it…Can you…" Kieron started to say something but never really got the words out.

"What?"

"Never mind." He said softly. I knew he wanted to ask about what happened, why I reacted that way and asked for permission even though Kieron offered. I could see his question in his eyes, but honestly, I wasn't ready to tell him everything.

He put the medication back and then, thankfully and without any prompting, he put his hand back in mine.

The rest of the car ride was quiet as Kieron drove us quickly through the city and pulled into the underground parking of a nondescript, mirrored skyscraper.

"This is headquarters?" I asked, looking around at all the millions of dollars of sports cars in the parking garage, expensive cars lined up one after and another. Lamborghini's, Porsche's, Maserati's, Ferrari's. Dear god. Have any of these people even seen a Ford or Chevy?

I think Kieron's Mustang, as beautiful as it was, was the cheapest car there. "Wow."

"I know." He said, pulling into a free space between a Rolls Royce SUV and a sleek black Ferrari. "Let's go." Kieron smirked and I tried to smile back. I watched him stand up and climb out of the driver side, his ass perfectly encased in his jeans.

Yum.

"Let's go, Talia." I heard Kieron say from outside the car and I swear, I heard a smile in his voice.

Like the jackass knew I was looking.

* * *

Kieron led me to an elevator and pressed the top button, meaning his dad's office was in the penthouse.

He leaned against the side of the elevator, crossed his arm and ankles and looked at me with a dangerously sexy smirk as he looked me up and down.

"What are you looking at?"

"You. You're beautiful, you know?" He said, pushing off the wall and standing right in front of me, his back to the door.

"Oh, I don't know about that." I said softly. I knew he was trying to be nice and help me, but I knew how I looked, especially with my caked-on makeup to cover the bruises that were impressively gross looking today.

"You are. Always have been." Kieron brushed the back of his knuckles over my cheeks so softly I wouldn't have felt it if I hadn't seen his hand touch me. His eyes were dark brown and locked onto mine. I could feel my heart beat faster. The way that he was staring at me… It was like he wanted to eat me alive, in the best way, but also that he understood my hesitance.

Before I could say anything, the elevator doors dinged and light illuminated Kieron, bathing him in bright light. He took both of my hands in his and then his expression changed. His facial features turned down; became more serious, more dangerous. The light and joy in his dark eyes went out and he looked every bit the mobster he said he was.

If he hadn't been holding onto my hand and giving it gentle squeezes, I would have backed away.

"Trust me," He mouthed to me before turning around, still using his body as a shield between me and the rest of the room.

"Kieron." I heard from within.

"Father."

"Please, come in." Kieron started to walk forward and brought me with him. Our hands were joined, but the way that Kieron had positioned himself, I was still hidden.

"Did you bring her? I would like to meet the woman who has captured my son's attention so totally." The man spoke with a heavy Irish accent, and my nerves started to take over my body again. My spine started to tingle and my heart was beating too fast. I could feel the palm of my hand clasped in Kieron's start to sweat.

"I did. Father, this is Talia Jones. Talia, this is my father, Kellan Tavish." Kieron stood aside and rested his hand on my lower back so I could shake his fathers outstretched hand.

"Nice to meet you, Mr. Tavish." I said. I tried to sound strong and confident, but it was hard when I was acutely aware of how I was shaking hands with the head of the Irish Mob.

"Please, lass. Don't worry about calling me Mister. Kellan or Skipper will do just fine. Please, have a seat." He took my hand in both of his and shook it. I looked around the office and was shocked with how cozy and welcoming it was. I don't know what I was expecting, but it wasn't the comfy grey couch with an adjoining loveseat that looked equally as inviting to sit on. The space was a proper living room set up with a dark coffee table in the middle and a lamp on either side of the couch that gave off soft light. On the other side of the wall was a TV that was mounted up high, muted and playing a soccer game.

"Coffee, tea?" Kellan asked, walking over to a little coffee bar set-up and I was so surprised I just shook my head.

"I'll have a coffee, Dad. Thanks." Kieron said and guided me to the large grey couch before sitting down close to me. His hand never once leaving my back. I just shook my head, declining.

I was surprised that there wasn't anyone else in the office with him, no security or right-hand man. It seemed to be just Kellan working here.

"Don't you guys need security?" I asked Kieron quietly while Kellan was pouring two cups of coffee and bringing them over.

"There is, just not in here at the moment. Dad wanted you both to meet without a bunch of sentinels hanging around."

"Sentinels?"

"Workers, soldiers. The men that are out on the streets working or the ones ranked below our generals." He explained.

"Oh."

"So, Talia," Kellan said as he handed one of the cups to Kieron and sat down on the love seat. "Tell me about yourself."

"Um, if I'm being honest, there isn't much to tell really." I confessed, not exactly sure what he was looking for. Did he want my education background, work, special talents? Should I just recite my resume?

"Now, lass, that's simply not true. Where did you grow up?" Kellan said and took a sip of his drink.

"Here in Boston. I went to Pryde University for college and now I work in an electronics store."

"Is that where you met my son? At University? I tried to get him to go to Harvard, you know, but the fool is stubborn and wouldn't accept any help so when he didn't get in on his own accord, that was it. I offered."

"You know I wanted to get into a college on my own, by myself. It was important to me that I have that accomplishment for myself. Besides, I'm proud of going to Pryde University. It's a good school." Kieron cut in.

"But not as good as Harvard."

Kieron rolled his eyes and stared at his father over the rim of his coffee cup.

"Anyway, that is neither here nor there."

"I did meet him at school, but if I understand right, he was out of school when we met. He had just come back for a party with Trenton and we met at the party." I wanted to try and help Kieron get his father off the Harvard topic. Obviously, it was still a sore subject for the both of them.

"Ah, the classic college party hook-up." Kellan said with a laugh. "Well, you made an impression. I don't think any of the women my son has taken to bed in the last five years have even gotten a call back. But here he is now, starting a war for you."

"I didn't ask him to." I said strongly, defensively.

"I understand that, but lass, please don't misunderstand. You and my son are wanting me to put my men on the line to protect you and our clan. In order to do so, I need something from you."

"Dad," Kieron started, moving to the edge of his set, but his dad put up one hand to silence him.

"What is that?" I asked, sitting up straighter.

"You've been living with the son of the Italian don for years. I need intel on him. Preferences, habits, routines. I need information on his father and their operation. That is the price."

I sat and thought back to Luca and the good times we did have back in the beginning. Could I do that to him? Could I betray him in such a way?

But then I remember the nights I laid awake in fear that he would use my body for his own pleasure regardless of if I wanted it. I remember the bruises on my ribcage from kicks so hard I didn't think I would be able to breathe right. I remember the vile words yelled in my face for so long.

"Easy." I said to Kellan, then I looked to Kieron who was watching my every move. I nodded once; sealing my fate and giving allegiance to my Irish savior.

Chapter Nine

Kieron

I knew he would love her.

Even through the bruising, I knew my dad would see her beauty and be a goner.

Kellan Tavish always was a sucker for beautiful women. I could see his eyes sparkle at the prospect of getting more information on his enemy and having Talia around longer.

I pulled Talia closer to me.

We might not be anything right now, but I will not let anyone else, least of all my father, try to take her from me.

Apparently, the movement didn't go unnoticed by my father, who leaned back in his seat and spread his thighs in an aggressive gesture and smirked at me.

My father wasn't an unattractive man; he takes great care of his body like he had taught me to do, his hair is dark brown and peppered with grey streaks and he did have a sharp jaw. I'd heard from girls in high school that he was a total DILF and I'd had a few girls try to get to him through me.

That was a great experience that I wish to never repeat again. And he knew it.

"Before I have you answer my questions about the Garzino's, I need to ask you one question. And do not think of lying to me." He asked Talia.

I could feel her shrink into my body and press into me. I knew she was nervous and on a very real level, I was happy that she wasn't into my dad. That she came to me for comfort.

"Forgive me for the bluntness of this question, but what happened to your face?"

It was obvious that Talia had tried to cover the marks, I had been looking for them because Trent told me. I don't know if I was necessarily surprised that Kellan asked her point blank, Dad wasn't exactly known for being delicate.

"I fe-" Talia started to recite the same lie that she had told me, that they had told Trenton. I put my hand on her thigh, right about her knee, and squeezed. She needed to tell the truth.

"I was hit." She said softly, looking down at her lap.

"I can see that. By whom?" Kellan asked roughly.

"I… It's…Please…" Talia started, her voice started to shake and I could tell she was fighting within herself on if she should say the words and place blame or not.

"Luca did this to her." I said, doing it for her. Talia turned to me and her eyes were lined with tears.

"Luca did this to me." She whispered.

I turned to my father and without a doubt he can see the rage and violence in my expression.

"Well," Kellan took a deep breath and leaned his elbows on his knees. "That just won't do."

"I'm going to make sure that he never does something like this again. I'll make sure that he never comes close to you, never breathes your name." I snarled, gripping her fingers tighter as if I could take back every rough awful, malicious touch from that son of a bitch with my own.

"I agree." My father said.

Talia's sobs were audible and I could feel the shakes that she was trying to hide.

"I'm sorry." She said softly, wiping the tears. "This is so nice of you and so comforting to know that I have someone in my corner. But you don't understand everything. He has evidence on me and I can't let anything happen to my family. I could…I could go to jail, but he is threatening my sister."

I turned to my father, trying to hold back a smirk.

"Oh, we know, lass." Kellan smirked as well.

"I told you, Talia. I kept my eye on you." I said and squeezed her thigh again.

"What do you mean-"

"I mean," I interrupted her "We know how your sister was being beaten, badly. We know how you saved her and how you protected others from his *deadly* abuse."

Her jaw dropped and the sobs were immediate. Talia cried and cried and cried.

My dad might be a horny asshole, but at least he is a sensitive guy as well because instead of looking at me with annoyance that my girl was weeping, he simply grabbed a box of tissues and brought it over. He sat on the edge of his seat and held them out for her to take.

"I'm sorry," My beautiful girl said through her tears, "I just, I never meant for it to get this far. I was just trying to protect my family."

I smiled and put my arm around her. "And that's why you keep attracting these mafia men like moths to a flame. Going to the enth degree to protect your loved ones, that's sacred. It's what we do."

"I have to tell you, lass. This might no come as a shock to you, but I've done much more for much less to protect my family. And anyone that is in my clan, I consider part of this family." Kellan said to Talia and I watched her shoulders relax, like the weight of the world seemed to lift off her shoulders. "What does he have on you exactly?"

"I don't know what kind of evidence he has on Auggie, or me, rather." She said.

"What does that mean?" I asked.

"Luca, he thinks that my sister Auggie killed her boyfriend."

"How?" Kellan asked her, picking up his coffee cup and taking another drink.

"When I walked in on that man hitting my sister as she was laying on the floor in a puddle of her own blood with him still hitting her, I lost it. I saw my sister being killed and I stepped in. I didn't mean to kill him at first, but then he turned on me. He got a few hits in, I got away and got him away from Auggie. But then he started talking about how I needed to stay out of it, mind my own business. Auggie still hadn't moved. I don't know what came over me. But in that moment, I could feel myself losing consciousness and I couldn't let her die."

"What happened then?" Kellan asked her.

"Instead of running and getting help, I charged at him." Talia crossed her arms over her chest and shrunk back into herself. "I wanted him away from us. I was smaller than him, weaker than him, and beaten up pretty badly. We were fighting, and I just - I just went crazy and tried to get him to stop. He tackled me to the ground and I hit my head but while I was on the ground, I fumbled around for something, anything to get him off me. I grabbed the fire poker by her fireplace and just started hitting."

"Damn it." I seethed. My rage, that had already been simmering, turned to a full inferno. "The fucker is lucky that he's dead. I would have fucking shredded his goddamn skin from his bones."

Talia looked at me with surprise and her eyes looked even bigger with the shimmer from the tears pooling in her eyes.

"Calm down, son. Your girl took care of it already." My dad looked at me with a chuckle and a knowing look.

"I trusted Luca." She said and it felt like a knife twisting in my gut. The jealousy that he had been trusted by her, had gotten to hold her and be there for her and then the anger that he dared to betray that trust.

"He had been my person. I thought…He hadn't let me down before, that's why it was so hard for me to accept the abuse and leave. That night, after I realized that my sister's ex wasn't going to wake up, I called Luca to help. I knew that his family was powerful and… I don't know what I was thinking. I thought he could help. And he did. But not without a price." She said sadly.

"The price being your wellbeing and happiness?" I asked sarcastically.

"He never explicitly said what he wanted from me. Just that I follow his rules and be there for him. It started so slowly that I didn't realize it and when I finally did, it was too late. The sweet moments and affection had gone, leaving only the pain and fear."

"What were his rules, lass?" My dad asked, pushing through to get the answers he needed. Thank fuck for that because I was seeing red.

"Don't talk to other men. Don't accept phone numbers, compliments, anything like that. Only dress in grey, beige or black unless it's been pre-approved. Don't be late home. Don't leave the apartment unless given permission, with him or for work. He would decide what I ate or drank when out. He was in total control of the food in the house as well. I wasn't supposed to text people, I was to only have his phone number in my phone. Don't drink to excess. Don't talk to him unless spoken to. Don't let anyone know about the abuse or how his family is. And always, *always* put out when he wants it. There's more, but those are the main ones."

"And if you didn't follow?" My dad prodded gently. I felt my hackles raise even more, hoping that what I already knew was the only thing that was going to be divulged.

"It started with tight grips that left bruises but he always followed by apologies and gifts. Then that turned into shoves and pushes, hard enough to knock me over but again, apologies and gifts. Promises that it would never happen again." Talia put her hand to her mouth and she looked so…broken. But I would help her put herself back together again. I would.

"After a few weeks, it moved onto slaps, hits, always hard enough to get my attention and make me afraid, but never hard enough to leave lasting marks. I finally started drinking when I got home in case he needed to use me to get off, I wouldn't remember it. This last time though, this last time was the worst. It became so bad that I needed a drink to stand the sight of him but not drinking to excess was one of his rules. I ignored it."

"So it was escalating. The whole relationship." I said roughly.

"Yes." She whispered.

"That son of a bitch." I said through clenched teeth. I could feel my molars protest, but if I unclenched my jaw, who knows what I would say and the last thing Talia needed was me going off the rails.

"If he finds out…" She said and I could see the stress and anxiety start to manifest. She was wringing her hands together, her foot started to bounce.

"What did you think was going to happen by coming with my son? You walked right into the lion's den of his enemy. Luca will know if he hasn't found out already and then his father will as well." Kellan said with a wave of his hand as if that piece of information didn't matter to him. I knew it didn't. Kellan Tavish wasn't afraid of anyone.

"I… Kieron said… I can't…" She stuttered.

"I told her I'd protect her. Like I told you before." I said to my father.

"I know what you said, Kieron. But I need her to understand that there are consequences to what has happened now. Not that I don't relish a chance to take the Garzino empire to the ground. She will stay here at headquarters."

"Wait, Dad," I started to cut in. She was meant to stay at my beachfront with me where we could relax, where we could just reconnect and be. Not surrounded by all this violence and planning that went on in headquarters. Sure, it was locked up tighter than Fort Knox, but mentally, she needed to be free. Looking over the waves as they crashed on the water and breathing in the fresh salt air.

"My decision is final. She stays here where there is more protection." Kellan said strongly, his tone leaving no room for any discussion. It was the tone I'd heard many times, usually accompanied by a kill order. "And I can keep an eye on things."

"Yes, Skipper." I said, my anger was thinly veiled and I knew that even though I'd tried to hide it. Talia sat beside me, her eyes cast downward.

"Talia," I turned to her and took her hands in mine once more. "Trenton, my father and I, we've all discussed a plan. It won't be immediate because we need to do this smart. My father wants to completely take them down, I will settle for serving you Luca's head on a silver platter."

"Talia, you need to understand that this is going to get much worse before it gets better, but I can promise you that no harm will come to you." My father said and walked back over to his desk.

"What about Auggie? My parents?" Talia asked, her voice was small but I could hear the bit of hope that had started to bleed through.

"No harm will come to them either. Right, Dad?" I said louder, a clear signal to my father that I meant business. This was important to me and he would respect her wishes.

"On my honor."

Talia sobbed once and then a smile broke out. One that looked bright and light like she hadn't felt any kind of relief in years and I felt myself mirror her.

"Thank you. Thank you so much." She whispered and brought her palm to my cheek. I couldn't help it; I leaned right into it.

"Of course." I whispered to her, wrapping my fingers around her forearm to keep her hand on me.

"As touching as this moment is for the reunited lovers," my father interrupted. If I had my gun on me, I would have shot him for interrupting us. "We need to discuss what happens from here."

"Yes, sir. Thank you." Talia said respectfully and I rolled my eyes at her use of a title. A little jealous too.

"As of now all our business dealings with the Garzino's and their affiliates are done. We were one of their most prominent suppliers for their laundering business front, but now they are going to be scrambling. I will discuss with Trenton if he still wants to continue with his part of the plan to infiltrate and tear down from the inside. Kieron, you take Talia to her room here in the building and have her settle in. I gave her the apartment next to yours since I'm certain you would want to be watching over her yourself regardless of what I say. Talia, my dear, please leave a few hours open tomorrow morning and we can have a meeting to really discuss Luca and what you know. It was nice to meet you, lass." My father said, a clear dismissal as he went back to studying the reports and papers in front of him. Orders given, I stood up and put my hand on her lower back as she also stood.

"Thank you." She said softly and I took her hand to lead her through the room back to the elevator. Talia was silent as we walked, as we waited for the elevator, as we entered the elevator and I pressed the button to her, our, floor.

"Are you-"

"Is it over?" She asked me, those bright, wide eyes looking at me with disbelief.

"Is what over?"

"The fear. The pain." I walked up to where she was leaning against the metallic, shiny wall of the elevator and took her face in my hands. The bruises are awful; purple and yellow, they stand for such hate, but they are a testament to how far this beautiful woman would go to protect someone she loves.

"On my life, I will never let him hurt you again." I whisper with as much emotion as I can imbue in that promise.

She doesn't speak, doesn't move, but her eyes are looking at me, darting all over my face and I'm not worried about her silence. It's expected even since I seemingly came out of nowhere and rescued her.

Just as the bell is about to ring telling us we have reached the right floor, Talia surged forward and kissed me. This kiss was passionate and oh-so-welcome. Her small hands wrapped around my waist and she pulled me closer into her. She started to pull away from me when the door opened, but I couldn't let her move yet. I slid my fingers up to her hair and gently tilted her head up so I could deepen the kiss.

I licked her lips and she opened her mouth so I could taste her and heard myself groan.

Just as I was about to push her back towards the wall so I could lift her up, I felt her entire body freeze and tense.

Something was wrong. I'd done something wrong.

"Talia?" I asked her, slowly releasing her from my space and trying not to move in a way she thought was threatening.

"Yes?" Her voice was monotone and dull, like all emotion had left her. My heart dropped and I immediately backed as far away from her as I could.

"Talia?" When she noticed where I was standing, her light came back to her eyes and she started to tear up.

"I'm sorry. I'm sorry. Please." Talia wrapped her arms around herself and turned to the wall of the elevator, leaning her head against it.

"Don't be sorry, baby. I'm sorry. I got carried away. Please, don't be afraid."

I whispered. I wanted to go to her and hold her, kiss her tears away and promise that everything would be okay.

She didn't say anything back to me, but her sobs made the guilt I felt turn ten times worse.

"Want to see your apartment?" I asked after a moment. Maybe giving her her own space will make her feel safer.

Talia turned to me with wonder in her eyes and I saw a transformation take place before my own eyes. Her shoulders straightened, she held her head high, she stood with more confidence as she swung her blonde hair over her shoulder.

"Yes, please." She said with a smile and pressed the open button before she walked out of the elevator and left me in her wake.

Chapter Ten

Talia

I watched Kieron's back muscles move with his motions to open the apartment door. The hallways were like a hotel; weird ass carpet, plain walls, and doors every few feet from each other.

I tried to push down the weird feeling that had taken up residence in my chest after the almost dissociative state that I entered in the elevator. I don't know what I had been thinking, kissing him like that. But fuck, was it a good kiss. A kiss that I would definitely be thinking about later when I was all alone. He was so strong and so kind, but then he gripped my hair and turned my head up swiftly. I don't know why, but I entered some kind of trance that made me emotionless. Like when Luca wanted sex and I just had to do it.

I felt awful after seeing the look on Kieron's face when he realized that I'd mentally gone into hiding because he'd moved too quickly. How could he even want me like this? I don't want to be around myself.

"Your palace, my lady." Kieron said, pushing the door open and standing aside. I smiled at him and stepped through the door. I stepped through and felt him right behind me.

The light flickered on and I couldn't believe my eyes.

The apartment that he promised was beautiful and simple. There was a bed, a living room set, a massive TV that was much too big for me, and a simple, yet inclusive kitchenette. The entire place as far as I could see had a modern grey, white and stainless-steel look.

"Wow," I whispered and stepped farther into the living room.

"It's not much, I know. But it's yours. I can take you shopping to decorate it and we can make it how you want." Kieron said behind me. I could hear the hopefulness that I wouldn't be disappointed with what he was offering.

"Kieron, it's beautiful. It's more than I need. Then I deserve." I said softly as I walked farther into the room.

A large, warm hand took wrapped loosely around my forearm. I knew I could break the hold if I wanted to, but instead I turned and looked at the person who held onto me. Kieron was staring at me so intently that I could feel the anger from him.

"Don't say that."

"What?"

"Don't say that something I'm giving you is not what you deserve. You deserve far, far more than you've gotten, and I intend to give you the world." He said, his eyes locking onto mine and not letting me go.

"Thank you,"

Kieron let go of my arm, letting his hand slide into his pocket. The other hand went to the nape of his neck. My eyes flickered down, with the movement, Kieron's white tee had risen and I got a peek of the toned v of muscle he had. He'd obviously not let his figure go in the five years we'd been apart. If anything, the giant of a man I knew five years ago had grown even bigger.

"Of course." Kieron smiled when he caught my eye and I could feel a blush heat my cheeks.

"What happens now, Kieron? Do I just stay here and hope that Luca forgets about me? Do I give you and your father all the information I have on his family and wait until it is taken care of? Do I get my family out of here? How do I keep everyone safe? What about my job?" I started to ramble. The repercussions of everything started to come to the forefront of my mind now that things had calmed down just a bit again. Luca would kill everyone, not because he wants me, but because he wants me to suffer.

"Talia, baby, take a deep breath." Kieron said calmly over my heaving breaths. "We will figure it out. I promise."

A knock on the front door sounded loudly and I jumped closer to Kieron, who caught me with open arms.

"Mr. Tavish?" A male voice called out.

"Jonny, come in." Kieron pulled me closer and whispered softly in my ear. "That's just one of the guards. No need to be frightened."

A shorter man with cropped brown hair wearing an all-black ensemble walked in and shut the door behind him.

"Kieron, we have a problem. Mr. Garzino is here and demanding to have Ms. Jones back. We have him contained, but there have been a few injuries." Jonny told Kieron.

Kieron's whole demeanor changed. He was still cradling me and still put me between him and any harm, but his expression, his energy. It all became sinister. A smile creeped on his gorgeous face and it became intimidating.

"Good. I'll be right there." Kieron said calmly. Jonny nodded and left the room silently.

"Do you want to be there for this?" He asked as soon as the door shut.

"Will he see me?"

"Never again." Kieron vowed.

"What are you going to do to him?"

"What am I going to do or what do I want to do? Because those are two very different questions, baby."

"What are you going to do?" I asked.

"Ask him to leave. Tell him your debt has been repaid three or four times over and he needs to forget you exist."

"Do you think that will work?"

"No, not a chance." Kieron said with a chuckle.

"What will you do then?" Kieron sighed. He probably knew what I was trying to get from him. I didn't want Kieron to get hurt, I didn't want anyone else to get hurt because of me.

"I won't be the one to strike first." He promised me and led me out of the room.

* * *

Luca was shouting so loudly that I could hear him the moment we stepped off the elevator. Kieron assured, promised and vowed to me that Luca would not see me through the glass, but I was still terrified. This man who had been my own personal Devil, my own torturer for months, for years, was angry and my body was conditioned to cower and protect myself.

"No one but me comes close to her, understand me?" Kieron barked at one of the guards next to the room I guessed they were holding Luca in. His curse words were flying and free intermixed with Italian. He was livid.

"Sure man." The guard answered and gestured for me to follow him to the next door. I had a death grip on Kieron's hand, holding it so hard I was surprised he hadn't gently pried it off yet.

"He's good, you'll be safe." Kieron whispered.

"What about you?"

Kieron chuckled and kissed my forehead softly. "No harm will come to me. Go with Cillian. He will make sure you're safe and you will be able to hear and see us."

I nodded slowly, scared to let him go into the same space as my abuser. What if they talked and Kieron changed his mind?

"Go, baby." He whispered and gave me a nudge to the man he called Cillian.

"Be careful."

"For you." He flashed me a panty-dropping smile and walked through the door, making sure that no one could see out of the room.

"Miss." Cillian said, holding his arm out to have me enter the adjoining room.

Kieron promised.

So, I went in.

Chapter Eleven

Kieron

I knew she was nervous. How couldn't she be? But I needed to do this, for her and for myself.

The fucker had turned himself over basically, walking into his enemy's lair with minimal protection and I was itching to give him the beat down he deserved.

"Well, well, well. You must be Kieron Tavish. The little crybaby of the Irish mafia. The bitch must have whored herself out in order to get in here with all of you hiding her from me." The sad sack of shit was seething, his anger making his words difficult to understand with his accent. Fuck, that was annoying. I'm sure that it didn't help that the two of us were next in line for our respective, proverbial thrones and I was rising through the ranks quicker and more respected than he was.

"Well, Luca Garzino. What brings you here?" I said, crossing my arms over my chest and choosing to try and go as long as possible without bringing up Talia.

"You fucking know why I'm here. You have her. She's mine, give her back."

"I don't know who you're talking about. But if you've lost a woman, I think it's best to just cut your losses. You obviously aren't great at keeping them…satisfied." I said with a smirk and sat in the chair across the table from him. My men hadn't cuffed him, but he was roughed up. He obviously put up a good fight. His oily hair was all out of place and his nose was bleeding. It definitely looked broken.

"Don't fuck with me, Tavish. I tracked her phone and her GPS tag. She's here. Little bitch ran and cried wolf. Now turn her over."

That was interesting. I figured about the phone, as much of a pain in the ass he was, he wasn't stupid. But the GPS tag; was it an implant, a piece of jewelry, sewn into her clothes? I'd have to look later.

"Now, now, Luca. That's no way to talk about a lady. Tell me, who are you looking for?"

"My girlfriend."

"It definitely doesn't sound like she's your girlfriend. It doesn't sound like she's anything of yours. Especially not with those bruises you've left on her pretty face." I said, my cocky demeanor changing to show him that I was pissed and ready for war.

"What does it matter to you? She's my girlfriend." The fucker spat at me.

"Not anymore. She's mine."

Luca stood up and lunged for me, but I sidestepped his attack.

"You don't know her. She's not worth starting this war over. She's a worthless cunt; a used-up piece of ass who means nothing. She fucking *owes* me." Luca said lowly with a sadistic smirk.

I saw red. My entire line of vision narrowed to his slimy face and I cocked my fist. But wouldn't let it fly. It took all of my willpower to hold back. But I promised her I wouldn't start a fight. I was trying to earn her trust and this was how it would start.

"So, she sucked your dick too. Fucking slut." He said, his eyes taking in my cocked fist.

"Shut your motherfucking mouth or I will shut it for you. For at least eight weeks." I said through clenched teeth, my promise to Talia still fresh in my mind.

I wouldn't break a promise to her. Too many men have done that to her and I will not be one of them. Not again.

"Talia Jones is mine. And I will tell you right now, if she is not back in my apartment tomorrow by 8 am, I will take it as an official call to war. You have been warned."

"Take it however you want, Garzino. You won't see her again, you won't touch her again, you won't think about her again. Do you fucking understand me?" I leaned in closer to him and grabbed the collar of his shirt, twisting the fabric and forcing him closer. I had a good five inches on him and basked in the satisfaction when he shrunk back, trying to get away. Luca brought his hands up and shoved me away with as much force as he had, but I barely budged. I wasn't going to give him the satisfaction of moving me around.

"You don't know what you're doing. You don't know her. She's not some little girl that needs protecting, she is a wolf in sheep's clothing. You're starting a war over a nobody."

I was so sick of his voice.

"I know exactly who she is. I bet I know her better than you do. And regardless, you're a piece of shit *abuser*."

He just chuckled darkly. "Your loss. I've given you my terms and if she's not back by 8 am, we will be at war."

"Understood. Now get the *fuck* out." I seethed and shoved past him to open the door.

Luca didn't say another word, and I was fucking glad because I was barely hanging on to my self-control. When he walked out the door, I let my fist fly.

I felt the pain when my knuckles broke through the drywall, but in that moment, letting myself hit something - even an inanimate object that was a poor substitute for the real source of my anger - felt amazing.

"Kieron?" I heard her twinkling voice that immediately brought some relief to my anger that was burning brightly in my chest.

"Talia? What are you doing in here?" I turned around quickly to face her but also to hide the hole in the wall.

"Cillian said it was safe to leave the viewing room, that security told him Luca had left the building. Are you okay?" She asked, walking into the room and coming up to me.

"I'm fine, are you okay?"

"I am. You did what you promised." She took my hand and pulled it from behind my back to stare at the damage I'd done.

"I did, I tried." I felt my shoulders drop with the statement. I didn't hit him, I wanted to, but I didn't. But I still hurt myself and she was going to take that on herself because *I* needed to let my anger out.

"You still got hurt." She whispered and took my already bruising hand in hers. It was covered in a fine dust but thankfully no cuts or broken skin. Talia brought my fist to her lips and gently kissed my knuckles.

I couldn't help but watch her and hold my breath as she freely gave me affection. Being very cognizant of what happened last time, I froze.

"I'm okay. Just a bruise, it's nothing."

"What happens now?" She asked me softly, still holding my hand close to her face.

"Now, we are at war." I said with a soft smile and I slowly moved my hand to cup her cheek.

"What happens to my sister? To my parents? I haven't talked to them in months. How do I protect them?" She looked at me with her big dark eyes full of concern.

"Cillian!" I barked, not moving my hand or out of her arms.

"Yes, cousin?" Cillian said as he rushed into the room.

"Get with Jonny and have a guard detail be put on both Augustine Jones and her parents. It is a 24-hour guard shift with absolutely no access to anyone new and if there is any deviation in schedule, routine, or familiars, I need to be notified immediately. There is no room for error on this, do you understand?" My voice was strong and sure, I knew what needed to happen now and I wasn't going to have my girl be scared anymore.

I look back at Talia and see her awe. Her big, brown eyes were open and trusting, something that I know she hasn't felt in so long, her pretty pink lips are parted slightly, and I can see her tongue dart out to moisten her lower lip. My attention zeroes in on that motion.

I cannot get hard right now.

"Yes, understood." Cillian said. When I looked at him, I saw a fondness, an understanding of some kind, in his eyes when he looked at Talia.

"Make it happen by 8 pm tonight." I could tell my jealousy was seeping through my tone, but I did my best to keep it in check. What had happened between the two of them in the 20 minutes I was in here dealing with the asshole? Granted, Talia did have that way about her that caused most people to like her instantly. Even as demure and scared as she was now, she still shone brightly.

"Will do." He said. The fucker still hadn't left.

"Dismissed." I said roughly.

"If I may?" Cillian said. Cillian is one of the guards, a good soldier, and my second cousin. He'd grown up in this life just like I had so usually when he had a question or idea, he shared it freely. I always heard him out because, unfortunately, the fucker had good ideas and was skilled at what he did.

"Yes?"

"Talia needs a detail on her as well. Someone outside her apartment here and with her whenever she leaves."

I knew he was just trying to help. He knew about how I felt and he knew about the dangers she would truly be in now. But what I couldn't stand was the thought that he didn't think I knew how to properly protect her.

"Excuse me?" I seethed, turning my back on Talia and putting myself between them.

"Kieron," I heard Talia say but my attention was focused on Cillian.

"You think I don't know how to protect her? Like those things weren't the first things I was going to do once I left this room?"

"Kieron, no disrespect meant." Cillian said, his hands up in front of him to calm me down. "I simply was wondering if you wanted me to get that started as well. I know how much she means to you."

That made me feel better.

Slightly.

"Kieron, I was just talking to Cillian while you were with Luca. To take my mind off of what was going to happen and I mentioned that I was scared what he would do if he ever got me alone. That's why Cillian was offering. Granted, he should have phrased it better." She said with a pointed look to Cillian, then looked back at me with soft eyes. "I know you're going to protect me. I knew it back then and I know it now."

"I was just a cheeky fucker back then, but you knew?"

"I did. No one had ever made an impression like you and I never stopped thinking about you even when it would have saved me a lot of heartache." She confessed and I wanted nothing more than to kiss her, but the memory from the elevator was still fresh in my mind. So instead, I brought her hand up to my lips and kissed the back of her hand softly.

"I never stopped thinking of you either."

"Lord, don't we all know it." Cillian said from the side.

"Fucking leave, Cillian! Get the protection detail on Mr. and Mrs. Jones, Augustine Jones and Talia started." I ordered, throwing up my middle finger behind Talia's back to him.

"I'm going, I'm going." Cillian walked out the door with his hands up and laughing.

"Have I thanked you today?" Talia said, looking up at me as she stepped closer into my body and rested her head on my chest. I was positive she could hear just how fast my heart was beating for her.

"Yes, you have. Only about a hundred times. You don't have to thank me, baby. I'm making up for all the times I should've been there." I confessed.

We walked out of the room and I could have sworn Talia felt lighter. Her shoulders weren't as tense and she had a confident look in her eyes. We walked hand-in-hand towards the elevator and I pressed the number for our floor, I needed to get her sorted for the evening; maybe order some food and get her comfortable clothes and then I would leave. It's been a long fucking day, even for me.

"Will you come over for a bit? I have questions." She asked after a few moments of silence.

"Yeah, of course. I'd be surprised if you didn't." I said with a chuckle.

When the elevator doors opened, she led the way to her apartment door. I still needed to get her a copy of my apartment key. I hoped that it would make her feel safer here, but I also, selfishly, wanted to pretend that we were in a relationship.

Pulling her key from my jacket pocket, I handed it to her and let the cool metal drop in her hand. It had a small keychain on it made of cheap plastic, but it said number 15 for her apartment number here.

"Are you sure?" She asked.

"Without a doubt."

"We barely know each other now."

"True. But there is plenty of time for that." I said with a smile and waited for her to turn the key and accept that this was her home now. If she wanted it.

"That is true." She replied and turned the key, accepting the shelter.

"Home sweet home." She whispered.

***

"I'm going to run next door and get you some clothes and tomorrow we can go get you some new ones. Also, I was thinking of getting pizza for dinner. Do you like a certain kind?" I asked her after she settled in on the couch. I showed her how to work the remote for cable so she could watch some TV and unwind.

Today had been taxing.

"Whatever you want is fine." She said softly. But I remembered what she had told me about how Luca controlled her food and I wanted to be sure that she knew that wouldn't happen with me, ever. I walked back towards the couch where she sat nervously, picking at her nails and eyes flitting around.

Kneeling in front of her, I put one hand on her knee and one under her chin, forcing her to look at me.

"What do *you like*? It can be anything. Pepperoni, onions, mushrooms, sausage, plain cheese, any of the combinations, hell I'll even get you pineapple if you want it. But please, Talia, know that here, with me, you will have access to any and all food you want. You will never go hungry or wonder if I'm going to allow you to eat. I want you to. I want you to be healthy and be happy." I said earnestly. She was a beautiful girl, but she was skinny, almost too skinny. Her curves that I remembered and lusted over were gone and her skin, even bruised and swollen as it was, looked pale. Luca had used food as a training weapon and the thought of what he put her through made me sick.

"Are you sure?"

"Yes, baby. I'm 100% sure. So, what pizza do you like?" I said with an encouraging smile.

"Pepperoni." She said in a small voice, but I could see the smile on her lips start to form with the prospect of getting a food I'm guessing she hadn't gotten in a long time. My heart warmed with the realization that she trusted me just a little more.

"You got it. I'll be back in five minutes." I said, standing and cupping her chin.

"Please," She said, the smile disappearing from her face and she jolted up. "Be quick."

"I will. Promise." I winked and walked towards the door.

Chapter Twelve

Talia

"He said he would only be five minutes, he said he would only be five minutes, he said he would only be five minutes," I whispered over and over to try and keep myself calm. Truthfully, I was so thankful that Kieron had offered more comfortable clothes and food. I was starving after not eating all day and barely anything last night. Plus, I was still in my black jeans and standard-issue 'Electrodes' polo from the store I worked at.

Did I work there anymore? Was I going to have to quit? Luca knew exactly where I worked, when I worked and who I worked with. Were they safe?

"He said he would only be five minutes," I started whispering and pacing the length of the apartment again. Would Kieron expect something from me for his kindness? Would he expect me to put out or work for his father? Oh god, would he pass me around to the guys in his gang? I started to feel nauseous.

Had I traded one jailor for another?

"That's not him," I argued out loud against my inner thoughts.

I heard a knock on the door and I cautiously walked over to the dark wood, sturdy front door with a peep hole in the middle. Leaning up on my tiptoes, I looked through the small glass and hoped it was Kieron.

"It's just me, Talia." I heard his deep voice and saw him standing, waiting patiently for me to open the door and let him in.

"If you need some time by yourself, I understand. I can leave the clothes out here and I'll bring you some food when it gets here." He said loud enough for me to hear through the thick wood separating us.

He looked as if he had changed into comfier clothes as well and I eyed the pile of clothes he was holding.

Ripping the door open, I took the clothes from his arms and held them close as he laughed at my movements.

"I just brought some of my comfy clothes, if that's alright." He explained. "They are going to swim on you, but I always thought that too-big clothes were comfier to sleep in anyway."

"Me too."

His hair looked like it had been brushed and so smooth as it flowed to his shoulders. I always knew Kieron was attractive, I'd been drooling after him since the first moment I heard his voice all those years ago. But seeing this side of him; the sensitive yet powerful side that proved that no one would dare go against him, the side that would do anything to bring me comfort was breathtaking.

"So, pepperoni pizza is on its way for you, meat lovers for me, and then we can watch a movie. Sound good?" He asked and walked over to the couch, picking up the remote and flipping through the channels.

"If that's okay with you." My response was immediate, causing Kieron to look at me.

"Is it okay with you, baby?" He asked. I loved when he called me baby. I'd never really felt taken care of; I was- or used to be - a strong, independent woman who was fearless in the pursuit of what I wanted so I didn't need anyone to take care of me. But the rare times where I felt vulnerable enough to be taken care of, no one was there. My sister was younger so she always needed to be taken care of, my parents decided I didn't need them once I hit 18 years old and Luca tried but always seemed to fall short. Then the abuse started and it was my job to care for him solely.

The times that Kieron has called me baby today, I felt cherished. Like I could depend on him and he would take care of me. Like I could be vulnerable.

I nodded and smiled at him softly.

"Good. Now come over here and help me pick a movie. Then when the food gets here, you can ask me all your questions and I'll answer them as honestly as I can." He said, holding his hand out and dragging me towards the comfortable couch.

* * *

"What's your first question?" Kieron asked me as I rested my back against his front, at his insistence.

"Are you seeing someone?" It may have seemed like a stupid question, but I needed to know. He was surely acting as if he wasn't attached to anyone, but I needed to hear him say the words.

"No." He said with a chuckle. I let go of the breath I wasn't even aware that I'd been holding.

"Why did you leave that morning?"

"I told you why."

"But why didn't you say anything back then, tell me a reason? I would've understood." I said earnestly and took a sip of my beer. Kieron had brought a six-pack over from his apartment while I got changed. He was right, his clothes were enormous on me. I had to roll the waistband three times to get it to even stay on my hips and cuffed the pant legs three times as well just so I wouldn't trip over them.

"I couldn't just open up to someone about my family running the mafia. Can you imagine if I had said 'Oh hey, Talia. By the way, no matter how much I want this to happen, it can't. My father is the clan leader for the Irish mafia running here in Boston and he is grooming me to take over so this can't happen because of that. At least not right now. Wait for me? But please, I need to know how you feel just once so I can jerk off to the memory for years to come.' That would've gone over greatly." He said with a chuckle and his hand went to the nape of his neck. A nervous tick, I've noticed he does quite often.

"True, it wouldn't have gone over well." I chuckle, wrapping my arms around myself. We were still waiting for the pizza to be brought up, but it was nice. A nice break between dramatic and scary episodes, I knew it was only going to get worse before it got better.

"It was one of the hardest things I've had to do." He said looking down at his feet that were propped up on the table. "But I did it for you."

"Really?" I said with snark.

"I know it doesn't seem like it. But you had such adventurous, hard goals that you had worked for and you were so close to finishing. I couldn't it from you. If I'd told you about my family and what we did… you'd have to give it up in some way. Big or small, I couldn't say. So, I didn't say anything, I couldn't do that to you." Kieron said. My jaw dropped and awe filled my chest. The fact that he remembered how important my dreams of being an engineer were to me was enough to touch my heart. That added to the fact that he put aside his wants in favor of mine, that's something that I haven't had in a long time.

"I know it was selfish," He started to say after a few moments of silence. "To take you home. But I felt such a strong connection to you, I just…I needed to know you."

"I'm so glad you did." I said softly, reaching over to take one of his large hands in between my two small ones. "The memory of our night together was what kept me sane. It would play in my head like a movie and remind me that not all people were like him. That I had been cared for, even for a moment."

Kieron looked at me with wide and vulnerable eyes.

"You know," he said with a slight smirk playing on his lips. "when you say things like that, it makes it very hard not to kiss you."

"Do you not want to kiss me?" I ask, inching closer to his warmth on the couch.

"I do, very badly. I have for years. And now that I have you, I want nothing more than to tear your clothes off and worship you like I should have been doing for years." He looks at me and I could see the fire, the want, the desire, burning brightly within him.

I wanted that. Him. All of it, anything he will give me.

I was also terrified.

"I saw how you reacted to the kiss in the elevator. I never want you to be scared, or flinch, or feel like you need to retreat into your mind ever again. Especially because of something I did." He said, his expression turning guilty. His dark brown eyes were thoughtful as he smoothed his beard down and then put his hand behind me to rest on the back of the couch.

"You don't have to feel bad about that." I whispered. "It was just a reflex."

"A reflex you've been trained to have because of someone hurting you and forcing you to do things. I don't ever want you to feel that way with me. I want to bring you happiness and safety, love and passion. I want you to feel like you. The good, the bad and the determined." He smiled at me. I moved close enough to him that our sweatpants-covered thighs were touching.

"I'm sorry."

"Please, don't be sorry. I'm sorry that I didn't get to you before. That reminds me, I need to knee-cap the jackass motherfucker that decided that you being with Luca Garzino was an alright idea and didn't tell me." Kieron's expression turned completely furious, murderous even. I'm so used to Luca's raging, his violence and throwing, that Kieron seemed almost serene as he sat by me; breathing heavily and clenching his fist on his knee.

"It's my-"

"I swear to god, Talia, if you say it is your fault that that motherfucker abused you and that the PI solider I put on your watch didn't have any fucking common sense to realize what was happening to you, I will scream." He said, his words coming out quickly and passionately.

"Okay."

"I promise you, none of this is your fault. Not one thing."

I so badly wanted to kiss him, wanted to relive the moment from the elevator and climb onto his lap and devour him. But I couldn't.

Not yet.

"Okay," I said softly. "I believe you."

The look on his face when those three words left my mouth was enough to make my heart feel lighter and brighter than it had in… years.

"You do?"

"I do." I said, feeling more confident by the minute.

Kieron and I sit there for a moment, letting the enormity of what I'd just admitted and decided on sink in.

"Good." He said with a smile and wrapped his arm around my shoulders, bringing me closer to his body so I could lean on his chest while we waited for the pizza.

* * *

I had forgotten what being full felt like. I had forgotten how amazing pepperoni pizza tastes.

Kieron had ordered two pizzas and breadsticks for us to share and was very encouraging whenever I started eyeing the box for another slice. I tried to not let the insecurities get the best of me.

Luca was never shy about telling me just how horrendous he found my body and how he was hiding and restricting food for me for my own good.

"No one wants to look at a fat slob. Much less live with one." He would say it over and over. Then the taunts got worse and more cutting. "If you put one more bite of food into your mouth, I swear to fuck you will regret it. Can't you see yourself? Aren't you disgusted? I'm disgusted and I have to look at you. God, it makes me sick. Just look at yourself!" He would scream and throw my plate across the room, throwing food everywhere.

I shook off the memory and grounded myself with Kieron, looking at the monstrous TV that was playing some car-chase movie.

"I'm full." I said and pushed the half-eaten pizza away from me, falling back on the couch.

"Okay, well I'll put the leftovers in the fridge before I leave and you can snack on it whenever you want. Sound okay?" He asked, sitting up and throwing a crust onto his empty pizza box. That man could put some food away. Granted, he was like 6'5" and covered with muscle. All that muscle needed food to grow.

I nodded and pulled my long hair back into a ponytail.

"I've been meaning to ask you. I know five years is a long time, you could have changed your mind, but why did you change your hair? Last I saw you, you were rocking black hair and a shaggy short bob with bangs. You told me all about how you didn't want people to think you were the typical blonde, sorority girl and you felt more like yourself with your edgy hair. Don't get me wrong, I think the blonde waves look amazing, but I just wondered why you went back to blonde." Kieron asked. He pulled on the end of my pony and then twisted his fingers in the strands.

"Luca wanted me to, made it a rule and so I had to obey and keep it. When we first started dating, I had grown my hair to my shoulders. It was still dark, still…me. But then he made a comment about how much more attractive I'd be if my hair wasn't so dark. So, I stopped coloring it black and went a bit lighter. That cycle continued until I became this. Complete Barbie and a doll for him to throw around as he pleases." I said softly.

I knew I had fallen far, had given up so much of myself but it wasn't until now that I realized I wasn't even a shadow of who I used to be. Of who I am inside, somewhere.

"You're not a doll." Kieron said. One of his fingers came under my chin and he slowly moved my face up to meet his eyes. "You're strong, so strong, and you've done what you've had to do to survive. That's a badass motherfucker right there."

I chuckled, the sound between a laugh and a sob.

"It's true. Don't feel bad because of what happened. Heal, grow and move on. Once it is safe for you, if you want to leave, you can. You can go and be whomever you want to be, with me or by yourself. But don't forget just how strong you really are." He said, his words ringing with sincerity.

I surged forward and kissed him. His soft lips were still, they moved against mine but he didn't try to overpower me. He was letting me set the pace.

I moved closer to his side and put one leg over his lap and wrapped my arms around his neck. I wasn't ready to sit on him like my core so badly wanted, but I needed to hold him, to be held by him. When I broke the kiss, I could feel the flush on my cheeks and the answering smile on his face made my heart beat even faster.

"Was that okay?" I asked shyly and Kieron groaned.

"More than okay. I really like kissing you." He said, one of his large hands sliding up my leg and resting on the outside of my upper thigh.

"I like kissing you too."

We sat there in silence, wrapped in each other and watching the movie.

Content.

Comfortable.

Finally, I felt safe.

Chapter Thirteen

Kieron

I don't know when Talia fell asleep but I wasn't going to wake her up. She looked peaceful, finally.

I looked down at her face studying the bruising of her skin and I couldn't help the surge of anger that she was marked in such violence.

I won't lie, I love leaving marks during sex. Bites, hickeys, their ass red from my hand. But the marks are always left in lust, always because I want to bring my partner more pleasure. The marks, if any, are consented to. I have never left a mark from anger on a woman. It's something I was engrained with, to never put my hands on a woman in anger.

Talia's eyes fluttered as she dreamed, a slight smile ghosted across her lips, and I smiled back at her, even though she couldn't see it. I pulled her in closer so one of my hands was supporting her back and the other wrapped around her legs. She was swallowed in my clothes, our foot of difference in height to blame. Some primal part of me was purring with the image of her in my clothes. Mine.

The action movie was playing softly in the background and I had no intention of getting up. Talia was asleep comfortably on me; she was safe, full and content, so I wouldn't be waking her up anytime soon. Who knew the last time she slept well.

I needed to get it together. I was so head-over-heels for this girl and I was falling for her quickly. But I needed to get more information. More basic information. Actually get to know her for her, not just a file that my soldier gave me. How did she take her coffee? What is her favorite childhood memory? Did she sleep on the left or the right side of the bed? I wanted to know more about her than just her file and the few precious hours I got five years ago.

Speaking of the file, I needed to rip Sion a new fucking asshole. I gave him very specific instructions about how his surveillance was meant to go, what to bring to me, what to do and the incompetent motherfucker let this happen. Sion is my father's PI that works for the clan so I assumed he would be trustworthy. My fingers curled protectively into Talia's skin, grounding me so I could calm down slightly.

The bruises were on his head.

The pain she'd endured was on his head.

Talia muttered in her sleep, tightening her hold on my shirt and her head dropped into the side of my neck. With each breath she exhaled, her warm breath tickled my skin and made a lock of my hair move. She was softly snoring and I felt so protective of the soft woman in my arms, it was kind of amazing.

The movie that neither of us cared to actually watch started to roll the credits and I was faced with a choice. Do I move her into the bed and then respectfully leave her to her own apartment, or do I stay here, let her sleep on me and watch over her? What would she want?

After a few minutes, far more than I needed, I picked her up and started walking over to the door that would lead into the small bedroom. After getting over how pissed I was that my father decided she would stay here and not at the beachfront, I was glad he gave her this apartment because I knew it came furnished with a king-sized bed. This girl, my girl, deserved all the luxuries in the world.

I lightly kicked open the white door and made my way through the darkness until my shin hit the edge of the bed. Leaning a knee on the edge, I tried to lay her down gently so I didn't wake her up. Her blonde hair fanned out and as soon as my hand left her body, she immediately curled in on herself protectively.

I clenched my teeth and felt my hands make fists at the fact that that monster had hurt her so much that even in sleep her body tried to protect itself.

Walking back into the front room, I sat back down on the couch. I wanted her to have a good nights sleep, but I also wanted to be here in case she had nightmares or woke up in a panic. A lot had happened today.

I turned the channel to some comedy show and made sure to turn the volume down low so I could hear if she made any kind of noise.

My eyes started to close and I finally let myself succumb to slumber, knowing that my girl was okay and safe.

* * *

Did I not shut the blinds? Why the hell is there one annoying beam that will not go away no matter where I move?

Then my memory snapped into place and I sat straight up. I looked around and saw Talia, curled up on the lounge chair next to the couch. Her arms were crossed under her head, and she lay leaning on the arm of the chair with her feet tucked under her and her head rested over her arms. Sometime during the night her hair had come free from the ponytail she'd put the golden waves back earlier.

"Talia?" I whispered.

Her eyes opened slowly, as if it was hard for her to be pulled back into reality. She blinked a few times and lifted her head.

"Hi," she whispered.

"Are you okay?" I asked. "What happened?"

"I woke up and you weren't there." She said softly. I sat up, shifting on the couch to sit closer to her.

"I didn't think you'd want me to sleep in the room with you. I was trying to be a gentleman." I chuckled and pulled my hair back into a low bun so it was out of my face. I wondered what time it was, I felt as if I hadn't slept much at all. The TV was still going and a different program was on. Talia yawned and let her head fall back onto her arms.

I looked down at my watch and found that it was only five in the morning and with the late night we had after everything, we couldn't have gotten more than two or three hours of sleep.

It also meant we only had three hours until Luca expected Talia to be back in his life.

How sorely he was mistaken.

"Why don't you go back to sleep in the bed? Is it comfy enough for you?" I asked her. I was up now, I needed to make sure the men were prepped and my father had some kind of plan for us.

"It's very comfortable. Thank you." She said, her eyes closed.

"Then let's get you back in it."

"Will you lay down with me?" She asked me quietly. So quietly that I thought I might have imagined it.

I kneel in front of her chair. Her hair had fallen in front of her face, just slightly. I let my fingers slide over her soft cheek, as gently as I could so I didn't hurt her bruising, and pushed the strands back behind her ear. I had to.

"Mmm," Talia moaned and moved her face in time with his hand.

"I'll lay down with you baby, just until you fall asleep." I said softly and slid my hands under her, lifting her into my arms.

"No, stay." She muttered. Talia's head fell back against my shoulder as I stood. I swear, my heart was trying to beat out of my chest. As she moved I could smell her sweet vanilla and lavender scent. It was intoxicating.

"I have to get some things prepared for today. But I'll be here until you fall asleep."

"Promise?" She whispered. I carried her back into her bedroom and let her slide under the covers before I climbed in after her.

"Promise." I whisper and hear her sigh happily.

The standard issue sheets that the clan put in all of the apartments were sterile and overly starched, but the duvet was heavy and crisp as I lifted it to cover us both.

But none of those things mattered. The only thing that mattered was the woman who turned into my warmth and put her forehead to my chest.

"Thank you." She muttered sleepily.

"Anytime." I kissed the top of her head. I felt her breathing even out after a few moments of silence and her body relaxed.

I couldn't fall asleep, I had to get the troops ready and figure out how my father wanted to handle this. I knew how I wanted to handle it, but as Second-In-Command, I still needed to defer judgement to the Skipper.

I just didn't want to leave this bed.

For the first time, in a very long time, I too felt at peace and whole.

Unfortunately, life especially in the mafia doesn't work like that. It's eat or be eaten, be smarter than your competition or die. So, I pulled her in tighter, savored the moment of Talia in my arms and then slid out of bed, replacing my body with one of the pillows.

She looked beautiful. Her long blonde hair wrapped around her like a glow coming from within. Her face was soft and she looked every bit like the girl who stole my heart all those years ago.

My heart clenched as I knew I had to leave her alone but I forced myself to turn away from her and walk out of the bedroom, slowly and quietly closing the door. My forehead rested against the white wood of the door as I pulled myself together.

One deep breath and I turned to the front door, walking with purpose so I could go be the leader I was.

This war was just starting and I was going to fucking win.

* * *

I slammed the door to my office closed after taking a quick shower and changing into my usual black jeans, fitted tee and my motorcycle boots with my black leather jacket over top. Stomping over to my desk; a dark, heavy wooden thing that I barely used if I'm honest, but sometimes its usefulness had its moments. I looked over the piles of paperwork that I refused to touch where in the middle of the desk was one solitary file with 'Garzino' labelled across it. At least not all of my men were incompetent.

Before I even opened the file, I pressed the intercom button and waited for Marcellie, the assistant we have for the clan, to pick up.

"It's a little early for mafia thug business, don't you think?" Marcellie's hoarse voice sounded fuzzy through the receiver. She was the kind of lady who smoked a pack of cigarettes a day, every day since I'd known her. And she'd been working for my family since I was a baby.

"Oh, shut it. I know you're awake, have smoked three cigarettes, and on the clock already, so don't be harping on me for calling you at 6 in the morning." I rolled my eyes. "I need you to get Sion and have him here in thirty minutes."

"That's asking a lot, boy." She rasped; muffled coughing sounded from the other end of the receiver. "Fine. Anything else?"

"Not at the moment, you old bat."

"Love you too." She said with a wet laugh and hung up the phone.

The very first thing I had to do today was sort out the bullshit with Sion because something wasn't sitting right.

I opened the file that had surveillance for Luca that I'd ordered once he left our building. I needed to know exactly where he went, who he met up with, what he did, in order to take him down. Inside were pictures of Luca, black and white, zoomed in photos obviously taken from a far-range lens. I had a perfect picture of every moment of his night from when he left to about an hour ago.

Flipping through the pictures, it was mostly as I had expected. Luca was a fucking asshole who had been rejected when he thought that he held all the cards. The first few photos were of him stalking out of the building, pushing bystanders and storming through downtown. He'd gone straight to the bar about a block away, the next few photos were of Luca power drinking and screaming into a cell phone. I was sure that he was going to go to some strip club or go start a fight, but the rest of the photos were of him sitting at the bar, getting sloppier and sloppier the more he drank.

He did hit on some bystanders, even taking one into the bathroom by the looks of it. Thank fuck there are no pictures of that. But he didn't leave the bar until about four in the morning based on the timestamp at the bottom of the photo. The next one, and the last one, was of Luca unlocking the front door to their apartment.

No. Not theirs. Not anymore.

Talia wouldn't go back there ever again.

A knock sounded on my office door interrupting my thoughts and Sion walked in. Sion was an older gentleman. He was a short man who took care of his body and even though everyone knew he was greying, Sion continued to color his hair and his beard brown like when he was younger. He had an impressive talent of being able to blend in anywhere, which is what made him such a good investigator.

Except for this time. When I was counting on him.

"You wanted to speak to me, boss?" His old Irish accent came through very strongly and still laced with sleep.

"I do. Come take a seat." I gestured to the chair in front of my desk. Unlike my dad, my office was really only for show. The walls and bookshelves were bare, I didn't have a comfortable seating area or personal touches. But in this instance, I don't think it really mattered.

"How can I help you?"

"I had some questions for you regarding my...outstanding project." I leaned my elbows over onto my desk and clasped my hands in front of me, looking over them at Sion.

"Yes?" Sion asked, picking an imaginary piece of lint off of his black slacks.

"The girl, Talia. There seem to be quite a few things that you left out of your reports."

"Kieron, I assure you that everything I discovered, aside from the details you specifically specified that you didn't want, was given to you."

"I can assure you," I said pointedly, his lack of ownership was going to cost him. "That that is not the case. Can you tell me again what details I told you I didn't want to know?"

"Place of residence, place of work, any lovers or repeated hook-ups unless in a relationship." Sion recited immediately.

"I believe I asked you to tell me anything else. Am I right?"

"Yes."

"Then why don't you tell me how *the fuck* this goddamn asshole got away with beating and raping her for months before some twist of fate put her back into my life!" I bellowed, throwing the photos of Luca's surveillance at him.

"Kieron, I can-"

"Explain? Yes, please, fucking *try*." I yelled at him, cutting him off.

"You didn't want to know about lovers! She had been living with him for a while and it started out as if it could be a kink, you know? I didn't think much of it!" Sion stood up and backed away with his hands in the air. As if that would stop me from beating his ass.

"You 'didn't think much of it'?" My anger and rage were growing in my chest, my fists were begging me to fly out and knock him out, and I couldn't think of anything except the bruises on her face, the marks he left on her and how I could have interceded long before now. I could hear myself snarl at him as my voice lowered dangerously.

"You must be getting complacent in your old age. Consider this your retirement." I said strongly. I couldn't kill him, no matter how much I wanted to. The bastard knew too much and if I killed him, there would be hell to pay from my father. And I needed to keep Kellan happy right now. "Do not ever come near Talia or myself again."

"Kieron, let's talk about this." Sion started; his body language reeked of desperation. "I didn't do anything wrong! I followed your orders for years! I did what you asked!"

"Do you honestly and truly believe that? You were meant to warn me if she was in any danger. You were meant to keep an eye on her safety. And what did you do? You did nothing. You sat and watched her get beaten and broken and you thought that was okay. For a man to abuse his woman like that. I can't believe you, you piece of shit. Get out of my face!" I yelled at him.

"You can't fire me, you fucker! I work for your father." Sion's true colors were showing through the façade he'd built with me. I'd been patient, I'd asked my questions and had given him a way out peacefully, but he refused.

So, an ass-kicking it was.

I shot over the desk and tackled him to the ground, my fist flying out and connecting with his jaw. I must have surprised him because once he realized what happened, he was trying to block each of my blows. My fists continued to rain down on him, one after the other, over and over, and all I could see was Talia's lifeless expression in the elevator after I'd kissed her.

"You fucking piece of shit." I hit him "You sad excuse for a man" I hit him again.

"Stop this!" He roared from underneath and one of his fists flew up and hit my jaw. Sion was in the Irish mafia as an investigator and a spy so he made sure he knew how to fight and he made sure to keep his punches strong.

I brought down two more punches in quick succession and then sat back, satisfied with how bloody and how in pain he looked.

"Do you understand me now?" I snarled in his face and got up. I wiped my knuckles, a few had opened on each hand and I knew I was going to have deeper bruising on the hand I'd punched through the drywall.

Sion wheezed as he rolled over and tried to stand up.

"I expect any and all information for your current cases, including mine, to be handed over. Originals and copies. If you do not comply you know what will happen to you. To your family." I said, standing tall and confident behind my desk. "You are dismissed."

Sion looked at me with disbelief, betrayal, and revenge heavy in his eyes.

"I will be speaking to your father about this." His last attempt to get me to quiver. I barely contained my eye roll.

"Go right *the fuck* ahead. He doesn't take too kindly to assholes who think abusing women is okay." I snapped back.

I knew my expression must have been near murderous because as the blood from his nose ran down his face, his mouth dropped and disbelief filled his eyes.

"Is she worth this? I've been working for your family for decades."

I put both of my bruised, crimson-stained hands flat on the top of my desk with a slap.

"Absolutely." I answered without hesitation. "Now get the fuck out."

Chapter Fourteen

Talia

The sheets were warm against my cheek and I cuddled into the pillow a little more. It had been such a long time since I'd actually gotten a deep sleep that wasn't induced by alcohol. I wanted to savor the feeling before I had to get up and face the day.

Today, sometime soon, the deadline that Luca had given Kieron and I was going to expire. I needed to know what that really meant and what Kieron and Kellan were thinking of doing about it.

I wasn't going to claim that I knew more than the head of the Irish mafia or his second, but if there was any way to not go into a bloody war, I wanted to try.

I rolled over and opened my eyes slowly, letting the filtered sunlight warm my skin and the silence wake me up softly. My arm reached over to the other side of the bed and even though I knew I was going to find it empty, it still stung to not have Kieron here.

I threw the covers off of me and swung my feet off the side of the bed so my feet could touch the plush carpet. What was I meant to do? No one told me anything really except for how I was safe here.

I reached my arms up overhead to stretch and I went off in search of coffee. I really wasn't sure what I was doing; should I wait for Kieron to come back? Should I get dressed and go off exploring? That's what I wanted to do, but I don't think I should. It scared me a bit, just being free to do whatever. Like I would get in trouble for doing something wrong or not doing something.

Making my way back into the kitchen, I located a French press and some expensive, fancy-ass coffee grounds and got to work making the liquid of life. I didn't take off Kieron's clothes, they were beyond comfortable and really, I didn't have any other clothes except for my work uniform. As the microwave dinged and I turned to pull the boiling cup of water out, I heard the front door open quietly.

It had to be Kieron, but that didn't stop the terror that sprang to life.

"Hello?" I forced my dry throat to call out.

"Oh good, you're awake!" Kieron said with a smile and he came to give me a hug. He must have seen the scared expression on my face because he stopped mid-stride and looked around. He was on guard, his hand started to go for the back of his pants and I was sure there would be a gun there.

"Are you okay?" He said softly after a few moments of surveillance, deciding there wasn't an imposing threat.

"Yes, I'm okay." I said, putting my hand on his forearm. "You just gave me a fright when you opened the door like that."

Understanding dawned on him.

"I'm so sorry, baby. I didn't want to make a lot of noise if you were still sleeping. You were dead to the world when I left and I wanted to make sure you got some sleep."

"I know, thank you."

"I have one of my assistants bringing you up some clothes, just enough to get you through the week, but I wanted to see if you had any requests."

My heart fluttered, how was this man so thoughtful? I didn't deserve his attention.

"No, anything you think will be fine with me." I said honestly. I know that I should have been worried and having flashbacks or panic attacks about my clothing being picked out for me again, but this was different. Kieron was different. He wasn't doing this out of a need to control me, he was doing it to help me. To take one more stressor off my plate. To take care of me.

"Are you sure?" He asked me, his eyes boring into mine in search of any hidden feelings about it.

"Yes," I smiled brightly at him and took both of his hands in mine. "I'm sure. Now, do you want some of this extremely over-priced coffee I'm making?"

Kieron just chuckled and sat at one of the bar stools adjoining the small kitchen island.

"You pay for what you get. I get good, smooth, rich coffee." He explained with a smile and a shrug.

"Folgers is pretty decent, you know. And it won't make you take out a second mortgage on you house to afford it every morning."

A good night's sleep was bringing me back to life. A good night's sleep, a full stomach and a feeling of safety.

"Try it. If you try this and you don't think it's any better than your Folgers," he said with a grimace, "I'll never buy it again. But, if it's the best coffee you've ever had, I win."

"And what do you win?" I asked, my heart beating quicker at his deep melodic tone.

"A kiss." He said, standing up and walking over to stand right in front of me. I couldn't help but notice that even in the face of our intense tension, he still made sure not to crowd me, not to make me feel like I couldn't escape if I needed to.

"That's all?" I asked him.

"That's all." He smirked down at me and he was so close that I could smell his cologne, his shower gel and his crisp leather scent on him.

"Well, you drive a hard bargain." I teased. "But I accept."

"Great. Now, pour me a cup please and let's see who wins."

I opened a few of the dark grey cupboards before I was able to locate the coffee mugs, but I found two and poured us each a cup.

I lifted the white mug to my lips and saw Kieron smile a knowing smile at me as I took a sip.

Fuck.

It was the best coffee I'd ever had. Even better than the coffee I had tried at Luca's father's restaurant which, before now, I thought was the best. I set the mug down and tried to school my face to reveal nothing.

"Well?" Kieron prodded, taking a drink from his own cup.

Instead of answering him, I walked over to where he had sat back down on the bar stool and rested one hand on his chest. I could feel his heart beat pick up and beat faster as I got closer to him. I tried not to smirk too much. I slid my other hand up and pushed my fingers through the back of his hair where it was tight from being pulled up, his gorgeous curls were still slightly damp from the shower he must have taken this morning. Now that he was sitting, there wasn't such a big height difference so I leaned in and pressed my lips strongly against his.

Kieron was still for a moment, then his lips were returning my kiss with fervor.

I groped at him trying to touch and caress as much of his body as I could reach. I loved the black leather on his torso, but I wanted to feel his warm chest against me and feel the strong cords of muscle that laced his back beneath my hands.

Kieron was letting me set the pace while also showing me that he liked what I was doing by nipping my lower lip softly, by his hands wrapping around my waist and holding me lightly. Not to mention the groans and heavy breaths that were leaving my mouth that made my core start to heat even more. At this rate he was going to be able to tell just how much he affected me by a wet spot on my borrowed grey sweats.

Kieron's hand lightly twisted the white shirt and his other hand slid up my back, his warm hand spanning my entire lower back. He simultaneously pulled away while keeping my body close. He was so gentle, so hesitant but at the same time, I knew he wanted more and he wasn't going to pressure me for it.

"I won, yes?" He said, his voice was husky and low and I couldn't get enough.

"Smartass." I said with a smirk that matched the one on his lips.

"That was…one hell of a kiss, baby." He said, completely sincerely. "But we need to talk about what happens now."

I could feel my body stiffen at his words, they made what he wanted to tell me sound like he was going to toss me back to Luca. "What do you mean?" I whispered in fear.

"I mean, it's a quarter until 8 o'clock. We have fifteen minutes until Luca's little threat of war is enacted. I wanted to know what you thought, what you wanted." He said with a sigh. I could see in his eyes that he was in protective mode.

"I was thinking about that when I woke up actually. If there is a peaceful way to handle this where no one gets hurt, I'd like to try it that way." I said quietly, but confidently.

Kieron looked at me with something akin to awe. He opened his mouth and closed it a few times, but no words ever came out of his mouth. He was staring at me with wide eyes, and still holding me tightly.

"What?" I asked after a few silent moments of weird awkwardness.

"You realize what he did to you makes it incredibly difficult for me to not want to cut his head off with a machete."

"I know."

"You know that I should. That he deserves it and more."

"I know."

"Then why?" He asked me, his head cocked to the side.

"I'm not saying that I don't want him to suffer, because I do. That might make me a shitty person, but it's the truth. But what I don't want is a bunch of people getting hurt because of me. Innocent people."

"Baby," Kieron said sweetly, and ran a hand through my tangles. "No one is truly innocent."

"Kieron, I will forever feel guilty and terrible if any of your friends get hurt over me. Don't even get me started on if *you* would get hurt. I couldn't stand it."

"I won't get hurt." He tried to reassure me.

"You don't know that." I said loudly, getting tired of him not listening to me. "And I'm not willing to take that chance."

Kieron looked at me, his eyes were unreadable. I didn't know what he was thinking or if he was mad at me, maybe he was thinking how to make me get out of the apartment and out of his life when he pulled my mouth to his and kissed me. This kiss was sweet but had an edge of violence. Just like him. His hands were loosely holding onto my wrists, keeping me in place but I knew I could pull away if I wanted to.

"You're amazing." He said breathlessly as he pulled away.

"No, I'm not."

"Yes, you are. Not many people who have been through what you have, would tell the Second of the Irish Mafia Clan, who is completely willing and able to do anything they want to the perpetrator of your nightmares, would try to have a peaceful resolution. Most people would see my power and demand that I start a war, that I use every foot soldier I have to try and bring them down, to kill them in the most gruesome way imaginable. But not you. My angel." He explained softly as he cupped my cheek softly.

"I'm not an angel. Not even close."

"You're my kind of angel."

I shook my head softly and smiled.

"I don't know how peacefully we can handle this, baby. That's not how it works in the mafia. Any mafia; the Italians, the Irish, the Russians, hell, even the Polish Mob here in Boston doesn't work that way. In Luca's eyes, and therefore his fathers, I have taken his property regardless of how awful that sounds. He fully believes that you were his property, not your own person. In the Clan, the rules for theft are simple. If it is found that you did indeed steal, regardless of who you are, you are beaten until you pass out. If the person you've stolen from is feeling generous. Theft between the different mafias, though? That's grounds for murder."

I gasped and could feel the panic, the fear and the dread set in.

"No," I gasped. "No, no, no. I'll go back, I can live like I did before. Before you walked into my life, I had resigned myself to living like that anyway. If it saves people from being murdered over me, over nothing, I can't, I can't…I don't…" I started to feel myself hyperventilate.

"Talia," Kieron's voice was stern but I could hear the fear in his voice. "Talia, breathe." He ordered.

"I… can't…" My hands went to my chest and to my throat trying to claw it open. I needed air, I needed to be able to take a free breath.

"Baby, breathe with me. Please." He crushed my chest to his and I could feel his heartbeat, beating strong and sure, against mine. Kieron took a deep breath and I tried to follow, then he exhaled, and I tried to as well.

"Good, good. Again." He breathed in deeply and waited until I did too. Then he exhaled slowly.

"There, keep breathing." He ordered, keeping me held tightly against his chest. I was starting to come back into myself, he'd caught me before my panic attack became too much. I could hear his heart keeping time in his chest and I let myself get lost in its rhythm.

"I'm only going to tell you this one time, so I need you to listen, okay?" Kieron said softly in my ear and I nodded. His voice was deep and his words laced with a growl so his chest vibrated against my face as he spoke. His words were hushed, hurried but rang strongly with truth.

"I would burn this whole world down for you. Not that you'd ever ask that of me, but I would do it and I would fucking rejoice if it brought you joy. I don't revel in death or destruction, and I'm not going to lie to you and tell you that I don't enjoy the chaos though. But if you asked me to, I'd lasso the moon and bring it to your feet. I was going to take you from that hell, regardless of the consequences, and I did. And I don't regret a moment of it. I don't now, and I won't later."

"How do you know? Kieron, he won't show mercy, he doesn't have any boundaries." The fear of Kieron being hurt, injured and bleeding, bringing the panic back into my heart. After so long of being fearful of Luca, I couldn't help but worry even though anyone could see that Kieron could take Luca in a fist fight. Kieron would probably punch Luca's face once and it would explode.

"And in regards to him, I don't either." He said. His tone was low and dangerous, his eyes narrowed and unfocused as if he was looking off into the future, trying to plan exactly what he was going to do to Luca when he saw him next.

"I don't want you or anyone else to get hurt because of me. Please," I said softly, gripping the lapels of his jacket tightly.

"And I promise you that I will do everything I can to make sure that no one but him does." He said as he brought his hands to cover mine. "Just for you." He added with a smirk.

"I'm serious, Kieron."

"I know you are. But baby, I'm the Second of the Irish Mafia. I am in danger just breathing right now, simply for being who I am. By being born who I am. If I am dancing with some more danger by protecting you, I will *gladly* take it on. Do you understand me?"

I hadn't thought about it that way. He had always been in danger. He must have had to learn how to protect himself from such a young age. Always been sought after and used because of his father's position. A vision of a small Kieron, just a small boy who had to grow up so quickly, formed in my mind and I wanted to scoop him up and hug him tight.

"I'm sorry." I whispered, hoping he knew why I was apologizing.

"I've gotten stronger." He said simply with a shrug of his shoulders.

"Still."

"I wasn't telling you that to make you feel badly, Talia. I wanted you to realize that danger, politics and always watching over my shoulder is second nature to me. It's always happened and it always will until the day I die. So, again, I say that you coming into my life again has made me so much fucking happier regardless of the danger. Do you understand?"

"I do." I nodded, accepting what he was saying and trusting that if he really wasn't okay with this, he would have to tell me.

And that was hard to accept. To trust.

"Good. Now, can we agree that we won't bring me or my soldiers in danger up again? I won't intentionally try to get people hurt but I won't let that maggot intimidate me, take you back, or try to crumble my family's business. Trust me."

That word again. Trust. Every bit of trust I'd had, had been stomped on and lit on fire by men over and over. The man in front of me included. But, something deep inside of me did trust him. It always had.

"I do," I said strongly, looking at him. The immediateness of those two words struck a chord with me. It brought me right back to five years ago as he asked me to trust him and pulled me into the backyard, into the little nook he'd made and listened to my fears and dreams. I swear, I fell for him right then.

Kieron leaned in and kissed my lips softly before leaning away. I took a few breaths, then picked up my coffee mug and tried not to dwell on how fantastic it was.

"I take it that you have no intention of going back?" Kieron asked carefully, not making eye contact with me at all.

"No. I don't. And I doubt you'd let me even if I did." I said with a big smile when his dark eyes found mine.

"No. I don't think I would." He tried to hide him smile from me, looking down at his watch quickly, but I saw it. Just for a moment, but it was there and it was beautiful. "In two minutes, Luca will call his father and the ball will start to roll. We are already pulling out business and we've put on additional security detail at all our businesses so there shouldn't be any fallback there. There is one thing that I would like to talk to you about regarding your family."

"Okay."

"I have people watching and guarding them for now, but only short-term while the shit hits the fan, is there any way you could get them out of Boston?"

That was a great fucking idea. One I should've thought of the moment I got here.

"Yes! I can try. I just need my phone and some time. They haven't heard from me in months. Luca had me cut ties with everyone. Everyone but him."

Kieron stood up and walked over to where I stood on the other side of the island. Silently, he took the mug out of my hands and set it down before wrapping me in his arms and pulling me up into the air. I wrapped around his waist and I held onto his broad shoulders, my fingers digging into the leather.

"Never again, baby. I'll make sure of it. From now on, you're free. I promise." He said softly in my ear.

"How will I ever repay you?" I asked, my mouth lightly touching his neck with every word. I swear I could feel a little shiver run through him as my lips brushed his neck.

"Just be happy and live your life the way *you* want to. Please."

It was the 'please' that got me. This big, strong, tough man who looked like a fucking motorcycle model imbued with dangerous power could have anyone in the world. Literally anyone.

And he picked me.

"I am now." I said with a smile that mirrored his own.

"Be with me." He said against my lips, his forehead touching mine.

"Aren't I already?" In my head, the moment he had called me baby and held me through the panic attack at the electronics store, I'd been his again.

"Officially, then." He said with a wide smile.

"Are you asking me to go steady with you?"

"Brat." He pinched my ass and I rubbed against him which earned me a tight groan.

"What are you asking, Kieron?"

"Talia Jones, will you be my girl?" He asked with such sincerity and such adoration that I could feel my heart exploding. A wide smile crossed my face and I'm sure he could see every emotion cross my face. My guards were down, everything was genuine.

"Yes." I said softly and pulled his lips to mine by holding the back of his neck and pulling him towards me.

"Thank god." He whispered right before our lips touched. The kiss that followed was addicting. Like lightning bolts crashing, it was so powerful. Everything seemed to change in that moment.

I knew where he stood, and he knew where I stood. We wanted to be together and he was well-aware of my trauma. I felt...loved and protected.

"Baby girl, kisses like that are dangerous." He whispered hoarsely as he pulled away but rested our foreheads together.

"But so good."

"But so good." He repeated with a groan and kissed me again. Kieron's hands were on my ass, holding me up and against him before he moved the mugs out of the way and sat me down on the kitchen island.

"Have I told you how much I love seeing you in my clothes? So fucking hot." He muttered as his lips went from my mouth to my neck and he left hot, wet kisses all around it.

I moaned when he got to the particular spot I liked and I could feel his grin against my skin. My hands went to his jacket and I started to push it off, I needed more of him. Thankfully, Kieron seemed to catch onto what I was wanting because he pulled it off and let it fall to the ground.

It was like a switch had turned inside me and I no longer felt like I couldn't have him touch me without spiraling into fear. I wanted his touch, needed it, craved it.

"Listen, baby," He pulled back and physically stepped out of my space, leaving me feeling cold and dripping for him. My legs were spread wide still to accommodate him and I was desperate for him to step back in between my thighs. "We can go as fast or as slow as you want. Nothing will make me change how I feel about you and how badly I want you. We don't have to rush." He said as he cupped my cheeks with both of his hands.

"Promise?" I said, cursing how weak and small I sounded.

"Absolutely I fucking promise."

"Thank you." I let a breath go, and could feel my shoulders relax as a weight I didn't even know I was carrying dropped from me. I wanted more, I wanted us to finally be together, but I needed more time.

Kieron stepped back in-between my thighs and pulled me in for a hug. Knowing I was accepted, flaws and all, was something I hadn't felt with someone other than my family before. I wanted so badly for all of this to be true and real. I wanted it so badly.

Kieron bent down and kissed me softly before walking over to the small fridge in the corner of the kitchen.

"Now that all that is decided…can I make you some breakfast?"

Chapter Fifteen

Kieron

An hour later, after feeding my girl, *my girl*- I couldn't keep the smile off my face, pancakes and eggs until she was full, I had to leave to go to get the report from the guards on Talia's family. She said she was going to think of a way to get them out of town for a little bit like I'd suggested, but she needed a little bit of time to figure it out.

I walked down the hallway towards my father's office, nodding to Franny, his secretary, as I walked right into his office. My dad has always been and always will be a workaholic. I'm sure that I'm just like him in that way but I had a much better work-life balance than he did. I rubbed my temples in preparation for listening to my father lecture at me for at least thirty minutes.

"Kieron, I'm glad you're here. I need to discuss some things with you." His business voice was in full effect signaling that this talk was going to be a big one.

Fuck.

"Good, I would like to discuss some things as well." I said, putting bravado in my tone. I wasn't going to cower on this. I wasn't going to let him push me around because of my dismissal of Sion or how I handled it. That fucker had it coming and I stand by that.

"Very well, lad. Have a seat."

I went to the seat in front of the desk and got comfortable, crossing my ankle over the knee and putting a hand on my boot to refrain from it bouncing.

"First, how is Talia doing?" He asked politely, not making eye contact with me and looking through the papers in his hand.

"She's doing well. As well as can be." I said and could feel myself getting mad again. Kellan looked up at me, the papers still in his hands but his focus now on me.

"I don't doubt it one bit. I remember when you two were younger and you tagged along to a meeting of mine with the Don. Luca was in his office and he was out of control. Throwing tantrums, breaking things. And Lorenzo just fed into it. When you did that at a younger age, you got the belt. And now look at you, a well-rounded, well-behaved man who knows how to treat others."

My eyebrows shot up at the compliment. My father was not one to dole out compliments frequently.

"Thank you."

"At the very least, you're better than him. If only in that regard."

And there it was. I pursed my lips and nodded.

"I try to be." I said softly with a chuckle.

"Does she have the things she needs? Clothes, toiletries, shoes?" He asked, looking back down at the papers.

"Yes, I saw to that. Before we left her workplace I asked if she needed anything specific and she said no. I am sending Cara out to get her a few outfits and toiletries." I explained.

"Good. It's not a good idea for her to be out right now."

"I assumed that. But why do you think that?" I cocked my head and asked.

"It is 9:30 in the morning. An hour and a half since Luca's deadline and he will be furious. I've already heard from a few of our scouts how the Italians are snooping around here waiting for a glimpse of her to take her out. It doesn't seem as if Luca cares about bringing her back, there is a kill order out on her." My father said, no dressing it up or trying to sugar coat it. Most of the time it bothered me how bluntly he spoke about business, but now, I appreciated it. I needed to know what lay in wake for Talia in order to protect her from it.

"Any word on how the businesses are doing?" An hour and a half was a long time in our world. Once the Italians knew we had pulled our business with them, which they no doubt knew by now, they would get vicious.

"There has been no retaliation thus far. But that doesn't mean that it isn't in the works." He said with a sigh.

The Italian mafia was bloody, they believed any malfeasance against them needed to end with blood and pain. We tended to only go to bodily harm and murder if provoked, that didn't mean that we would let people walk all over us, far from it. There are more ways to break a man than simply drawing some blood.

For example, you sink his businesses, his way of making a living and see how it hurts. Especially when they depended on our help in business to continue to provide drugs and weapons to their associates. Those of who would not react kindly to their shipments being delayed.

"Understood." I nodded. "Anything else?"

"Yes. In fact, there is more." He dropped the papers and crossed his arms over his desk. "I need to know how far you're willing to take this. I understand she is important to you, or she was, and you just need to get her out of a bad situation. But we are using a lot of resources, a lot of men, and some of them are asking questions."

"What does it matter if the foot soldiers are asking questions? As long as they are doing their job, that's what I care about." I shrugged, leaning back in the chair.

"Kieron. This is serious. I back your decision to take her from them, but you ultimately committed a form of theft in their eyes."

"I know."

"Good, then you realize that this is bigger than just you because of your position and the position of the Garzino boy. If the grunts are asking who this girl is, why we are doing all this, it is important to keep their support and dedication. Even if that means giving them a bit of the story. So again, I ask you, who is she to you?" The words came out as a question, but I knew it was more of a demand. He would find out or he would make it so.

"She's my girl." I said simply. "She's my girl and she deserves all the protection of being such."

"Your girl? Didn't you just meet her?"

"No, I was just reunited with her. And you know that, old man. There is a difference. She is," I took a deep breath and tried to explain it as best I could. "She is the girl who got away. Like she told you yesterday, we met while she was in college. We had one night together and I was a goddamn coward who walked away because I was so convinced that I would put her in danger by being with her. If you recall, I wasn't allowed any lasting relationships back then because of the trials and the requirements of the Clan. But I always kept an eye on her." I ran a hand down my face as I was reminded of Sion and his betrayal.

"Speaking of, I fired Sion." I said quickly, no nonsense about it. My decision had been made and there wasn't any reason to prolong it.

"You what?" My father snapped.

"He had looked the other way when Talia started to have visible marks on her. He knew what was happening and he looked the other way. Then when I confronted him about it, he had no reason as to why he did it. He 'assumed it was a sex thing' and directly broke an order."

My father sat back in his chair with a thoughtful expression. His anger had been replaced as he scratched his face in thought. He wasn't angry or I would be being yelled at. But he was thinking it all over.

"Interesting. There have been small things that have been leaked. Things that were only privy to certain groups. Sion was always on the outskirts of that information, but it is possible he would have been able to hear it."

"Why didn't you tell me we had a mole?"

"It wasn't anything big, yet. Small strategy moves, businesses we were going to buy or try to move on, but all of it was information that the advisors and I hadn't made a full decision on yet." He rubbed a hand over the scruff on his chin in frustration.

"Damn him." I muttered. "At least he is gone now. Fucking traitor." I said with venom lacing my words.

"Yes, I agree." Kellan said, still thoughtful and like he was trying to solve a puzzle in his head. "Anyway, if she is indeed your girl, I take it that you have honorable intentions? Moreso than any of your…overnight guests."

"Yes, she's it for me. The others were just a distraction until I could find her again." I confessed. I wasn't ashamed by my words, if anything I was excited by them. I wanted her in any way she would have me. It was much, much too soon for marriage, but I would be steady and true and sometime in the future, Talia would understand that I would never hurt her. Then maybe we could move forward.

"I'm glad to hear it. It was time for you to start thinking about finding someone to settle down with. I'll have Franny start getting the preparations made and you will need to make a formal announcement. I understand that you have purchased a home and no doubt that you two want to move out there, but I think at least until after the wedding you should stay here where there is more security." Kellan said, he was talking quickly like he did when he had already made a plan and was trying to get it executed.

"Wait, wait," I sat forward and put my hand in the air. "What wedding?"

"You two are going to be married are you not?" He asked me like it was the simplest thing in the world.

"No, not yet at least. We've only been back in each other's lives for a few days."

"Yes, but if you're serious about her and you want to marry her anyway, getting married will provide her with the protection of a mafia wife. There will be certain lines that will be drawn that would stop others. Even the Italians would stop and have to reassess."

"Dad, she is not ready for marriage."

"Have you asked?"

"Of fucking course not. I've been in her orbit for a few days, I don't even think she is ready to fuck let alone get married. I told you Garzino was horrible to her. I'm working on helping her heal and regaining her trust." I said, I could hear the desperation in my voice.

"Think about it, son. When she becomes Talia Tavish she will have the complete and total protection of the Clan. She would be recognized as the second's wife and you know that has more sway and power than the

Second's 'girl.'" He said, raising an eyebrow and cocking his head.

Truth be told, it wasn't a terrible idea. She would be protected no matter what, she would have the power and strength awarded to the wife of the prince of the mafia. But I selfishly wanted her to *want* to marry me for me and not for the benefits it would bring.

"I will think about it. But I'm not going to force her. She's had enough of that for more than a lifetime." I said. I knew in my heart that I could ask her, I could present her with that option, but I'd never force her into anything. She'd been forced and manipulated too much in her life and I'd die before being one more person to force her into something, especially something this big.

"Understood. My next point of discussion was what we needed to do in order to ensure Talia's safety along with her family. I heard through the grapevine that you've put them under a protective detail as well."

"I did."

"Okay, so let's talk strategy. I would prefer not to have this end in lost lives of our men or her family, but if we do this smartly, then we can destroy the Italians from the inside."

"And how do you propose we do that?"

"Simple. Trenton, could you come in please?" Kellan called out.

It was brilliant. Trenton will continue to pose as a recruit and we could undermine them so simply. Without putting Talia in danger.

"Are you sure about this man?" I clasp his hand in greeting. This would be a high stakes, long-term undercover job. Stress and danger with every breath.

"I am."

"It's an honor for him, Kieron. And a way for him to move up within our own ranks." Kellan interjected.

"I can't ask you to do this for me." I said, ignoring my father.

"I'm not doing it for you. No offense." Trent's normal humor seeping through. "I'm doing this because even though we are mobsters, we still have a code. She's your one, man. The one you've been after forever and if I can do something to help keep her safe, I will. So, maybe I am doing it a bit for you after all." Trent smirked, holding up his fingers in a pinch gesture. This guy, always able to wrap a sincere gesture in a joke to make you smile.

"Okay." I nodded gruffly, accepting his reasoning. I shook his hand, and the moment was charged because we both knew what he was taking on to do this for her, for me. He'd be undercover, putting himself deeper into the Italian den. If anyone suspects anything, he'd be killed without question.

I wouldn't let that happen.

"No one is to know about this. Trenton will leave through the tunnels, just like he came in case of surveillance. We will only communicate through burner phones and all messages will be ran through an encoding system. This top secret, utmost priority to ensure success and Trenton's safety. Understood?" Kellan said in utter seriousness. He looked every inch of the Mob leader that he was.

"Yes, sir." Trenton said.

"Understood."

"Good. Now, lads, let's talk strategy." He smirked and sat back in his desk chair.

Chapter Sixteen

Talia

"You're a beauty!" A petite woman cried in a thick Irish accent as I opened the front door after loud, incessant knocking just a little while after Kieron left.

"Thank you," I said with a reserved smile. Her accent told me that she was one of the Clan and to be trusted, but I was still weary. The woman's arms were weighted down with shopping bags, much more than a 'weeks' worth' of clothes like Kieron had said. This woman was sweet and had a very welcoming energy about her. Like a mother who was excited to see her daughter after a little while apart. That's what she reminded me of with her bobbed hair, curled under and her large, thick rimmed glasses.

"Kieron said you needed some clothes. He only gave me the size of the pants and the size of the polo you were wearing. And other than that, I had to guess your size. Let's have a fashion show!" She pushed forward into the apartment, and I kept the door open for her.

"You didn't have to do that. I just needed a shirt. If you could point me in the direction of a laundry mat or machine, I can wash my clothes." I didn't want to take advantage in any way of their kindness.

"Oh shush." The woman said, dropping all the bags without ceremony. "Our Kieron would never go for that. You're his girl, and therefore will be treated like Clan royalty."

I could feel a blush heat my cheeks. It was true, Kieron wouldn't let me walk around in a borrowed t-shirt that was four sizes too big for me and black jeans. He made it very clear how much he wanted to give me everything he thought I deserved.

"Oh goodness, I'm so sorry, dear. I'm Cara, I work for Kieron as his assistant but between you and me, I've been working for the family since he was a little tyke. I used to change his diapers."

"I'm Talia." I said with a smile and went to shake her hand.

"I know. Little Kieron has been head-over-heels for you for years. He doesn't say much about anything in college or the trials, didn't tell me about any of his girls, like he was trying to protect my delicate senses." Cara rolled her eyes and I couldn't help but laugh. "You're different. He's never talked about a girl, let alone brought her home and willing to take on the Italian mafia single-handedly to keep her safe." She laughed while patting my arm. I had absolutely no idea what to say. He was different for me too. Always had been, but I had just assumed I'd never get more than that one night.

I smiled softly, letting her words build confidence in me.

"Now, let's get you some clothes." She said, bending over to pick up one bunch of bags and taking them to the couch.

"Okay." I said softly, a big smile on my face.

* * *

"He's going to love it!" Cara clapped her hands from where she sat on the sofa chair after I came out in my favorite outfit from the bags. A black mini skirt that stopped a few inches above my knees, showing off part of my thigh tattoo of a portrait of the goddess Athena. It hadn't seen day in years. Luca always deeming it inappropriate and said it made me look like a whore. But I loved it. On my top I wore a tight white tank top with an almost see-through cozy blue sweater that I had tucked into the skirt. Cara had brought a few different shoes for me to try on as well; a pair of heels - ick, a pair of motorcycle boots that looked perfect for kicking some ass, and a pair of black ballet flats. Luckily, they all fit me so I could take my pick and slipped the boots on.

I had to walk over to the bathroom where there was a mirror, but when I looked into the mirror, I almost wanted to cry. I felt more like myself than I had in forever.

"Are you okay, dear?" Cara came in and stood behind me, looking at me in the mirror too.

"Yes." I whispered, my voice getting caught in my throat.

"It's one small thing, choosing clothes, but it can express how you feel inside. You don't have to hide anymore." She said softly and she moved my long hair over my shoulder. I nodded and looked at her with a watery smile.

"Are you hungry?" She asked and I let out a noise that was a mix between a sob and a laugh. These people were intent on making me gain weight by feeding me often and feeding me well.

"No, I'm okay. Thank you though."

She nodded and turned as if to go to the massive pile of clothing she'd bought me and start tidying up, but I stopped her.

"Cara? Can I ask for something? I will pay you back." I asked quickly before she left the bathroom.

"Of course, dear! What would you like?" She turned and looked at me with enthusiasm.

"Can you find me some permanent hair dye? Maybe a dark blue or a deep purple?"

Cara's smile brightened and it made me wonder just how much Kieron had been talking about me.

"Yes, dear. I will go grab some for you right now." She came and gave me a hug before she walked right out of the apartment and I was left looking at the crazy amount of clothing they'd gotten for me. All things that were complete opposites of what I had been forced to wear for Luca, to keep up appearances. Nothing was pink, nothing was lacy or flowery. It was all dark colors and soft fabrics. All of the pieces were sexy in an understated kind of way and I was almost overwhelmed with the different combinations I could make and how each and every one made me feel sexy.

A knock sounded against my front door and I hoped it was Cara with the hair color, I was going to keep the long hair. But I needed the blonde gone. I was starting to feel like myself again.

It was addicting. And I was scared it was going to be taken from me at any moment.

"Talia? Baby?" I heard the deep melodic voice and smiled when I heard how he closed the door loudly, but not forcefully. He remembered what I said earlier and was making sure not to repeat anything that would cause me panic. His loud footsteps sounded as he started to walk through the apartment in search of me.

"I'm here!"

"Did some of the clothes fit?" He said before the bathroom door opened wider for him to see me.

"They did. They're perfect, Kieron. Thank you." I said sincerely, standing a bit taller.

"Wow." He said, looking at me intently and one of his hands went to his forehead, the other went into his jeans pocket. "You look… I think you…I want…Wow." He stuttered, never taking his eyes from me.

"I hope the ends of those sentences were good." I teased him. Kieron still had yet to drag his eyes from me or my legs.

"You know you've seen it all before." I smirked to which he just groaned like he was in physical pain. "What? You have."

"Bringing up the best night of sex in my life to try to get me to calm down is not the best plan."

"That was the best night for you? Even with all of your other girls?" I asked, his words reminding me of how much more experienced he is. How many girls he must have brought home with him. I mean, he's gorgeous so they must have been too.

"100% that night with you was the best night I've ever had. And I'm sure that when we take that step again, it will be amazing and satisfying in a way that I haven't had in five years." He said bringing his hands to mine and folding them to rest on his chest. "And the other girls? They didn't mean anything. They were a distraction and a way to get the guys off my back.

But that doesn't take away any of my feelings and want for you."

"But…I'm broken." I said softly, trying to hold the soul-crushing inadequacies back and hidden.

"Baby," Kieron sounded like he had been punched in the chest. "Do you really think that?"

"Of course, I do! I have no idea how you don't and how you don't hold it all against me! For fuck's sake, I got scared when you tipped my chin up and I felt trapped. You could have anyone, Kieron. Don't you realize that? Anyone. But you've decided for some reason to latch onto me. To save me. Which I'm incredibly grateful for and I will always be. But you don't have to…pretend like I'm something better than I am." I said, my anger at the whole situation bleeding into my words.

Five years ago, I believed that I was worthy of someone like him. And that was back when I was just confident, oozed sexuality and was always willing to tell others were to fucking stick it when they tried to fuck with me.

God, how I've fallen. Look at me now.

"Talia," He sounded surprised and when I looked at him, his expression was puzzled. His eyebrows furrowed and his mouth was open slightly as if he wanted to say something but didn't.

"I can't do anything about the other girls I've been with. Just like you can't change how you were with Garzino. But we have a chance now," He took both of my hands and ran his thumbs over my knuckles. "That we didn't before. So, no. I don't think you're broken. I think you're a survivor and you've done what you needed to do to survive. I think you're brave and beautiful." He said and cradled my face between his strong hands. "I think you're ambitious and even though you don't see yourself how you used to, I see you. I see all of you."

"You do?"

"I do." He said with a smile.

"And you're sure you want me?" I asked, hating how my voice cracked.

"More than anything." He replied immediately, making me smile.

"Thank you."

"You know, I feel like you say that a lot." Kieron said with a smirk.

"Probably because I do. You do many things for me that I need to show gratitude for." I rolled my eyes and smiled at him.

"From now on, you don't need to thank me. Just be happy and I'll be happy as well."

Instead of replying with another 'thank you' like I wanted to, I stepped into his open arms and wrapped my arms around his torso, pressing my ear against his chest. His arms wrapped around me again, holding me close to him in the most loving, protective way. His strong arms felt like home.

"So, you like my clothing choices?" He asked. I could swear that his voice had a hint of nerves in it. Like he was worried about what I thought.

"I do, I really do. Thank you." I said, pulling back from the hug to look at him. When he heard my thanks, he gave me a pointed look which I ignored and continued. "It does seem like you have a type though." I smirked.

"What do you mean?"

"I mean, all the clothes are dark, bold and sexy. Very similar to what you wear." I said, very matter-of-factly and straightened the lapel of his leather jacket. Kieron looked down at my outfit and I saw his tongue swipe out and lick his bottom lip.

"I hadn't thought of it like that. Honestly, I just thought about things that would look sexy on you. And I was right." His hand went down to caress my thigh, right over my Athena tattoo and watching me intently to make sure I was okay until his hand up reached the curve of my ass and my breath caught. This time it wasn't from fear or nerves, there was no part of me that was nervous and didn't want him to keep going.

"This one is new." He said softly, moving his hand lower again to the tattoo.

"I got it a few years ago." My voice sounded shaky.

"I like it. I like them all." He whispered, bringing his lips closer to mine but stopping right before our lips actually touched.

"I like yours too. I want to…" I said, but my words cut off with a small moan as his hand went back to my ass and he squeezed slightly.

"You want to what?" He teased quietly.

"I want to…" I started, but I couldn't think with his hands holding me like this, with the tension between us so thick I thought I'd perish if we didn't close the gap between us so I could taste his mouth again.

"If you tell me, I'll give it to you." He promised after a tortuously long time, *finally* closing the distance between our lips. He was sweet and his kisses were gentle, but his hands… His hands were not gentle or innocent. The one hand was up my skirt palming at my ass and his other was wrapping around my waist, making sure I wouldn't fall because my knees were starting to grow weak. His fingertips moved from my ass to graze my inner thighs, no doubt feeling the intense heat coming from my core. It wouldn't surprise me if, no, when he pulled his hand back, it was wet and shiny.

"Tell me, baby. What do you want?" His voice was low and breathless. Sending a jolt of heat to my core. I swear, I can't handle any more teasing without being able to do something about it. I was used to not finishing, I don't think I've come in at least two years, but Kieron's words, his hands, his mouth, hell, just *him*, was making me more wet than I'd ever been. I'm sure that this brand-new underwear that I'd gotten were already destroyed.

"I want to see all of yours. Your tattoos. You look like you've gotten more since last time." My words stuttered as Kieron moved onto my neck.

"I have definitely added to my collection over the past five years." He said with a smirk and bit down softly on the juncture of my neck. If he hadn't been holding me up, I would have fallen. I groaned at the feeling of his teeth on my neck and my eyes fluttered shut.

"You like that, don't you?" Kieron said huskily in my ear and I nodded quickly.

He stepped back and ripped his jacket off his body, letting it fall to the ground with a heavy thump. The white t-shirt he was wearing was doing holy work, wrapping around his biceps so well and highlighting all the dark ink that graced his arms.

As I was ogling him, I heard him chuckle before he stepped completely out of my reach and smirked at me in that way that meant he *knew* what he was doing to me. Then again, it wasn't like I was trying to hide it very hard. He reached overhead and grabbed the collar of his shirt and pulled it up overhead.

Logically, I know I've seen his body before, but all I could think was Hot. Damn. And stare at his torso as my mouth started to water.

"You're beautiful," I said softly, walking up to him to put my hands over his chest and trace the intricate lines and details of the tattoos that covered his chest. It looked like he was sculpted from marble; his chest and ab muscles showed just how much time he spent honing his body into the weapon and piece of art it is. His arms and shoulders were thick, lined with muscle and I could not wait until they were wrapped around me. I could feel the sturdy, strong warmth of his chest under my hands and I traced the main tattoo that spanned shoulder to shoulder.

"Teaghlach go deo, anois agus i gcónaí." I tried to sound out the strange letters and combinations that were scrawled in elegant script across this chest with vines and roses sprouting from the words. "What does it mean?"

"It means, 'family forever, now and always'." He said in a gentle tone.

"It's beautiful."

"I got it when I was inducted into the clan officially." He explained. "Most of the original family still gets some kind of variation of that quote, to prove to the elders that they are in this life permanently."

My hand travelled along the tattoo, lightly grazing his skin. I looked up at his expression and his jaw was taunt, his eyes closed and his head slightly tilted up as if he was in pain.

"Is this okay?" I asked softly, continuing to run my fingers over his inked skin, memorizing the designs.

He nodded stiffly. I started to worry that I was bothering him or hurting him somehow, but then I felt his hardness press against me lightly.

He wasn't in pain; he was turned on.

Just by me touching him like this.

I felt powerful. This incredibly strong, giant, sexy, god of a man was turned on by me lightly touching him.

"You're so strong." I whispered, pressing a soft, chaste kiss to the middle of his chest, right over one of the words that bound him to his clan.

"You're so sweet." I whispered, pressing another kiss to the hollow of his throat and was rewarded with a shiver.

"You're so sexy." I whispered again, letting my hand trail down his chest, over his stomach and lightly dip under the button of his jeans.

"Don't tease me," He groaned, the words coming out more breathless and softer than I'm sure he was wanting.

"I'm not…Sir." I said in his ear.

It was like a dam broke because all of his control, all of the tension that was holding him back, released and he scooped me up in his arms, pressing his lips to mine almost violently.

"You know what that does to me." He growled, pulling the sweater and tank over my head aggressively, leaving me in just a bralette.

"I remember."

"Then if you don't want this, if you want me to stop, you need to tell me now so I can set you back on the ground, walk you to your room and go take a cold-ass shower before I explode." He said quickly.

"I… I'm nervous. But can we try?" I asked, my voice small again. I would have been embarrassed, but I was fairly sure that Kieron got off on taking care of me and being the big, strong protector, he naturally is.

His hand cupped my cheek and he rested his forehead against mine.

"We don't have to do anything."

"I want to." I insisted. I was done living how Luca wanted me to live. I was scared, of course I was, but I wanted to feel like me again. And what better way than to have my protector fuck the fear out of me?

"You're going to kill me." Kieron groaned. I could feel his hardness pressing against my thigh as he stood between my thighs on the bathroom sink.

"But what a way to go, huh?" I joked and brought his lips to mine, hoping to distract him enough to continue ravishing me.

"I'm going to take care of you." He said.

"I know."

To prove that I was serious, that I wanted this, I reached my hands around my back and unhooked my bra letting my tits free, and the bra fell to the floor.

Kieron's mouth dropped ever so slightly with his gaze and I felt like I was on fire from his stare. In all the times my breasts had been looked at in the last five years, never once have I felt so alive from a look. My skin tingled and I could feel my nipples turn to peaks from his gaze.

Kieron stepped forward with his hand outstretched, cupping my breast softly with one hand and putting the other hand on my lower back, causing my back to arch slightly in his hands. I let out a very soft whine when he brushed my stiffened nipple with his thumb.

There was such a distinct difference between Kieron and Luca, not just in looks of course, but in energy and attention. Kieron gave me everything, his whole presence was tuned to mine and I knew that if I breathed a word of discomfort, he would stop.

In the beginning, Luca was sweet. He was kind and had a playboy type swagger about him. As time went on, Luca became cruel, he was indifferent and mocking. His touch would repulse me and make recoil in fear.

I shook my head slightly, opening my hooded eyes to look at the man in front of me. He pulled me back into the present by moving one of his hands up to my neck and somehow moved even closer into my body while his other hand pulled on my nipple hard. It was a very confusing mix of pain and pleasure. His body heat wrapped around me, and I was quickly becoming drunk on the clean, masculine scent of him. I was putty in his hands.

"I know they're small. Or at least, smaller than before." I said, self-consciously, trying hard to not cover my chest as the memory of how curvy I used to look.

"You're perfect." He said sharply, his eyes narrowed as if offended I'd said that. He took one of my nipples between his lips and started to suck.

"Oh god, Kieron." I moaned, arching my back to try to get more of his mouth on my chest. He sucked, hard, on my nipple before switching his attention to the other one and repeated his worshipping.

"Please," I started to beg. I didn't know exactly what I was begging for, but whatever it was, Kieron knew what I needed. He stood up straight and pulled me to his body before sliding his hands under my thighs and lifting me into the air. Where he had been lavishing my breasts were still wet and made them extra sensitive when my nipples rubbed against his bare chest.

"I know, baby." He said and laid me gently on my bed. My back hit the comforter and I crawled back so quickly that my head bumped the headboard.

"Please," I said breathlessly and tried to shimmy out of my skirt and tights.

"Ah, ah, ah. What are you doing?" Kieron's hand shot out and grabbed my wrist.

"Do you…is this…I don't…" I started to stutter.

"That's my job, to undress my girl." He let go of my wrist and put both of his hands on my hips, gently moving his hands across the space between my hips to where the zipper was before peeling it down. He looped his thumbs in the waistband and slid the skirt and the thong down in one, slow, sensual go.

And there I was, I laid bare before him.

Not a stitch of clothing on, just waiting for him to take me.

I wasn't nervous, I wasn't afraid. I felt free and sexy under his gaze. Kieron was pinning me to the spot with his eyes and the more he drank his fill of me, the more turned on I got.

"Well, are you going to do anything or just stare?" I let an innocent smile cross my lips.

"Don't be a brat." He shifted off of me slightly and sat upright on his knees. A curl fell from his bun, falling into his eyes and he quickly pushed it back behind his ear.

I wanted nothing more than to pull the tie from his hair and let that wild mane free. I swear, my mouth started to water.

"I wasn't, I was simply asking you a question." I said innocently, making sure to keep my eyes wide to complete the overtly innocent look.

"That won't work on me, baby girl. I think that you need to understand something." He said, his breath fanning my face as he leaned in closer. "I make the rules here. You can stop me at any time, but if I want to stare at your gorgeous body underneath me," He slid a finger into my heat and I moaned. "all wet and wanting, I'm going to. It's been five long, miserable years and I'm going to savor this." He said with a growl, his face hovering right above mine and his impossibly long, thick finger was still sliding in and out at a torturously slow pace.

"Please," I whimpered into his neck, hoping he would pick up on my desperation and take pity. I wanted to come and I wanted to come because of him.

Chapter Seventeen

Kieron

I wasn't going to last long. I knew that the moment I realized this was going to actually happen.

Seeing her in that outfit, happy, and relaxed was enough to make me want to pull her into my arms and have my wicked way with her, but I knew I couldn't. Not until she was ready.

Imagine my surprise when she said she was ready now.

"Please," Her breathy voice whispered against my neck, giving me goosebumps as her breath warmed my neck.

"Please what, baby?" I asked.

My finger slid in and out slowly, giving her time to back out if she wanted. I wouldn't hold it against her, things were moving quite quickly by anyone's standards and if she shoved me off, I'd kiss her softly and leave her to collect her thoughts. Then I'd run next door and jack off as fast and furiously as I could, all the while sucking on my fingers and imagining her coming all over me.

"Please, fuck me." She whispered, her eyes closed tightly and her head tipped back in pleasure. She was close to coming. I could feel it, her walls tightening and beginning to flutter around my fingers. Her walls seemed to pull me back in as if they didn't want me to leave.

"Fuck, baby girl. You're so goddamn tight. The moment I slide into you, I know I'm not going to last." I groaned and laid my head in the crook of her neck to suck a dirty mark. My mark.

"I just want to feel you." She said quietly like she didn't want to break the bubble we had made.

"I need you to come first, then I'll make love to you until you can't walk and your cunt will be molded to fit me. You're mine, and every part of you knows it." I muttered. And I meant every word.

"Please, I want it, please." She begged. Oh, how I loved it. That needy tone in her voice, the breathiness, the darkness in her features, the way her cunt tightened.

I crooked my fingers up in a 'come hither' motion and felt for the magical spot that would make her legs shake. Making sure to keep a close eye on her facial expression to see what she liked and what she didn't. Talia was like an open book, never hiding how a certain drag of my fingers made her feel.

"Fuck," I whispered and I bit down on her neck again. I wanted the mark I left to be purple and huge before we were done, then it would be no mistake to anyone that she was *mine*. "Do you like that? It feels like you like that. God, I missed you so much. Missed you, missed your body. I can't fucking wait to get inside your perfect little cunt and make it mine. Do you want that?"

I couldn't help the words tumbling out of my mouth, but based on a new wave of wetness on my hand, she didn't mind.

"Yes, Kieron, yes. Please, I want it." At her words I reluctantly withdrew my fingers and got on my stomach, sliding down her body until I got to the apex of her thighs.

"I can't wait any more to taste you."

Her shocked expression told me just how long it had been since anyone had gone down on her and I was going to rectify it right now.

"You don't-" She started to say and I nipped lightly, teasingly at her thigh.

"I want to."

At that, I dove in, licking and sucking at her lips and her clit. Suddenly, my shy, quiet girl was no longer there. In her place was a loud, sexual goddess who sat up, holding herself up with one arm and held the back of my head with the other. She was keeping me there, right where she wanted me and right where I wanted to be.

"Fuck Kieron. Fuck, please, more, right there." She moaned and muttered, pulled at my hair which had fallen from its tie at some point. I could feel her tighten around my tongue and Talia started to rock her hips against my face.

"Please, almost, please," Talia continued to whisper, broken pleas mixed with my name was music to my fucking ears.

I sucked on her clit and slid a finger into her, finding that spongey spot and started to thrust in and out, making sure to rub that spot each time. It only took two movements and she came with a scream.

Her hand was locked to the back of my head as she continued to grind herself hard against my face. I didn't think I could get any harder and then I looked up at her. Her golden hair falling in waves around her shoulders, her skin flushed in pleasure, and her beautiful lips parted, before she bit her bottom lip.

"Kieron," She moaned, closing her eyes and fell backwards onto the bed completely spent.

I sat up, flipping my hair over my shoulder and I made sure to look at her as I stuck my middle finger in my mouth and sucked off the come.

"That was…unbelievably hot." I said. I didn't want to assume that she actually wanted to fuck me now after she had come, but when her eyes opened once again, I saw that sexual goddess that had been hidden, peak her head out.

"You're not getting away that easy." She said confidently, sitting up quickly and pulling me to her by the belt. "Here's what's going to happen." She looked up at me and smirked. Talia knew what she was doing.

My girl from five years ago was back.

"I'm going to suck you off because I need to be reminded of how you taste and then you're going to make love to me. Nice and slow. Gently, until I tell you." She demanded, peeking up at me through her eyelashes and pouting slightly all while her fingers pulled my belt through the loops on my jeans.

"Is that what you need, baby?" I purred, giving her my best panty-dropping smirk. Her dark eyes flashed and I knew that I had turned her on all over again.

"Yes. I need you to be sweet to me, gentle with me. Until I ask for something otherwise." She bit her lip and I wanted to do that.

Truthfully, I'm glad she put some boundaries down as well. I wasn't planning on fucking her roughly or overly dominant, but the fact that she told me what she wanted was a great step in the right direction. As confident and glorious as she seemed, I knew she was telling me something real here. This was important to her, the way that we proceeded with our sexual relationship and I didn't blame her. But I was going to make sure she knew that she never had anything to worry about with me. That she could relax and trust that I would take care of her.

I wouldn't be rough with her. Until she was ready, that is.

"Always" I whispered and kissed her lips gently. "I fall at your feet, ready to be whatever you need."

I waited for Talia to pull my pants down, to take that final step to do this. It felt like the right thing to do. I wasn't going to push her and she needed to feel like she had the power here.

Her small hands moved quickly, rolling the black leather of my belt around her hand and unbuttoning the snap of my jeans.

I could see her fear start to creep up and it turned the sexual goddess in front of me into my shy beauty as her fingers started to shake slightly.

"Are you sure this is what you want?" I asked her softly, putting my hands over hers to stop her. As my chest filled with anger at just how far that Garzino motherfucker had hurt her, I tried to breathe deeply. I didn't want her to think that I was upset about stopping, but I wanted to kill the man that had done this to her.

"I do. I want you. I want us. I'm just nervous." She said, her words coming out with more strength behind them than I expected. I looked down at her and in her eyes, I could see conviction.

"My strong girl." I said, hoping to convey to her just how much I worshipped her. I leaned down to cup her chin in my hand, and I kissed her softly. Just a graze of lips, a brush of our mouths.

She didn't reply, and she didn't need to. Talia got back to work and very quickly she pulled the waistband of my pants and boxers down in one motion, just like I'd done with her.

My cock was standing at attention, ready and weeping for her. It bobbed slightly when it was released from the denim, and after watching her fall apart for me, I was pretty sure all she needed to do was breath on my cock and I'd explode.

"You're gorgeous." She whispered, her face at level with my cock and I swallowed audibly.

"Not as gorgeous as you."

I had wanted to say something more profound, something that showed her just how much I cared about her regardless of the next step we were going to take, but every single thought left my mind the second her mouth touched my cock. It was warm and wet and the way she was sucking me was shy and tentative, but shit, was it arousing.

"Yes," I hissed, tipping my head up towards the sky in pleasure. "Goddamn, baby girl, you're going to make me blow my load as quick as a fucking teenager again."

She didn't say anything, she couldn't, but I looked down at her on her knees like a dirty angel and saw that she was smiling.

"You're mine. You're never fucking leaving." I growled, trying to hold onto the razor thin line of my self-control so that I didn't start fucking her mouth. I had to remember to let her set the pace.

Talia must have liked that idea because her eyes fluttered closed and she moaned. The vibrations from her moan were almost enough to send me over but I gripped the base of my cock, hard, and pulled out of her mouth.

"Lay down." I ordered. Normally, I have to keep stroking myself to keep me in the moment, to keep myself as hard as I was, but with Talia, I couldn't. If I stroked myself right now, I was going to come all over her.

She followed my directions quickly and I wrapped both of my hands around her thighs before I pulled her body towards the edge of the bed. She shrieked a little before I reached behind her and grabbed a pillow.

"What are you-" She started before I stuffed the pillow under her ass to raise her higher. I was going to make her come so hard she'd see stars.

"You'll see."

I leaned over and kissed her lips, giving her a taste of my tongue before I grabbed my cock and ran it through the wetness that had pooled at her entrance. I made sure to let the slickness coat the head and I rubbed my cock around her clit a few times, earning me a deep moan from her.

"Are you ready?" I asked her.

Talia nodded.

"You want this? You want my cock?"

Talia nodded again.

"Words, baby girl. I need words." I said sternly, pulling my cock back and slapping her pussy with it. The warm wetness made a satisfying sound when our most intimate parts connected. She was shocked but her mouth opened.

"Yes, I want it. I just want *you*."

And I pushed in.

"Oh my god, fuck." I muttered. I knew she was tight; I had just felt her around my fingers, but it was absolutely nothing compared to how she felt like a vice around my cock. I could barely move.

I heard her moan and before I could do anything, her hand shot out, grabbed the back of my neck and she smashed our lips together for an explosive kiss.

"Just. Like. That." She said roughly. She was panting and I swear, I could feel her cervix with each thrust. The pillow under the ass was a great way to hit all the best spots and she seemed to be enjoying it. I pulled back and thrust in again slowly, encouraged to go harder and stay rubbing those same spots.

"I'm not going to last long," I said through clenched teeth as I tried to keep myself from thrusting, wanting to stave off my orgasm until I had gotten her there first. I was holding her legs, her knees in the crooks of my elbows, and watching her tits bounce in time with my powerful thrusts.

"You better come, you better fucking come all over me. *I* need it." I muttered, I could feel her walls tighten, but she needed more. And I could give it to her.

I took one of her thighs and secured it around my waist so that my hand was free to move to her clit. I started to rub the little bundle quickly but not too hard.

"Kieron! Fuck, Kieron!" Talia started to cry out my name loudly and I fucking loved it.

"Come on, baby, come on my dick." I said, in a strained hush, before leaning down and giving her a deep, devouring kiss. It was all teeth and tongue but it still had an edge of vulnerability to it that almost took my breath away.

I was starting to lose rhythm as I chased my orgasm, rubbing her clit quicker and muttering all my dirty thoughts to her.

Talia came with a cry and she crashed our lips together harder as her pussy seemed to suck me in with each wave of her orgasm and I lost it.

I came harder than ever as I emptied everything I had into her with a deep groan and her arms wrapped around my shoulders.

We stayed connected, laying with each other for just a moment before I pulled out gently and laid next to her while we caught our breath. I took one deep breath and let it go slowly before I walked into the bathroom to get a warm washcloth to clean her up.

I promised her I would take care of her, and I always wanted to keep that promise.

When I came back in, not even a five seconds later, Talia was crying softly. Her face stuffed into a pillow to try and muffle the sound.

"Talia?" I asked, fear lacing my voice as I set the towel on the side table and climbed into the bed with her, pulling her flush against me so that her small body was encased with my large one.

I didn't know what to do, but I was fucking terrified. Maybe I'd gone too far. Maybe she felt forced or rushed. I was too pushy and fucked it all up. My mind was spiraling with fear and doubt, but I needed to have her explain what was wrong.

"Was it…Are you…I'm sorry." I finally settled on. Maybe we'd gone to fast, and she was regretting it now.

"Kieron, that was perfect. I needed that, I needed to prove that sex can mean something with someone you care about. That someone else touching me sexually can mean pleasure and not pain. I can't thank you enough." She flipped over so I could see her face. She was staring at me completely open and vulnerable, honest in every word she said.

"You mean the world to me." I confessed, pulling her body into mine and I loved the feeling when she nestled into my chest. Her ear rested right on my heart, and I was sure she could hear how loudly it beat for her. "I'm so sorry I left you alone back then. That will never happen again. Like I said before, you're *my girl* now."

"You may have left me back then, but you came back." Talia placed a kiss right over my heart before she relaxed further into our embrace, and I heard a small, muffled yawn. "Not only did you come back for me, but you saved me all over again."

Chapter Eighteen

Talia

I'd done it.

I'd slept with someone and *enjoyed it*. And I'd slept with Kieron again. Something that I never thought I would ever get to do again.

My head rested on Kieron's broad chest; my fingers were tracing over the words in his tattoo as he held my body close to his side. He had picked up a few tricks since the last time we'd been together. And I tried to not let that thought take me into a spiral.

I'm sure that I'd lost some tricks I'd had, I couldn't think of anything or do anything because I was trying so hard to be lost in Kieron that all I could do was react.

"I can practically hear you thinking, baby. Want to talk about it?" Kieron asked, his gruff tone was quiet. His large, tattooed fingers made their way through my blonde hair, gently detangling the knots from his fingers. It was rhythmic and soothing. Something that would put me to sleep if he kept it up.

"It was just a big step. For me. And I'm trying not to freak out about how fucking magnificent you are at sex." I answered honestly, turning all my attention to the swirls and tribal designs etched in dark ink over his chest. His skin rumbled under my skin as he chuckled.

"And that's a bad thing why?" He asked. I had to roll my eyes because despite not being able to see his face, I knew he had a cocky smirk on his smug face. Sitting up and pulling the sheet around my chest with me, I let my hair fall over my shoulder so it partially covered my face and the bruises I'm sure were green and terrible by now.

"It's not a bad thing, Kieron." I said with a sigh. How could I explain this to him without coming off as needy or possessive, borderline jealous, especially when I'd *just* felt more like myself?

"Then why do you look so sad?" He sat up to face me, taking both of my hands in his.

And was he a sight to behold. All tanned muscle, tattoos and brave in his nakedness. He looked free and wild with his long dark hair falling around his face, his dark beard cropped close to his jaw and his dark brown eyes looking at me with such care. The sheet had fallen from covering my breasts, and I could see how hard he was trying not to look.

"I'm not sad." I ran my fingers through my hair. "It's just, you're so good at sex. You were last time too, and I'm sure I've backtracked. I have had one partner in the last five years, and I spent most of that time closing my eyes, hoping it would stop." I could see the fire of anger reignite in his eyes at the mention of Luca's abuse but he smothered it quickly.

"So, you want to know how many girls I've been with?" He asked slowly.

"I don't. I really don't need or care to know that number." I said, my tone tight. This is not how I wanted this to go. I wanted to keep cuddling and basking in the glow of the best sex I've had in years with the God of a man who wants to be mine. "I want to go back to cuddling and then take a shower, and then get rid of this blonde hair."

"If that's what you want, baby." He said softly, laying back against the headboard. He kicked one of his ankles out from under the white sheet and opened his arms wide, beckoning me over to and into his arms. I smiled softly, crawling back into his arms.

Kieron wrapped both of his tree-trunk of arms around me tightly, drawing me in even closer to his chest. I was engulfed in warmth and comfort and felt him kiss my head while taking a deep breath. "Just know that I will always tell you the truth. If you want to know, I'll tell you."

I turned my head to kiss him, our lips met for a brief kiss that took my breath away. I honestly didn't care about who he'd been with, how many people he'd been with. We weren't together then, so it wasn't my business really. But what I was really feeling was much more complex than just jealousy. It was a range of emotions. I was envious that he'd been able to gain all that experience and freedom to discover more about himself. Possessiveness over Kieron because of the women that he had fucked, knowing there was no doubt probably would've kept him. Fear that I wouldn't measure up to them. Anxiety because I'd finally taken that pivotal step away from Luca and I don't know how to classify it within myself.

"I know." I say quietly.

"I won't be upset if you want to know." He whispers softly.

"Do you want to tell me or something?" I ask with a chuckle. "You realllllly seem to want to." I tease him.

Kieron pinches my bare ass under the sheet, and I yelp in surprise.

"Brat."

"I'm just saying." I chuckle, snuggling closer to him.

"I've been with my fair share of women. No one that kept my attention for more than a few moments. No one that I spared a second glance at or could point out on the street again, if I'm honest. I'm a total dick and a pig or whatever other name you'd call someone that used women for just a fuck and then threw them out of their bed without a second thought for them or their feelings. It's terrible, and I own that." Each word he said was like a shock to my system. "The girls knew; I have a reputation both good and bad. But that's not an excuse for how I treated them. I just didn't care about any of them."

I wasn't shocked that he had treated women like that, but that he was so open about it. He wasn't trying to hide himself or making himself look more favorable.

Kieron was being *real* with me. Open, honest, showing the parts of himself I'm sure he'd rather forget.

"That was in the past." I said softly. "There isn't any need for me to know this. You were a free man." I tried to explain to him, but he wasn't listening. Too lost in his own thoughts.

"There is." He said strongly, running one of his tattooed hands through his dark curls. "You do need to know. I'm not a good man." He breathed deeply. My heart started to beat faster, worried that he was going to tell me something that would reverse all the comfort and sanctuary I'd found with him. I must have tensed or looked like I was starting to panic, because Kieron leaned over and kissed my bare shoulder.

"I've been with countless women in the last five years." He said, throwing those words out there harshly. "But out of all of them, not a single one made me feel anything like you do." He hands came up and cupped my face softly, brushing a lock of my hair behind my ear. "Even back then, I'd been completely infatuated with you. I had to make you leave when all I wanted was to hold you close and keep you. You were the one that got away. The one that I measured all other girls to because you *are* my dream girl, my fantasy."

With as sweet and loving and heart-wrenching as his words were, I couldn't help but feel stressed at them as well. I wasn't that same girl anymore. I wasn't who he'd been envisioning and even though he was saying how he wanted *me*... would he still when he realized that I wasn't her? I don't know if I could even be her anymore.

"I can see your brain turning. I can see you overthinking. Let me relieve your worries, baby." Kieron manhandled me and positioned me over his lap so our hips were pressed tightly together. His hands were spanned across my naked thighs, bracketing his thighs through the sheet. "I know we are both different people from when we were younger. But we get to know each other again. We get to take our time and pursue these feelings like we wanted to back then. Before I fucked it up." He looked so shy and hopeful, like a young boy who was scared to hope for presents under the tree from Santa.

I looked into his dark eyes; eyes that had new shadows in the darkness from the things he had been forced to do as his role in the Mafia, eyes that were begging me to understand.

"I want that too." I said confidently, trying to put as much comfort and conviction into those words as I could.

I guess we both had things we needed to work through, and I knew that we could do it together. That being said, I still was terrified I wasn't enough.

"I'm worried that I might be…too broken for you. What if I let you down or I can't be that girl that you remember so fondly? She's in here somewhere but I've had to hide her for so long. I don't even know to bring her back." I decided to tell him the truth, to be vulnerable and open in hopes that we could figure this all out and be on the same page.

"It doesn't matter if she is or isn't. I want to be with *you*, Talia. You're not broken. Cracked maybe, but we all are. I know I am." His fingertips bit into the flesh at the bottom of my hips possessively, rocking me forward so our heat was shared. I moaned at how he was already ready to go again and I felt myself clench around nothing to try and stay the feeling of emptiness when all I wanted was his cock deep inside me.

Kieron gripped my chin in between his forefinger and thumb, forcing me to keep my head still so he could look at me. "If you're cracked, that means you can be fixed and baby, I want to be the one to put you back together again." He whispered against my lips. "But I need you to promise to do the same for me. I'm cracked, broken wide open in some places and I didn't know how to be whole. Not until I found you again." His forehead leaned against mine. His words took my breath away.

"I promise." I whispered, our lips barely brushing against each other, but just enough to taste him.

"Good. Good girl." He whispered with a smile, a teasing smirk on his lips before pulling me even closer. Our chests crushed together as his hand wound in my light blonde hair, tugging slightly to hold my head against his.

I was positively dripping as soon as *good girl* had left his lips and he knew it too. He started to grind up against me; his thick, hard cock pressing just right against my lips. There was even more friction because of the sheet separating us, and I really liked it.

I wrapped my arms around Kieron's shoulders, holding myself up to grind against him as well because, damn it, if he was going to make me come from just dry-humping me, I sure as hell was going to make him explode with me.

I started to roll my hips against his and he groaned loudly. Kieron pulled his lips from mine and he looked wild. Feral. Like he was a predator about to attack and it made me shiver.

"Be careful what you start, baby girl." He growled in my ear, biting down on the lobe enough to sting, but not enough to truly hurt.

I ignored him completely, choosing to continue grinding against him. Groaning each time my clit rolled against his hardness. Kieron growled, his chest rumbled against mine as he reached down and ripped the sheet from between us, our bare skin touching once again. My eyes rolled back in my head as he very swiftly angled himself up and entered me quickly.

"That's it, baby. We have a lot of time to make up. Ride me like you so badly want to." He whispered roughly in my ear while his hands started to wander. One hand drifted to my tit to squeeze and pinch, the other to my ass to help me keep the movements going, his lips attached to my neck to nip and suck.

"Like *you* want me to." I said with attitude, rolling back and forth.

"Who wouldn't want a goddess to use them to fuck herself with?" Kieron said briefly before attaching his mouth to the other side of my neck.

"Yeah, whatever." I said with a chuckle and rolled my eyes.

That was a wrong move apparently.

Kieron stilled under me, his hands stopped moving, and he sat back to look at me. It was as if I had flipped a switch and he looked almost angry.

The difference between his anger and Luca's was that I knew in my soul that Kieron wouldn't hurt me. He might get mad, he might get frustrated, but I knew he'd never raise a hand at me or manipulate me emotionally. His anger and frustration still caused my anxiety, and body, to react.

I sat up, halting my own movements and waiting to see what the issue was. What I had done wrong. I felt my shoulders rise with tension and my head lowered slightly so I couldn't meet his eye.

"What?" I asked, my voice sounding smaller than I meant it to.

"I don't like that you put yourself down like that." He said, the frustration leaking through his words, into his tone. "I don't like that you don't see how amazing you are. If I call you a goddess, I expect you to say, "Damn right I am" or at the very least, "Thank you". If I give you a compliment, same idea.

Do you understand?" He said strongly.

"But, Kieron…" I started to say but he cut me off. He shifted forward slightly and his dick throbbed inside me. My walls were begging me to get to moving again.

"No, Talia. You're beautiful and amazing and all the good things that I or anyone else says about you. Don't let that motherfucker hurt you anymore."

"I…"

"Are you going to argue with me on my own feelings for you, baby? I think it's pretty fucking clear how I feel." He said thrusting up, pushing himself all the way inside hitting new spots that made me cry out in pleasure.

"Let me prove it to you." Kieron growled in my ear, bringing his hand up to cup the nape of my neck and hold me close.

His movements never stopped, never stalled. He moved like a man on a mission determined to ruin me for any other dick for the rest of my life. Just like he'd promised.

"You're mine now, do you understand that? *Mine.* And I take very good care of what's mine." He emphasized his words with a hard bite to my neck.

"Kieron!"

"It's true." I could feel his smug smile against my neck. Without warning, Kieron flipped us over and entered me again in one hard thrust that had my eyes rolling to the back of my head. "Fuck, I love it when you do that. I love seeing your eyes roll back, that means you're completely wrapped in the moment, only thinking about me and what I'm making you feel." Kieron grabbed my knee and wrapped my leg around his hips.

"Please," I gasp against his neck. A thin layer of perspiration covered our bodies as we moved together. I could feel my orgasm teasing me. It was so close, just within reach, and I doubled my efforts to get us both to the finish line. I wanted to see him lose control.

"I've got you, baby. I've got you." Kieron grunts into my ear, his noises and words bringing me that much closer to what was surely going to be a mind-blowing, life-shattering orgasm.

Kieron shifted his body up roughly, pulling me even closer to the headboard and his hand went up to grab it. With this leverage, he hit inside me so deeply I swear his cock was hitting my cervix. The image above me will, no doubt, stay in my mind forever.

Kieron's strong arm holding the headboard, his bicep and forearm flexing with every movement. His dark curls falling around his face, framing him like a curtain. His dark eyes never once leaving my face as he looks at me with clear love and determination in his eyes. The tattoos covering his body are so fucking hot, I trace my hands up over his shoulders, grabbing at the ink covered muscles to hold onto him as best I can while he fucks into me perfectly.

"I want you to come with me." I gasp as his thrusts speed up, making my eyes roll back in my head yet again.

"I want to fill you up with me. I need to feel your pussy fill up with my come and watch as it drips out of you." My pussy clenched around him, not wanting him to leave my body at all. His filthy words were going to push me over the edge, and I was going to take him with me.

Kieron moaned, his eyes screwed shut and his jaw clenched. "You're going to kill me, gorgeous. Come for me. Come all over my cock so you can show me what a good girl you are, taking all my come."

He continued to mutter in my ear, pushing me closer. I love how he let his mind and mouth run. Kieron wraps his hand around my hitched leg, squeezing tightly before bringing his hand to my clit and rubbing small, tight circles with just the perfect amount of pressure. It felt like a bomb detonating throughout my body.

My back arched, my nipples tightened, and the now-familiar sensation took over my body.

"Kieron, Kieron, Kieron!" I chanted, pulling him closer to my body, needing the weight of him on me.

Kieron dropped his arm and latched onto my neck, biting and sucking while he groaned loudly. His body tensed up and he gave me one last powerful thrust before I felt his warmth flood into my body. I moaned, tightening my grip around his shoulders, holding him close as possible while his body gave out.

We both stayed silent as our breathing evened out.

Kieron shifted himself off me, unfortunately, but kept me close, tucking me into his side and wrapping me in his arms.

"Do you believe me now?" He asked, kissing my head.

"I trust you." Was the last thing I remember before I fell asleep; stated, safe and relaxed.

Chapter Nineteen

Kieron

I must have fallen asleep with her wrapped perfectly in my arms. A loud knocking woke me up, and I quickly extracted myself so I could figure out who was here.

Standing up, I pulled my pants on while I watched Talia take my pillow and cuddle it close to her chest. A smile formed on my face. Her blonde hair spanning the white pillow and sheets, her bare shoulders peeking out from under the sheet. I loved seeing the tattoos hidden under her clothes, the rebel inside making herself known through her ink.

I leaned over to tuck a lock of soft hair behind her ear when the knocking happened again.

"Fuck," I whispered and quickly moved through the room to close the bedroom door so Talia would stay sleeping peacefully. Whomever it was at the door was going to be getting a pissed off Irishman.

"What?" I snapped as I ripped her front door open.

"Where are your manners, Kieron? Jesus, I thought you were raised better than that." Cara said with a smirk as she pushed herself inside Talia's apartment, past me and dropped the white plastic bag she was holding on the kitchen island.

"Sorry, I didn't know it was you. You woke me up from a nap." I said sheepishly, pulling my hair back into a bun to keep the strands out of my face and look somewhat presentable.

"Uh-huh. A 'nap'." She said with a chuckle and teasing look as she unpacked the bag. "Is that what you kids are calling it these days? Back in my day we called it an afternoon delight."

I felt my face heat up, but I crossed my arms over my chest and narrowed my eyes. I didn't want her to start making those jokes in front of Talia. She'd just started to feel comfortable.

"Har, har, har." I said sarcastically. "Don't talk like that when Talia comes out here, Cara. I'm serious."

"Well of course not, you big dolt." Cara slapped my bare arm. "I'm not daft. But that hickey you're sporting on your chest and the scratch marks on your shoulders do tell a tale." Cara said, pointing to my chest, which indeed did have marks.

I'm totally and completely okay with the marks, I love them actually. They prove that Talia marked me as hers. I looked down, seeing the deep purple circle peeking out around my tattoos on the empty skin. The scratch marks on my shoulders were fresh and red.

Fuck, just seeing them on me turned me on.

Running my fingers over the raised lines, I smiled softly. I always knew I liked leaving marks, but never wanted marks on me. Until her.

I pulled myself out of that train of thought and looked to Cara who was watching me with a knowing smile on her face. My smile and hand dropped.

"What?"

"It's nice. Seeing you like this." Cara leaned against the island with her hip and crossed her arms.

"Like what?"

"In love." She said simply.

I rubbed the back of my neck and put my other hand in my pocket. "She's something, isn't she?"

"She is. I like her for you. She brings out your softness, something that you've pushed away for so long in order to be the man who you had to be for the Clan. There was no room for weakness, for caring about anyone other than your soldiers. But since she's arrived… you're different. More open. Happier." Cara walks over to me and pats my beard-covered chin.

"She's good for you. And you for her."

"Thank you." Cara's opinion means a lot to me, I wanted them to get along. She was my pseudo-mother growing up, a nanny or caretaker that checked in on me when things got to be too much. As I climbed through the ranks, as I did what I had to, the things that turned me into a monster, her affection didn't waver.

When I turned to heavy drinking to numb the voices, the struggles of what I'd done for the Clan, and the girl I'd so cruelly left behind, Cara was there alongside Trent to bring me back to center.

Behind us the door creaked open, and Talia walked in wearing my t-shirt. My cock stirred at the image of her in my clothes and I had to restrain myself from walking over there and bending her over the edge of the sofa.

"You weren't there when I woke up." Talia said, her voice laced with sleep and her eyes barely open. My white shirt barely covered her ass, her tattooed thighs on display. Goddamn, it's like I wasn't just between her thighs, twice, a little bit ago.

"Cara was at the door and the knocking woke me. I'm sorry, baby." I said, walking over to her and hugging her tight to me, lifting her up a few inches off the floor.

"I brought the hair color you asked for, lass." Cara said, bringing one of the boxes over to where we stood. Talia pulled back from my arms with delight as she took the box from Cara.

"It's perfect. Thank you." Talia said with a bright smile, looking at the box of purple hair color in her hands like it was another lifeline.

"Do you need help coloring or are you good?" Cara asked.

"I can do it. I've done it before." Talia said with a smile, hugging the box to her chest.

"Very good." Cara smiled and looked to me. "Your father has been asking for you. I assume your phone is off."

"Shit." I dig my phone out of my pocket and see that Kellan has tried calling and messaging me, asking me to come to his office. "I have to go. Are you going to be okay here for a little bit?"

"Of course." Talia says with a smile. I can tell she wants to turn her hair color back dark. One more step away from that fucker, and a step back to herself.

"I'll be back a soon as I can." I say, resting my forehead against hers.

"I know." I take her lips in a quick kiss before going to retrieve the rest of my clothes, sans the t-shirt she's wearing.

"That boy…" I hear Cara say and can just imagine her shaking her head and smiling.

"I know." Talia says and both women start to laugh.

* * *

"Look who decided to join us with his presence." Kellan said from behind his mahogany desk.

"My phone was on silent." I say simply as I plop down into one of the chairs in front of his desk.

"Ah, I see." My father puts down the file and takes his readers off, letting them hit the desk with a soft thud. "How's Talia?"

"Good, rested. The clothes I got her were delivered and she was able to nap." I say nonchalantly. I'm not shy around sex, and my father and I have no issue discussing our sex lives. But I want to keep what Talia and I shared just between us. I don't need to flaunt the best sex that I've ever had in his face. Even though I want nothing more than to announce to the world she's mine and so fucking sexy I want to bury my face in between her thighs, making her scream my name, nonstop.

"That's good. I'm glad she's settling in well. Especially after having to see Luca the other day." Kellan stops organizing things on his desk and looks up at me sharply. "It's time for her to tell me what she knows. I expect her here in ninety minutes, understood?"

"Yes, sir." I say, turning around to go prepare Talia for what is to come.

"And Kieron," Kellan's voice calls out to me as my hand touches the brass door knob. I turn to face him expectantly.

"Make sure she knows what's at stake."

⁎

I let myself into Talia's apartment, calling out my arrival as I locked the door behind me. As I stepped into her space my nostrils were assaulted with chemicals. It was impossible to miss the smell of hair dye. It was like I was in a salon.

"Talia? Baby?" I called out, taking my leather jacket off and draping it over the back of the couch as I stepped through the apartment and into the bedroom.

"What do you think?" Talia asks me, stepping out from the bathroom and I'm floored, yet again by her beauty.

She colored her hair while I was gone, the blonde tresses long gone. Her hair is so dark, I would think it is black. She walks over to the bedside and turns the lamp on and I get a better look, the dark color is purple. A deep, rich violet that shimmers in the light.

"You look beautiful. The purple suits you, baby." I say, walking over to her, brushing the hair over her shoulder and pressing a kiss to the juncture of her neck. Talia moans softly, her body melting into my touch as I slide a hand up the back of her shirt to feel her warm, soft skin against my palm.

"I'm glad you like it. I like it too." She says breathlessly, her head dropping back to give me more access to her neck.

"I liked the blonde, I liked the black, I like this purple. I like *you*." I emphasize.

Talia pulled back, but I kept my hands around her waist. "I feel more like me. Like the me I want to be."

I honestly was at a loss for what to say. My heart was so full of her, how safe she seemed to feel and how light. I wanted to be the one to keep the fire burning in her eyes and the smile on her face. I'd do anything to keep her smiling.

"I'm so glad." I smiled softly before leaning down and capturing her lips with mine.

"What did your dad want?" Talia asks, snuggling into my chest so I could wrap my arms tighter around her.

"He wants to see you. Soon actually. He said it's time for you to tell him what you know."

"Oh." Talia says softly, her voice quivering slightly with just that one word.

"I'll be there the whole time, baby. Don't worry. And remember, we know your big, bad secret already so there really isn't anything to fear." I want her to realize that even though she will have to dreg through all the shitty parts, there is a reason for it. We are going to stop the Italians, take the son of a bitch's power, and with any luck, shove him six feet underground. I want her to realize that I know what she did to save her sister and I won't let anyone use that against her.

"That's reassuring to know, but not completely why I'm worried." She says softly. One of her small hands slips under my shirt and slides over my abs softly. Like she's tracing the ridges of my muscles to gain confidence and support in what she is about to say.

"Why are you worried?"

"If he, if they, find out that I've given information to you, there will be nothing stopping them from killing me on sight. What if we want to take a walk? I'm constantly going to be worried and paranoid about being shot. What if we want to order dinner from a new restaurant? There will always be the possibility that they've tampered with our food. What if they come after you to get to me? Fuck, Kieron. I couldn't stand something happening to you because of me. I'd escape right now if I didn't care for you so much. I don't think I could leave you even if I wanted to." She says quickly, her words tripping over themselves as she rushes to get them out.

"You're worried about the future. About our safety." I can't help but chuckle slightly. If only she knew just how influential and strong the Irish Clan is, she wouldn't worry so much.

"Yes. If I go to your father and tell him anything I do know about Luca and his father and their operation, the little, mundane information that I do know, I'll never be able to stop worrying that they will come after you. Me. Us. My family. Yours. And I'd never forgive myself if something happened to someone we love because of me. Because of the mess I've brought to your doorstep." She hangs her head sadly, and I can tell she's resigning herself to her fate. Or what she perceives as her fate.

"Let me tell you something, baby." I take her hand and walk her into the living room where I left my coat, before picking it up and draping it over her shoulders. It was adorably big on her and the vision of her in my jacket was speaking to the primal side of me.

Pulling the lapels closer to enclose her in my jacket, I leaned in close to her. She smelled vaguely like hair color, but the dominant scent was all her, all Talia, all mine.

"I won't let anything happen to us. I won't let anything happen to your family or mine. I know you don't have a good grasp on how this life works yet, but being the Skipper and the Second, comes with a lot of power. I have men guarding your parents and sister, I have men ready to guard you if we decide to leave the building. All of whom are highly skilled and dangerous. Please, trust me." I held her hands in mine, her soft, pale hands in my big, tattooed, calloused ones. A perfect fit.

"I do trust you, Kieron. I do." Talia moved one of her hands to my cheek and I couldn't help but lean into her touch. "It's Luca and his family that I don't trust. There is no mercy, no love lost between us, there's no chance he will go easy on me for old time's sake." I couldn't stand the fear in her eyes and I knew that it was only time that would show her she wasn't in danger anymore.

That I was always going to step between her and the bad from now on.

"They won't have to with how murderous I'm feeling, baby. They should worry about me, about the Irish coming after them with everything we have."

Chapter Twenty

Talia

Wrapped up in Kieron's jacket, I followed closely behind him through the building. He had linked our fingers together and pulled me along the maze of hallways and floors.

This building seemed to never end.

We got into the elevator and Kieron pushed the top floor button so we could meet Kellan. I knew the risks I was taking by giving Kellan and Kieron the information on Luca and the Italians. But I also knew I couldn't live like this anymore. Kieron was right, I couldn't let Luca take more from me.

I was free.

If what Kieron promised about his standing and the strength of the Irish mob was true, then I guess I really didn't have much of anything to worry about.

But that didn't stop me from worrying.

The insecurities and worries were running rampant through my mind. What if Kieron got hurt? What if Kellan decides I'm not worth the effort and Kieron agrees? What if the Italians are able to make it past the impenetrable defenses of the Irish?

What was the hardest for me to quiet in my mind was; what if Kieron ends up deciding I'm not worth all this trouble? That it'd be that much easier to drop me back off where he found me and high-tail it out of this messed up situation?

I don't think I would be able to survive him leaving me twice.

"Don't look so somber, baby. All he wants is to ask some questions and then that's it." Kieron pulled our linked hands to rest on his chest and pressed a soft kiss to my knuckles. "Have I told you today how beautiful you are?"

I rolled my eyes but that didn't stop a smile from crossing my face. The bruising had faded just slightly, but I was able to smile and show expression on my face without pain anymore.

"The purple hair is really sexy on you. I can't wait to take you back to the apartment and show you just how much." He whispered naughtily in my ear. He pulled back with a smirk like he knew *exactly* how his words affected me.

Let's just say the thin scrap of lace felt barely there now.

"And when will that be?" I bite my lip and look up at him through my eyelashes.

"As soon as I fucking can. Promise." Kieron bent his head down and kissed my neck in the perfect spot. The spot he'd found earlier that drove me crazy. My eyes closed and a small moan escaped my lips.

We were stopped outside Kellan's office; the hallway brightly lit and completely absent of any noise. Kieron looked down the hallway quickly, as if checking that there wasn't anyone watching us. Satisfied that the coast was clear, he turned his attention back onto me.

Before I could even make a sound to ask what was going on, Kieron pushed me up against the wall. My back hit the wall with a soft thud, and his mouth descended on mine in possessive dominance. I wrapped my arms around his strong shoulders and returned the kiss with as much passion as I could. I knew that we had a meeting, but I couldn't find it in myself to care when he was holding my thighs so tightly, when he was kissing me so hard, when my fingers were tangling in his dark hair that felt like silk.

He pulled away abruptly, still holding me up, but giving me the chance to chase his lips.

"I just can't keep my fucking hands off you." He said breathlessly. "But we have to go talk to my dad. He's expecting us."

"You started it."

"I couldn't help it." He chuckled. I'm sure I was pouting, but he slowly lowered me to the ground. His hands never leaving my body as I slowly lowered down, our eyes never leaving each other.

The tension between us was so thick and heavy that I was surprised he didn't rip my clothes off right now and take me on the carpet.

If he did, I certainly wouldn't stop him.

With a deep groan that sounded too much like a whine, Kieron stepped away and knocked loudly on the door, letting his dad know we were there.

This visit was much different from the first meeting I'd had with Kellan and Kieron. The energy coming from the office snuffed out the sexual tension the moment the door opened.

Kellan was sitting at his desk, staring at us as we walked in with his arms crossed. He was sitting back in his chair with a thoughtful look on his face. It was an odd energy that filled the room, and he looked every bit the ruler he was.

Kieron led me into the room with him closely in front of me. "Come on, baby." He whispered.

"Talia, your hair." Kellan said as he uncrossed his arms and leaned forward in his chair. "It's a mighty change but it's a good one."

"I agree." Kieron says, squeezing my hand before letting go of it and sitting in one of the chairs in front of the desk.

"Thank you," I say quietly and sit in the other chair, just waiting for the interrogation to start.

But it didn't.

It was awkward, no one speaking, and Kellan just staring at me like I held all the secrets to his success. I looked to Kieron, begging him with my eyes to save me from this attention, this unnecessary look from Kellan. Kieron looked back at me, nodded his head towards me in understanding and support.

Without warning, Kellan clapped loudly once and stood up from his chair. I jolted at the loud noise, my trauma from Luca still running my body even if I felt stronger mentally.

"Talia, Talia, Talia." Kellan drawled, resting on the edge of his desk in front of me. "I understand that this is a hard time for you. I really do, lass. But I'm going to need more information in order to continue to put my men in harm's way and start this war *properly* with the Italians."

I nodded, he'd told me what the price was for their protection and aide.

"Good." He said, pulling out a document from the pile on his desk. My eyes widened and I gulped softly at the length of the document. Holy fuck, we were going to be here forever.

Fear ran through me when I realized I wasn't going to be able to answer them all like I'm sure they wanted. My hands clenched into tight fists in my lap as I waited for the questions to start.

I looked down, staring at my lap and picking imaginary lint off my black skirt. A warm hand enveloped mine, giving me some strength to make eye-contact with Kellan. Kieron threaded our fingers together on my lap, staring down his dad as well.

"I need to know everything you know, Talia. Everything about Luca, about the restaurant front, about the Don. Let's start with how you met." Kellan said, his eyes peering into mine with all seriousness.

Taking a deep breath, I squeezed Kieron's fingers again and settled in to tell my story.

* * *

"How did you not know he was the son of the Don?" Kellan asked after I finished explaining how I'd met Luca, how our relationship progressed, when the abuse started, what I did, what I saw, everything. Kellan and Kieron had sat quietly while I told them the story. In hindsight, I should've known Luca and his family were sketchy. Our only dates out happened at the Italian Stallion, Luca was always on the phone with his family speaking in hush-hush ways, the way I'd felt almost scouted by Luca and had to meet his father before he would commit to me.

Fuck, if I'd only left him then.

"I don't know." I answer honestly. I wipe my eyes quickly, already embarrassed with how much I've broken down in front of them already. Reliving all of the hatred, abuse and fresh trauma was too much for me to handle. This interrogation had been going on for so long that now I felt flayed. I was cut open and bleeding in grief and pain at all I'd endured, at all the signs I should have seen, at how idiotic I felt for being taken advantage of.

"How often is he at the restaurant?" Kellan asks.

Kieron's hand hadn't left mine since this all started but I could tell it got more and more tense in mine as time went on. I stole a look at Kieron to make sure he was okay but when I looked at him…

Kieron looked murderous. His free hand was flexing over and over in his lap, his forearm covered in the addicting swirls of dark ink was rippling with each flex. His chest was rising and falling quicker. His nostrils flaring with anger.

His jaw was clenched so hard I could see his jawline underneath his dark beard showing through and his eyebrows were pulled together so tightly that there was no doubt he would have a deep line between his furrowed brows.

My mind immediately went to how he was mad *at me* but after a few moments I realized it was because of what I've said.

Turning back to Kellan, I took a deep breath. "What would you like to know?"

"Could you tell me how many exits there are? Entrances? Does he have an office? Is there a basement? Anything you know, I need." Kellan said, leaning forward on his desk.

"The dining room has at least two entrances, not including the door to the kitchen. There was two bathrooms, the ladies had three stalls so I can only assume that the men's was the same. I only went into the backroom once, when Luca had to talk urgently to his father but I wasn't allowed into the actual office. I don't think anyone was. There was always a guard on the door and the door had no windows so I couldn't really see if there was any inside." I pushed my fingers through my hair, letting them trail through the deep violet strands.

"There were at least three to four security cameras in the dining room. I think. But I can tell you about the kitchen or the backroom where the waitresses hung out." I offered. "If there was a basement, I haven't heard about it or seen it. But it would make sense if there was."

"And why do you say that?" Kellan quirked his eyebrow.

"Because I never heard Luca say anything about going anywhere for work other than the Italian Stallion. He never met his father anywhere but the restaurant or his house. After Luca let me in on the family business secret, he continued to meet his father there. We only went to the nightclub to meet Trenton because Luca set it up."

"They need a place to do their dirty work. Having an underground interrogation room is a necessity. We will have to start there." Kellan said, writing notes down on a notepad.

"When did he start hitting you?" Kellan asks out of the blue; his tone was clinical and cold. A huge difference from when we first met.

A low growl vibrated from the side of me and Kieron closed his eyes and dropped his head. I shook it off and focused back on the question.

"After I killed my sister's boyfriend." I whisper.

"That's enough!" Kieron roars, standing up quickly and tugging my hand and pulling me up with him. "She's answered all of your questions. You know when the abuse started, I know, she knows. We aren't going to go around and around in circles, forcing her to relive it more than once." Kieron snapped at his dad.

"We're leaving." He announces and pulls me towards the door. "If you need more information, you know where she is. But she needs a break." Kieron says softly.

I realize he's leaving a structured Clan meeting without the explicit permission of the Skipper and I hope Kieron isn't getting himself in trouble.

Kieron pulls the door open and I glance back quickly at Kellan in fear, but he didn't look angry, he didn't look like he was formulating a plan to punish us, either together or separately. He was just looking at me, with what I could only think was compassion.

Chapter Twenty-One

Kieron

I couldn't believe my ears.

I'm one more word away from having to go to the gym to obliterate the punching bag. Or better fucking yet, I want to go to find Luca and pull his fingernails out with pliers and cut his cock off then jam it down his own throat. Maybe disembowel him and watch him bleed out slowly in *our* interrogation room.

It was more of a torture chamber and I wanted to inflict some goddamn torture.

I pulled Talia through the hallway, away from my father and his horribly necessary questioning. My heart is beating so fast and so strong I'm starting to get scared that I'm actually having a heart attack.

"Kieron," Talia said softly and she lightly tugged her hand from mine. I know she wants to talk about what happened, but I couldn't.

"Don't." I said sharply, dragging her towards her place.

I'm fully aware that I'm being a prick but I need to make sure she's okay. I needed to get her out of there more than anything. If I had to watch one more tear fall from her eye or listen to one more word as she tried to hide her sobs, I was going to pull her into my lap and hug her close to my chest, protecting her as best I can from the rest of the world.

But I couldn't do that in front of my father, not yet at least. It wouldn't be appropriate for his Second when we were meeting in an official sense.

Holy fuck, it took all my willpower though and I'm sure as shit that Dad knew it too.

"Kieron…" Talia's sweet voice tried to get my attention again, and I kept pulling her.

"Please, Talia. Just a little farther."

I got no response, and when I looked back at her, I knew I fucked up. Again.

Finally, we arrive at her door and I tug her inside. Looking back at her, I see her curl in on herself; shirk away from me and her shoulders curl forward as she tried to make herself smaller. Less of a target.

I keep fucking this up, especially when I'm so overwhelmed with all the different emotions that keep showing up. I push my hands through my hair, getting the rings on my fingers get tangled. I deserve the sting of pain as I rip the rings from my hair.

"Are you mad?" She whispered and the guilt made me clench my teeth a little harder.

"Baby, I'm sorry. For all you've had to endure. For all you've suffered. And I'm sorry I just made you feel like you had to try to hide." I took a deep breath and let it out slowly, trying my best to calm my beating heart. "Yeah, I saw that." I stepped into her, and wrapped my arms around her.

It felt like forever of silence, of her arms not around me, and just when I was going to lean back, fearful that I'd officially done more damage than I could salvage with my words, her arms wrapped around my shoulders.

"This isn't your fault."

We would be going round and round in circles of blame if I brought up just how much it was my fault. How much it *felt* like my fault. How even though I'd done my best to make sure someone was watching over her, I'd failed. We'd already spent too much time in the guilt/blame game.

Instead of saying that, I just burrowed into her embrace further.

"After hearing what he made you do…what you had to do to survive…how could you be okay with being intimate with me? With anyone?" I felt sick to my stomach about how she must have been so uncomfortable when we were together. Luca had used her, humiliated her, abused her, raped her forcefully, and hearing the specific stories correlated with awful thing…

"That's what's bothering you?" Talia said incredulously. Her hand lifted my chin and those gorgeous eyes met mine.

"Kieron…" She said softly, her hand cupping my beard-clad chin. "I didn't want to tell you those things."

"I know. And that's another reason I'm so fucking pissed off because you were forced to. By my dad. Some of those questions weren't necessary."

"To help keep you guys, my family and myself protected, it's okay." She argued.

"But that doesn't mean you should have to expose every single horrid thing that has happened to you to basically a stranger. You should've been able to tell me those things when you were ready. It was just another thing taken from you, baby and I'm sorry for that." I explained.

"I would've told you eventually." She said softly, her eyes flinting to the side quickly before returning to mine. "You know that, right? I'm not embarrassed."

Relief coursed through my body, drenching the red-hot fear and brought me back to neutral.

I press a kiss the top of her head.

Neither of us spoke, but the air was charged with electricity of want and need. I *needed* to show her I loved her. I *needed* to know she was okay. And on a primal, possessive level, I *needed* to be inside her to show her and prove how I'm not-a-fucking-thing like that piece of shit. That I'd take care of her, and be gentle with her always.

Talia leaned into me the same moment I bent down and we met in a simple, sweet kiss.

I poured as much love and adoration as I could into that kiss. But, of course, as like any time I'd had my lips on Talia, I couldn't keep it simple and sweet.

I picked her up, keeping her pressed as close to my chest as I could. As she wrapped her thighs tightly around my waist, I ground our hips together and she gasped, her head dropping back against the wall giving me access to her neck.

"Tell me this is okay." I whisper as I graze her neck with my teeth and lightly suck.

"More than okay." She groans and I can feel her body shiver slightly as her back arches. "In fact, if you don't take me to bed right now, I'm going to scream."

"My name?" I didn't need to take her to the bed, in fact, I don't know if I could physically part from her that long. I grabbed her ass and held her in position as I walked us the three steps over to the couch. I'd have no problem taking her against the wall, but I also want to lay her out and feast on her.

"You'll have to earn that." Goddamn, this woman is perfect.

"Don't you worry, baby. You'll be hoarse from screaming my name soon." I place her on the cushions, but not letting my body move too far from hers. In fact, I pushed in closer, letting my weight rest on her as I slipped my hand up her skirt.

And I groan.

She's so wet and ready for me that I meet no resistance as I slid a finger inside, she mewls and arches her back.

Without warning, I pull my finger out and look at Talia. I want to see her big, beautiful eyes staring at me and know that it is *me* who is making her feel this way.

"Take your shirt off." I growl, sitting back and reaching behind my head to take my own t-shirt off and throwing it to the side. Talia sits up with hooded eyes and her black hair resting behind her shoulders, down her back as she pulls the material free from her body.

I drink in the pale skin she's exposed, contrasting so beautifully with the deep red lace bra she's wearing. And I snap.

I rip off her skirt and pull the boots she's wearing off. I bit my lower lip and both of us were staring at the other. Her eyes were raking over my torso, lowering and lowering until they stopped at the waistband of my jeans before her expression matched mine and she smirked at the wood I was sporting.

My dick was pissed as fuck at being trapped in the denim prison, yet again, when all it wanted was to be free.

Talia licked her lips and looked up at me with a teasing, confident gleam in her eye. Suddenly, I was thankful for the denim tape down because otherwise I would have blown my load with that one look.

I bent over and inhaled at the apex of her thighs, breathing in the intoxicating scent of her.

"You smell so good." I groaned as I moved her lace thong over gently, and licked her from top to bottom, gathering as much of her moisture as I could on my tongue. "You taste so good."

Talia groaned loudly, and I watched, momentarily entranced, as her tits moved up and down with her quick breathing.

"Don't stop." She whispered and I got right back to work. I started circling her clit with my tongue, pushing down just slightly and was rewarded with a sharp tug of my hair.

I chuckled, getting the hint, and set to work. I threw her thighs over my shoulders and dug in. I fucked her with my tongue, working her towards another one of the many orgasms I've brought her today. Quickly, I could feel her muscles tense up, her abs contracted and she started to lift her hips in time with my strokes.

"Fuck, Kieron. Yes, yes." She chanted, making me harder than fucking steel. A gush of heat coated my tongue and I groaned, never letting up on the momentum and pressure to keep her orgasm going as long as I possibly could.

The moment I felt her shakes start to subside, I let her legs fall from my shoulders and shed my belt and jeans. Letting my cock spring free, I wasted no time at all in lining myself up with her entrance.

"Please, Kieron." Talia whispered, running her hands down my biceps before gripping onto my forearms as I held myself over her.

"You're mine, baby. Tell me you know that." I slid into her heat inch by inch, slowly and methodically. I felt the familiar sensation at the base of my spine that told me a powerful fucking orgasm was on the precipice.

"Harder." She demanded, completely ignoring my request.

"Tell me you're mine."

"Fuck me harder." Oh, that shit wasn't going to fly. I smirked at her and when she looked at me straight on, I knew she was playing with me. My sweet Talia's talons were coming out.

I pulled out completely and Talia whined. "Now, now, baby. Tell me, tell me you're mine and I'll make love to you like you deserve, fuck you like you want."

"Kieron," She whimpered and her eyes rolled back.

Holy fuck, I wanted to see that look of passion and pure, unfiltered need cross her face every day for the rest of my life. I wanted to be the one to put it there.

"Say it." I growled, sliding my fingers into her hair at the base of her neck and tugging softly. "Please, baby."

Talia surged up, wrapping her arms around my neck and we met in an open mouth kiss that was dirty and desperate and full of lust. Our kisses turned deeper, I couldn't tell where she ended and I began. It was messy and all-consuming.

Breaking the kiss, I looked at her softly as our breaths mixed. "Even if you won't say it because you're being a brat," I said as I slapped her ass, "I know it. I know you're mine just as fully as I'm yours. Always have been. Because the two of us, baby? We are fate. Destined. And I'm never letting you go again."

I slid into her again, but didn't fuck hard, rough and fast like she asked for. It would've been great, like always, but there was something about going slow that was exactly what we both needed.

Every thrust was slow and meaningful, charged with tension. Talia didn't stop touching me; her nails dug into my back and shoulders, her calves hooked around my waist or thighs, keeping me close, her fingers tangling in my hair. I kept a slow pace that was fucking torture of the best kind. Slow enough that I could feel every ripple of muscle, every time she clenched or fluttered around my cock, but deep and hard enough that I bottomed out with each thrust. I bite her neck softly and she moans in my ear, pulling my weight onto her fully. Her soft breasts are still encased in lace but the dusty rose of her nipples are intoxicating to see and feel against my bare chest.

"I'm yours, Kieron. Yours." Her voice is hoarse and quiet, proving her words meant only for my ears and I know that this girl is it for me. I take her lips in a deep kiss full of meaning and love while I deepened my thrusts.

"Fucking right you are. And I'm yours." I said and kissed her passionately.

Talia started lifting her hips up, meeting my thrusts so damn perfectly that I had to reposition myself to keep from coming. With a growl, I sat up, resting my weight on one my knees, putting my other foot on the floor, and yanked her hips up to meet mine. Her hair fanned out on the grey couch as her body shifted backwards and a delicious yelp escaped her lips.

My eyes rolled back in my head at the new angle.

"If you keep going like this, I'm going to come again." She warned. Like that was a fucking problem.

"Challenge accepted." I wrapped my hands around her hips, holding onto her hips and using them to bring her to me harder and thrust over and over.

Her pussy starts to clench tightly around my cock and I can feel myself losing it. The tingle sensation at the base of my spine was feeling like a rocket beginning to ignite and I was powerless to stop it. I can tell we both are close and going to reach the end together.

"Right there, right there," Talia cries and after a couple more hard, deep, grinding thrusts she peaked pulling me into the abyss with her. I groan out her name and I lean over to hold her as we both come closer together.

I know that she is still struggling with all the abuse she's suffered, all the pain and protection she'd had to endure. And the way that my father had to poke and prod at her emotions and memories had only made her cry and shake.

As I lay down next to my girl on the couch, I wrap her tightly in my arms and vow that nothing and no one will ever make her cry again.

Chapter Twenty-Two

Kieron

"Kieron," I hear a soft whisper pull me from sleep. "Kieron, wake up."

Peeking through one eye, Talia's big brown eyes are staring right at me with a sweet, longing look. During the night we'd shifted and Talia was on top of me, her light warm body creating the perfect pocket to fall into a deep sleep.

"Why?" I groaned, wrapping my arm around her and trying to go back to sleep.

"Your phone won't shut up."

Fuck. That probably meant something was going on. They'd discovered something we could use to take the Garzino's down. Hopefully it was something that would end up with Luca tied to a chair and me standing over him with a bloody serrated knife as he took his last breath.

I scrambled off the couch and found my jeans, pulling the buzzing phone out. Sure as shit, it was Skipper.

"Hello?"

"About goddamn time, Kieron. I understand you're infatuated with this girl but you still have fucking responsibilities and need to be accessible at all times. Do I make myself clear?" My father's voice boomed through the speaker.

"Yes, sir. Won't happen again."

"Now, pack a bag for you both and get the fuck out of the building."

My face paled and I felt my heart stop, my hand gripped the small phone a little harder. "What happened?"

"The Garzino's, that's what fucking happened. They infiltrated the security system and one of the grunts saw an unknown man leaving the basement structures. I'm not taking any chances. Get out and take anything of…a sensitive nature…with you." With that, he hung up the phone and I was left listening to the frustrating dial tone.

I jumped into action, pulling my discarded shirt on and walking straight into Talia's room.

"Kieron?"

I couldn't answer, we didn't have time. I didn't want to scare her, but I needed to get her out. Luckily in this apartment, there was a canvas go-bag in the bedroom closet. I grabbed it off the top of the shelf and threw in as many new clothes as I could. Just blindly shoving clothes into the bag and hoping for the best.

"Kieron, what's going on?" Talia's voice was worried understandably, but my first focus was getting her out of the building. If one of Garzino's men had infiltrated the building there is no telling what they did in their brief time here; poison the water, plant cameras and microphones, figure out a way to steal Talia from me…

"We have to leave. Is there anything specific you need to take?" I walk into the bathroom and pack anything on the counter I see.

"Why do we have to leave?" Talia followed me, stepping into leggings and throwing a dark crop top over her lacey bra that I loved.

"It seems at your ex somehow got one of his soldiers into the building and I'm not taking any chances. More than likely, we are going to evacuate the whole building in stages, then go over the entire thing with a fine-tooth comb. But right now, you and I are going to a safehouse. Your safety is my top priority. Now, hurry it up."

My words were all fact and true, but my tone was short. I knew the moment I opened my mouth that my stress was going to make me sound like an asshole. I cringed slightly as I look to her and see in her eyes that she looked like I'd yelled at her.

We would have time to talk it through later, right now I needed to get her out of the building. I still needed to grab my own go-bag and the documents in Kellan's office.

"Put on some tennis shoes, we're going to make a run for it. I have a few more things to go grab." I said, zipping up the bag and grabbing Talia's hand on the way out of the bathroom. "I'm going to go grab the stuff in my apartment and some things I need in my dad's office. Do not leave, do not let anyone in." I set her and the bag on the couch, holding her by the upper arms and kissing her forehead.

"Okay." Talia said softly, nodding and looking scared. She was looking around the room as if Luca was going to jump out from behind the door and her life would go back to how it was. Not on my watch.

"I'll be back in five minutes. Promise." I go to move away, those five minutes having had started, but my girl grabs the front of my shirt and pulls me in for a surprise kiss. It was quick and dirty, but filled with, dare I dream to think it, love.

"I love you." I whispered, fully expecting her not to return my words. At least not yet, even if I saw it in her eyes. Talia gasped softly and her mouth opened and closed like a fish before I put her out of her misery with a smirk. "Don't worry, baby. You take your time, but I want you to know how I feel."

The urgency to get her out of the building was growing stronger with every pressing moment and so I kissed her forehead, hovering there for the moment in hope.

"I'm serious, Talia. Do not let anyone in here. I don't know who is on our side at the moment." I warn her and walk out the door, determined to be back to her as soon as humanly possible.

* * *

After leaving my apartment with my always prepared go bag over my shoulder, I sprint to my father's office.

"What are you still doing here?" Kellan's voice booms as soon as I slip through the door. "I told you to get the fuck out."

"You told me to grab the documents." I snap at him, noticing that he's going through the sensitive documents and packing up the ones that would be the worst to fall into the wrong hands, but shredding the rest. Each document was getting a tenth of a second of contemplation before they met their fate.

"I told you to grab anything of sensitive nature. Not to break into my office."

"If you've got the documents, I'm going to go back to Talia." I say to him quickly and turn to leave.

"You need to make a decision and quick, Kieron. This is getting messier and if she had our last name there would be an additional level of protection for her." Kellan said, his eyes never leaving the documents in his hand.

"We've already had this conversation."

"And you didn't give it the proper thought." Kellan snapped. He wasn't my dad in this moment, he was the Skipper, the leader of the Boston mafia, the head of the Irish clan. "The only reason I'm giving you this much time is because you're my son. Otherwise, I would have had you marry her the moment you brought her into the fold and we decided to start this fucking war."

"I can't just force her to marry me."

"You'll think of something." He said, his voice changing again from Skipper to father. "This is about her safety."

"I understand." I hung my head slightly. It really was the only sure way I could protect her from all angles.

"Good. Now get out of here."

Not needing to be told twice, I turned to open the door to get back to my girl when the unmistakable sound of an explosion surrounded us. The sound and vibrations had come from underneath our feet… Right where Talia's apartment is.

"Was that…" Kellan asked, looking up from his papers. But I didn't answer him.

I ran.

I ran like there was a demon chasing after me. I ran like my life depended on it. I ran like *her* life depended on it.

Because it probably did.

Chapter Twenty-Three

Talia

He loves me, Was the only thought running through my head. My chest was warm, my cheeks were probably red with a blush that ran down my chest and they hurt from how hard I was smiling.

He loves me. My heart beat quicker at the knowledge that the man of my dreams, the man who I thought had gotten away…loved me.

I couldn't say those words back, no matter how much I wanted to. The last time I'd said those words to a man, my life went to shit. I know Kieron is nothing like Luca, but I can't help it. Something was holding my tongue as he shared his feelings.

I was too lost in thought to do anything but wait for Kieron to return, counting down the seconds in my mind until he would arrive. There wasn't a doubt in my mind that Luca had taken his threat 100% seriously, no matter the impending war between the Italians and the Irish. It didn't matter in his mind.

All that mattered was that I broke a promise and now my actions would have to be paid for. In blood. And since I wasn't readily available anymore… At the very least, I'm thankful he didn't go after my sister or my parents.

That I know of.

My anxiety started to spike and I twisted a flyaway lock of dark hair around my finger. Fuck, Kieron needs to get back here now so I can make sure they're okay.

I went to the kitchen hoping that there might be an old school landline but came up empty. I wish I had my phone, any phone. Some way of contacting them and checking in.

Pacing back and forth in front of the grey kitchen island, I run my fingers through my hair nervously.

I'm so fucking sick of being nervous, of being helpless. I used to be this motherfucking badass that didn't give two shits about anyone's opinion. I would be the first one to stand up for someone and for myself, by force if needed. But look at me now, cowering because of how an ex-boyfriend made me feel. It makes me sick to my stomach how much I changed for him, even when things were good.

Beep, beep, beep. Beep, beep, beep.

Where is that coming from?

Beep, beep, beep.

I walk through the living room, and pull the cushions off the couch in search for the noise. Nothing.

Going into the bedroom, the sound continued to ring out in illusive beeps.

The beeps were getting louder. I pulled the bed and sheets apart, searching for the sound and coming up empty. Getting on the floor and looking underneath the bed and through the bedframe, still coming up empty. I ran into the bathroom and the beeping got even louder.

"What is it?" I whisper, searching around but seeing nothing on the surface level. I tear through the cabinets, still coming up empty. Frustrated and now super over-stimulated with the continual beeping, I lean back roughly against the door and put my head in my hands.

The beeps echo slightly, still loud and there, I look over to where the sound must be coming from…

In the air vent I see a faint light, so faint I would've missed it had I not been on the floor.

I ripped the vent grate out unceremoniously and pulled the small clear bag containing a cell phone out. It was dreadful, freaky and scary all at the same time. A fog of suspense filled the air as I unwrapped the phone from the clear plastic, seeing the words 'Unknown Number' flashing on the screen.

It was an older phone; wouldn't have internet, was made only for calling and sending out the occasional text, and it was *still* ringing.

So many questions went through my mind. Should I answer it? How did the phone get in the vent? Who hid it within my apartment? But ultimately, *should I answer it?*

I took a deep breath and realized I would answer it regardless, I was too nosy. I needed to know who was on the other end. I pressed the green 'talk' button and slowly brought it to my ear.

"Hello?" I said strongly, hoping my voice sounded stronger than I felt.

"About goddamn time, you whore."

Luca's voice filled my ear and my body immediately went into protection mode. I curled into myself; my shoulders scrunching up higher, my arms wrapping around my torso and my feet slid up, bending at the knees to protect myself. It was so fucking stupid, just the sound of his voice sent me into this fearful state.

Not again. Never again.

"What do you want?" I sneered, forcing myself to relax and reminding myself that he wasn't in the room, he couldn't hurt me.

"I wanted to let you know, show you, just how inadequate you're protected with the Irish. I wanted to show you I could've killed you. I could've done so much fucking worse than kill you. You aren't safe. Not from me, not from my men."

"That's funny, Luca. It just seems like you weren't man enough to kill me. You never have been. Just a weak, pathetic excuse of a man who thinks hitting and raping women is okay."

I knew I was playing with fire but fuck, it felt amazing to finally tell him off. Finally show him he has no hold on me. I felt more powerful with the safety of the phone.

"I'll remember that." Luca said. I could tell he was livid by his accent thickening; in my mind's eye he was most likely grinding his teeth and his nostrils were flaring.

"You should, motherfucker."

"You're being awfully cocky for being such a whiny cunt."

"I finally have a partner who supports and cherishes me, not uses me as their emotional and physical punching bag."

Luca scoffed through the phone. "For now. He'll get tired of you like I did and kick you to the curb. Then you'll have no one to hide behind, *darling*. You're going to pay for what you've done, the war you've started and the inconvenience you've put me through for this. Just know this, you are going to get what is coming to you. What you deserve."

Before I even took a breath to respond to the vitriol, he was spewing my way, Luca hung up and I was met with a dial tone. One thing was for sure, he wasn't letting me go. What Kieron had said about Luca's ego being bruised and how he wanted to punish me for it, was completely true.

Luca wasn't going to stop.

I hope I could stop him before he hurt anyone I loved. I couldn't let that happen. Even at cost of my own life.

I walked out into the living room, sitting down next to the go-bag with the phone in my hand. It was scary that Luca had somehow gotten into my apartment and stashed a phone. It was terrifying that he had been here when I was sleeping and vulnerable without Kieron there for protection. Without anyone or anything for protection.

Wherever Kieron was taking me, wherever this safehouse was, I was going to have him teach me to fight. Maybe even have him train me on how to use a gun. I would not be left vulnerable like that ever again.

I tossed the phone across the room. Not hard enough to break it, but I needed some space. I needed to think and calm down before Kieron got back.

The view from this high up was incredible and I hadn't really given it the proper appreciation it deserves. With nothing else to do but wait, I figured no time like the present. Pulling back the gossamer curtain, it was like I could finally take a deep breath. We are so high above the fog up here, above the sounds of the city. The sun was brightly shining, illuminating the world in the best possible way regardless of any darkness or ugliness that was tainting my life.

I put my hand up against the warming glass, noticing for the first time just how thick it is. As I take a deep breath and then rest my head against the glass, I hear a zipping sound, like one of those fireworks on the Fourth Of July that zips around obnoxiously before disintegrating in noise and being.

Looking around me, I can't find anything in the apartment that was making any noise, let alone one as annoying as that. But then, I slowly look back to the window as I realize the noise isn't coming from inside. It's coming from the outside.

Through the air is whizzing some kind of pointed object, propelled like a rocket and headed straight for me. It hits the window and explodes with a deafening boom. I turn and dive for the floor with my hands over my head, bracing myself for impact and injury, but it never comes.

The glass is still standing, spider-webbed and cracked, but standing. A barrier between me and whatever bad thing was coming for me.

"What?" I whisper, lifting my head slowly and hoping that nothing else comes at me.

"Talia!" Kieron's voice roars from the hallway. "Talia!"

I climb to my feet, shaking slightly, I stand tall and strong, not willing to let Luca take anything more from me. He had beaten me, he had hurt me and abused me, but I'm not fucking there anymore. I'm strong and him trying to kill me *really* pissed me off.

The front door burst open and in ran my tall, burly, tattooed Mafia man. His eyes were wild, darting back and forth, as he searched the room for me while searching for a threat to protect me from. His heavy footsteps rushed over to me, sweeping me into his arms and holding me tightly against him.

"Are you okay? Fuck, Talia." His eyes rake over my body, searching for any signs of injury. "I heard the explosion and I swear to God, I've never run so fast in my life. Do you hurt anywhere?"

His chest was heaving deeply with the effort it took to get here so quickly, but that didn't seem to matter in this moment.

"I'm fine. I don't even really know what happened." My ears are ringing and I think I bruised my damn chin from diving to the ground. "Are you okay?"

"I'm fine, worried about you. I thought I'd lost you." Kieron says, his voice full of leftover fear.

"I'm okay." I immediately want to say hose three little words that will inevitably change my life. I want to prove to him that I'm okay and that our life will go on happily regardless of his job and family ties, of my past and how it's gunning for us. I threaded my fingers into his beard and cupped his jaw, keeping his eyes locked to mine. "I love you, too."

A stolen moment in a day that had erupted into chaos and fire, Kieron and I had been given clarity and understanding of our true feelings. I didn't want to wait any longer, I didn't want to give anything else to Luca by not giving Kieron my whole heart because I was scared.

"You do?" Kieron's eyes sparkled with emotion and disbelief but the smile he gave me was one I'll never forget.

"More than anything."

"Not as much as I love you, baby." He said and kissed me. One arm wrapped around my waist while the other hand went to the back of my head and brought me close to him. Wrapping me in his clean, masculine scent and I instantly calmed.

"As touching as this moment is, get the fuck out of here. Jesus Christ, what part of my orders are you not understanding?" Kellan yells at us through the door before disappearing back into the hallway.

"He's right," Kieron said, pulled completely out of the moment. "I need to get you out of here."

"Then let's go." I grab his hand and thread our fingers together before picking up the go-bag and walking as quickly as I could with him through the hallway.

Chapter Twenty-Four

Kieron

"I found the phone about five minutes before the explosion happened. Then got the pleasure of hearing Luca's fucking voice just being a prick." Talia talked quickly as I strapped her into my car.

As brave as she was sounding, as angry as she was, her hands were shaking. She was going into shock and not realizing it, so I'm just trying to keep her moving and talking.

"Do you still have the phone?"

"Yeah, I grabbed it before we left. It's in the bag." Her teeth start to chatter and I rip my leather jacket off, tucking her into it as quickly as I can before closing the door of the Mustang. I needed to do a quick sweep of the car and make sure there isn't any other explosives. I get down on the ground and look under the axis, then check the wheel wells, the trunk and backseat before being satisfied we were safe for the moment and running to the driver's side.

I didn't know if there are any more bombs or missiles in the building but I didn't want to stay around to find out. It was obvious that the missile had been meant for Talia and the next time, we might not get so lucky. I wasn't willing to chance it.

"That utter piece-of-shit." I mutter under my breath. Talia was quiet, the shaking hadn't gone away but at least it wasn't getting worse.

I was going to find Luca and his cowardly hideaway and when I did there was going to be serious hell to pay. I'd take my brass knuckles and bust open his head until that Garzino fucker couldn't get up. I wanted to see him suffer before I ended his life. I wanted to see the fear and remorse in his eyes before the life drained from them.

"He won't be living much longer, baby. I promise you that." I was speeding through the streets, pushing my Mustang to the max. I wanted to get us out of the city as quickly as possible.

"Kieron! You're going too fucking fast!" Talia cries out.

"Can you tell me more about the call? What did he say? Exactly, Talia, what did he say?" I took my foot off the accelerator slightly, still going way over the speed limit, but enough that it made her feel more comfortable.

"He just wanted to call me names and get all pissy that I got away from him."

"Talia, what exactly did he say?" I ask again. Putting my hand on her thigh I try to take a deep breath. She won't appreciate me going all Second-In-Command but my patience is wearing thin.

"I told you, he was just putting on a show of power like he used to. But it won't work on me anymore."

"Goddamn it, Talia, what exactly did he say!" I snap, a lock of hair fell into my eyes and I moved the hand from her thigh to move it back. Stress and anxiety felt like they were going to make my heart explode. I just needed her to answer the fucking question the way that I'd asked. He might have left a clue or a message within his evil words that we could somehow figure out his next move, figure out where he is hiding. Fuck, any number of things, but I needed to know what he said.

"Please." I say softly.

"He told me that I wasn't safe with you or in that building. That the phone proved it. He told me I am a whore and I am going to pay for what I've done to him. He told me you'll get tired of me and leave me. Then I'll have no one to hide behind. His words, not mine. He called me 'darling' like he used to before he would beat me. But he said more than once about how I wasn't safe with you or with the Irish and I'd be back with him and the Italians quickly." She rattled off, not looking at me, but watching the cars and buildings fly by.

The leather of the steering wheel creaked with the strain of my grip. How dare he say those things to her. How dare he put those thoughts into her head that I'd leave her, ever. How fucking dare he say I can't protect her.

"You know he's just being a dickhead, right? He's trying to get into your head and make you think those things. I'd never leave you, baby."

Talia nods offhandedly, still not looking at me.

I run my hand over my face and grip the steering wheel harder. I would have to deal with this, with frightening her or hurting her feelings but I can't right now.

Pulling my phone out of my pocket, I dial my dad's number and wait for him to answer.

"Are you guys there yet?" Kellan's voice asks through the phone.

"No, about ninety more minutes. Are you going to your safehouse?"

"ETA five minutes."

"Good, good. I have new information from Talia about what happened."

"Is she alright?" My dad asked and the fact that he asked about her before asking what the information was made me smirk.

"She's rattled, but the bulletproof glass on our floor saved her life. I checked the car for explosives, but there wasn't any. Garzino, or a man from their camp, somehow snuck into her apartment, hid a fucking cell phone and then called right before the explosion to keep her distracted."

"Fuck." Kellan snarls. "What did he say?"

"Nothing that needs repeating at this moment." I say into the phone, chancing a look over at Talia. She's finally looking at me, a look of gratitude in her eyes. "I'll send any pertinent information your way."

"Understood. Keep safe." Kellan said and hung up. Putting the phone in the middle seat, I saw the exit for my beach house and took it.

* * *

"It's beautiful!" Talia cried as she climbed out of the car. Watching her light up as she saw the beach, the water gently hitting the sand and the wind going through the trees was just what I wanted to bring to her. I wanted to give her relaxation and time to be herself. Once she saw the small one-story house right on the beach and looked back at me with a look of excitement on her face.

"Let me show you your new place for a while." I held my hand out with a smile on my face and she ran over to take it.

Thankfully, I'd been able to shoot a quick text off to Cara and she was able to stock everything for us.

"Oh my god, Kieron, it's beautiful." She repeats as she is looking around my house. I never wanted a huge, obnoxious house that would be too much space for just me. With the craziness and danger of my life, I wanted a piece of paradise, an oasis, that I could all my own.

The wooden exterior was painted a pale blue and weathered from years of salt spray hitting the paint. The exterior trim was a natural brown and the awning was just deep enough that I was able to put two white rocking chairs side-by-side to watch the sunset. With the sand that came right up to the front door, it was the perfect little home. And I didn't spend nearly enough time here due to the demands that come from being the Second.

Inside, I made sure to decorate, but honestly, I didn't care much for decorating. Who did? I made sure I had a few comfortable places to sit; an overstuffed couch and loveseat, a big ass TV and the bookshelves were lined with my favorites. Whenever I actually got to be here, I just wanted to relax and get out on the water.

I watched Talia take in everything. Her long violet hair falling out of the haphazard ponytail she'd thrown her hair in earlier. She looked absolutely beautiful. Natural. Like she belonged here, with me. *My girl.*

"There are no pictures anywhere, Kieron." She noted, dropping the go-bag in the middle of the living room.

"Who would I put pictures up of right now?"

"Your family, you traveling, you surfing, things you like…" She lists off. "I love having pictures up." Talia says wistfully, her eyes trailing along almost sadly.

"What's wrong, baby?" I can't take the look of sadness in her eyes. Wrapping my arms around her and tucking her under my arm, I wait for her to tell me what's going on.

"I had all these pictures at my, or Luca's, apartment. They were of my family, of my childhood and my life when I actually knew what my life was."

"We should've grabbed them before we left. We could've."

"They're just pictures." She said sadly. "Nothing compared to staying alive and keeping everyone I love alive."

"We'll take more. And then," I say, taking a step back and pointing to one of the blank spots on the wall "we put our favorite right here."

Talia smiles at me, bringing some of that light she had before comes back into her eyes. "I'd like that."

* * *

Call me through the encrypted line. We need to talk. My father apparently had something damn important if he wanted to talk through the encrypted line.

I pulled my laptop out of my go-bag, closing the door to the bedroom but leaving the door cracked so Talia could see me when she wakes up. After giving her a quick tour of the house, I offered for her to lay down and rest in my bed. Our bed. I'm surprised my stubborn woman took me up on it and she took her sneakers off and climbed right into the king-sized bed.

I reluctantly crawled out of the bed after holding her until she drifted off, after getting the message from Kellan.

Booting up my computer and plugging in the address to the deep, dark website that we used to hold meetings when we couldn't be together. His face appeared on the grainy screen, and then another box popped up with Trenton and Bryan sitting together.

"Kieron. Trenton. Bryan." My dad greeted us all before leaning back in his desk chair. He was in his honky-tonk, backwater town safehouse. It was his favorite one for some reason unknown to me, but the security pros were undeniable. It just wasn't my taste. Literally that house had nothing and no one around the small shack for fifty miles. Nothing around, nothing to look at, just open space and fields. It was like going out to a bunker.

"Skipper. What was it you needed to tell us?" I ask, leaning forward with my elbows on my knees. "Is there any new information on headquarters?"

"Preliminary sweeps are good so far. There has been no news of other explosives anywhere, and thanks to your report about the phone in the air vent I have made sure that the men doing the sweeps are extremely thorough. Every single nook and cranny is being swept. It may take us a bit longer to be able to move into headquarters but I'm working on a temporary place. Luckily, our businesses aren't reliant solely on the one property." Kellan opened a desk drawer and pulled a file out.

"The missile that we recovered, or the debris from Talia's window, show that the explosive was definitely Italian made. We have to assume that they knew that our windows were reinforced bulletproof glass. They don't want to kill Talia now, otherwise the phone would have been laced with an explosive as well."

I nodded and saw Trenton do the same.

"They don't want her to die with you. Luca is a sick motherfucker and has made it very known that the only harm to come to Talia is from his hand." Trenton speaks up and as the flames of my anger burned brighter in my chest. I could only imagine the terrible, awful things he wanted to do to her. I couldn't let that happen.

"Trenton has made progress through the rankings and earning the Garzino's trust." My father stepped in. "However, due to the attacks, I wanted another inside man and Bryan volunteered to have Trenton's back. Which I approved. Bryan is going to be looking into their financial situation more as Trenton is still climbing the solider rankings."

"You both are okay with that?" I ask. I know Trenton was all for it, he wanted to take the Garzino family down as badly as I do, but as much as I trusted Bryan, I wanted to make sure that he was okay with this change of this magnitude. Bryan hasn't had to go undercover before and with as stressed as I was about keeping Talia okay, I needed to take care of my men, *my friends* as well.

"Hell yes, man. I want to take these cocksuckers down." Bryan said, his enthusiasm making me feel better about sending him into the lion's den. Nodding, I looked to Trent, one of my oldest friends, who looked exhausted. He had dark circles under his eyes and his red hair was disheveled.

"One hundred percent." He said, through the obvious exhaustion through the stress and anxiety he no doubly was feeling, Trent knew what this means for me and he had my back.

"Have you discovered anything of importance?" Kellan asks, pulling the papers from the file.

"The things that Talia told me Garzino said on the phone correlate to what you've said already. Taunting, abusive, trying to put doubts in her head." I explain, the frustration clear in my tone but I do my best to keep my mind clear and focused on the problem.

"Lorenzo has pulled most of the underlings that haven't been sworn in onto surveillance. They've been tasked to your old apartment, the sisters place, the parents, any and all places of business and personal for the Irish mafia. If we thought they were watching us before, it's nothing compared to now." Trent ran his hand through his hair pulling slightly at the roots. "It took a lot of fucking convincing to get Bryan into the fold. They have absolutely no trust in anyone anymore."

No one said anything, knowing just how gnarly and condemning our own tests for new recruits are, I don't want to know what Trent and Bryan had to do. I'm sure they didn't want to explain it, nor should they have to.

"You know what I'm going to say, Kieron." My dad looks at me through the camera, his eyebrow arched and his head tipped to the side.

"I'll take care of it and let you know when it's done."

Chapter Twenty-Five

Talia

I know the moment I wake up that Kieron's been out of bed for a while. The bed at his house is amazingly comfortable and I thought the mattress back at headquarters was great. The setup at his house was more about comfort and ease than aesthetics and it was just what I needed. I felt safe. A feeling I was quickly associating with only Kieron.

Climbing out of bed, I pushed open the bedroom door and see the man in question. He sat with his back to me, hunched over his laptop. I didn't even know he'd been able to grab his laptop in the mad dash out.

"I'll take care of it and let you know when it's done." Kieron said strongly and slammed the top to his laptop down. He ran his fingers through his hair, the dark waves free from the tie. He seemed so stressed out.

"What do you have to take care of?" I ask, moving to sit next to my burly, tattooed, man who looked like the world was resting on his shoulders.

"I need to ask you something. I don't know how you'll feel about it." He says quietly, resting his chin on his clasped hands.

My eyes opened wide, a bit in shock and a bit in fear. "Okay, what is it?"

"Will you…Goddamn." Kieron chuckled, and turned to face me. He took a deep breath, staring at me with a look I just couldn't place. His deep brown eyes were open and showing me exactly how he was feeling. My problem was I didn't trust what I saw as being the truth.

"Talia, baby, you know I love you. I love you so much and I never want to not be there for you, with you, ever again. I understand we haven't had time to let this relationship grow, but I want to be the person who steps between you and anything that could make you upset, make you cry, even make you sad. It's my job to keep you happy and safe, a job I want so fucking badly I can't stand it." He said with so much passion I couldn't help but smile. "Will you marry me?"

"What the fuck?" I whisper, taken so far aback that it just slipped out. "I mean, Kieron, what the fuck?"

He laughed, taking ahold of my hands and kissing my fingertips. "Will you marry me?" He repeated. I don't know how or why it happened, but his nervousness seemed to have dissipated the moment I opened my mouth after his initial proposal.

"This is insanely fast. Are you sure *you* want to do that?" I didn't want to bring all the reasons why he shouldn't want *me*, but I was sure he knew. I hadn't exactly been quiet about my fucked-upness.

"More than anything." He smiles, and pulls me to standing and hugs me tightly. "I'm just worried that you'll regret it later. Regret being rushed into a marriage, regret me and this lifestyle that I have been in since birth. Being the Second-In-Command of the Irish Mafia, it's not something I can walk away from. Even if I wanted to."

I struggle not to roll my eyes or make a face that screams, 'are you crazy?'.

"None of that matters to me. What matters to me is that you love me and *you* want this, not that you're doing it because you've been told to." I say, gesturing at the computer. "Is there a reason you said you "would take care of it"?

"My father has been saying since the beginning that I should marry you."

"Really? Why?" That surprised me, I know Kieron and I had history, an intense connection, but even the two of us actually in the relationship might not have brought the idea of marriage up for a good long while.

"If you have my last name, it brings about certain privileges and safety. You'd be the Second's wife. Untouchable on pain of death. Not just for my crew, but for all. There's a bit of a code that all Mafia follow. But even the slightest bit of additional protection is better for you. Besides, Talia Tavish sounds pretty badass, doesn't it?" He cups my face and gives me a panty-dropping smile that I love to see. It's so infectious and you're powerless against it.

"It does sound pretty good, huh?" That makes his smile shine even brighter and my heart soars.

"Will you marry me, baby? Please?" He says again, proposing to me for the third time. This time though, his voice was strong, determined and it was different. The way he was looking down at me, holding me, the way he spoke, all of it showed me how sincere he was being.

"Yes." I say, cupping his jaw and pulling his face closer to mine, kissing his lips sweetly. "On two conditions."

"Oh, yeah? What would they be?"

"You teach me how to fight and you teach me how to surf."

* * *

He'd agreed, of course he had. Kieron was surprised but I guess it wasn't as much of a surprise as I thought. Kieron had been so ecstatic about me agreeing to marry him, he pulled me outside for my first fighting lesson on the beach. I'm all for it, wrestling with my big, strong, tattooed man on the beach? Sounded like the perfect foreplay to me.

"Do you know how to throw a punch?" Kieron asked, tying his hair back.

"Of course I do." I smirked, tying my long hair into a quick braid.

"Show me." Kieron put his hands on his hips and cocked an eyebrow.

"What, like punching the air?"

"Yeah, baby. Just punch straight out."

I make a fist and throw it out in front of me. Kieron nods, crossing his arms, making his biceps bulge in his fitted black t-shirt. "Not bad, baby." He walks around me, bringing the back of my body to the front of his.

His scent and warmth surrounded me, and I tried to not to be creepy by inhaling but the rumble of his chest against me told me he realized it anyway and was laughing.

"But make a fist again and when you throw it," One of his hands spanned the expanse of my stomach as he held it tight "keep your core tight and," he moved both hands to my hips and he gripped me close to him, "draw your power from your lower body, pushing through your tight core and shove it through your fist." His hands made a trail over my body as he explained, his words soft and low in my ear and suddenly the farthest thing on my mind was how to fight.

I took a deep breath and did exactly what he said, feeling the power flow through me. Just like he said.

"There you go, baby girl." He whispered in my ear and kissed my neck as my eyes rolled back.

"Maybe we wait a bit for the lessons, and go celebrate our engagement?" I turn my head to face him. I want to kiss him so fucking badly that I can't make eye contact with him for a good while, just staring at his lips.

"And how would you suggest we do that?" He leaned in a fraction closer, but holy shit, I felt like I was on fire.

"Kiss me," I whispered and he wasted no time in leaning in the whole way. I turned around and wrapped my arms around his shoulders as his arms found my waist, pulling me closer.

There wasn't any space between our clothed bodies and I loved it. But I needed more.

So much more.

"Take me to bed." I whisper when he pulls away.

"Anything for my bride." Kieron says with a soft smile, emphasizing the word bride before picking me up in a bridal carry and carrying me inside his house.

Chapter Twenty-Six

*K*ieron

Yet again, I'm pulled from my woman's warm embrace and her naked body pushed up against me, by my goddamn cell phone.

"This better be fucking important." I snarl into the phone, my voice husky from sleep, but I tried to keep my voice down to keep from waking up Talia.

"Call me on the encrypted line, ASAP, man. It's important." Trent's voice comes through the speaker and I am immediately pulled from any remaining dredges that sleep had over me. He hung up and I looked down at the beautiful woman in my arms.

Her mouth was pouted in sleep and her eyes fluttered as she dreamed. Her dark purple hair was twisted and tangled from our mind-blowing activities last night. I quietly and very quickly extracted myself from her embrace, shoving my pillow under her head as it slid.

I closed the door as quietly as I could, basically sprinting to the table and computer when the door latched.

Booting up the computer and logging into the encrypted line, I cover my face with both of my hands and sigh. Trent calling and demanding to use the safe line was not a good sign.

"Kieron, man. Shit's going down." Trent's face filled the screen and I could see just how stressed he was. I took a deep breath and let my shoulders straighten.

"I just got out of an emergency meeting the Garzino's called, they even demanded all their staff working on your case to attend. They've created a game of getting her back. Talia now has a bounty on her head."

"Fuck. *Fuck.*" I stand up and punch the back of the couch.

This means it's hunting season for the Italians, and I need to swath Talia in bulletproof armor even more. Before, I knew Garzino was gunning for her, but now it's *everyone.* Mercenaries, other charters in the Mafia, gangs. Anyone that wanted the bounty, or to impress the Garzino Don.

"Kieron, there's more."

"What?" I say through clenched teeth.

"They're scrambling to find ways to recover the income from the businesses we used to back. Not that they said that with those exact words. But Luca introduced a new income revenue."

"And?"

"I'm fairly sure they are planning on entering the human trafficking trade. Selling girls and guys for the right price to whomever can pay for whatever they want." Trent put his hands in front of his face like he was praying, his thumbs holding up his chin.

Shit just went from worse to catastrophic.

"Shit." I snarl, then throw a couch pillow across the room as hard as I can and it hits a lamp. The force causes the lamp to topple over and crash, breaking the light bulb. "This can't fucking happen, Trent. It can't. I know that we do some shady shit, some deplorable shit, but never, *never*, selling people. I want to fucking murder them."

"I get it, I do. I'll keep watching and learning, but we need to start planning and let the Skipper know."

"What's going on?" Talia's sweet voice carries through the room and I know in that instant that she heard everything. My head snaps around to see her standing there looking like a sex goddess, my t-shirt that's more like a dress on her, slipping off her shoulder with her long bare legs crossed at the ankle.

"Nothing, baby. Nothing you need to worry about." I say, reaching for her.

"It didn't sound like nothing."

"It's work stuff."

"Are you going to keep hiding the truth from me?" She asks me softly.

The way she said those words made me stop and pause.

That's exactly what I was doing. In my desperate hope to keep her safe mentally, emotionally, physically, I was withholding information from her because I thought it was best for her. And in doing so, I was taking a choice from her.

Sighing, I looked back at the computer and saw Trent just staring at me.

"The Garzino's have put out a bounty on you. Which means Luca no longer cares about him being the one to bring you in." I said, taking her hand in mine and walking her over to the couch to sit so we can all have this conversation.

"Oh." She says sharply, breathing in.

"They're struggling with money and have…" Trent started to say but I cut him off with a look.

"They're selling people. You said so yourself." She pressed, looking to Trent and to me.

"They are trying to get into that game. I don't have any more information at the moment. But I believe the Garzino's are going to have some kind of big event to…dip their toe into the industry. So to say." Trent said, looking as disgusted as I felt.

We sat there quietly, letting Talia think things through. The silence was unnerving and starting to grate on my nerves. The more we sat there in silence, the more my mind started to wander to the worst scenarios going through her head. I was worried because the more she sat there, the more her face fell, her energy shifted darker and her body tensed.

"Talia?" I asked, squeezing her thigh gently to try and get her attention.

"I'm going to kill him." She whispered, looking down at her hands as they clenched into fists. "*I'm* going to kill him."

Her words were so calm and quiet that I almost didn't hear her say them.

"What did she say?" Trent was leaning closer to the camera, obviously trying to hear.

Talia looked up slowly, her eyes entranced and burning. If I wasn't so fucking worried about her, I'd be turned on as hell.

Who are we kidding though, I'm always turned on when it came to her.

"I said, I'm going to *fucking KILL HIM!*" She screamed at the camera, at Trent, at me, at the situation. She stood up, bent over the computer, pointing at the computer like it and Trent was the source of all her problems. "He will die and he will die soon. I am not going to let innocent people get hurt because of me and my choices. After all he's done to me, done to my family and now this, hurting innocent people, there is no *fucking* way I'm letting him live longer than I have to."

My girl was fuming, murderous and I could tell she was 100% serious. An avenging angel in front of me, and my cock was getting harder and harder under my boxers.

I'm fucked up, I get it but she's beautiful and murderous and it showed me how much we were alike. And how much she was healing because she feels safe enough to let her true feelings out, without fear of retribution or punishment.

Goddamn, it is so fucking sexy. I have to move my dick to the side to avoid drawing attention to it quickly thickening.

Talia stands up quickly, pushing off the couch with fierceness and storming off to the bedroom.

"That, I was not expecting." Trent says, his mouth gaping slightly.

"Me neither." I really wasn't. I was thinking she'd curl into herself, get scared, or worst-case scenario, go silent and shut the world out in some kind of numb coma.

But I should've known not to try and shield her quite so much anymore. Because my girl, my angel, was a fucking badass.

"Where'd she go?'

"To the bedroom. I'll be right back." I needed to make sure she was okay. "Talia?" I knock on the bedroom door cautiously, and have to jolt backward because she opened the door so quickly.

She was dressed in an all-black outfit; tight leggings that showed off her shapely, little ass, and a black t-shirt that was just loose enough that she was comfortable and most alarming, black converse on her feet as she pulled her hair into a high ponytail. "Yes?"

"Where are you going?" My voice came out more demanding than anticipated, but really, where the fuck did she think that she was going? We were at the beach, a secluded location that I've kept a secret and protected for years, a few hours away from everything she knows. There's no goddamn way I'm letting her go anywhere.

"I'm going to go get Luca and knock some sense into him." She replies, pushing past me and into the living room. "Where's that backpack you had?"

"You're not going anywhere. Are you fucking crazy?" I snap.

"Talia, you can't leave." Trent's voice comes in from the computer.

"The fuck I can't!" She screams, throwing an arm behind her in both my direction and Trent's. "You don't know. You two don't know what it was like to be scared each and every moment for months on end. You don't know what it is like to be beaten and bruised and still have someone come at you with a closed fist or a kick or anything within grabbing distance." Her screaming anger turned to tears as she struggled to keep her emotions together. "You don't know what it's like…to be lying in bed and trying to pretend it's not real, that it's not happening."

I feel my breathing hitch and my hands start to clench tighter and tighter as I do my best to control my anger. She should've never been in that situation, should have never have experienced any of that. I'm trying to control my breathing and my anger because she sure as shit didn't need any of my issues while she was feeling this way.

"Baby," I say, holding up my hands slowly and taking the bag she was holding in a death grip. She steps back, ripping herself out of my embrace. "Baby, give me the bag. Please."

Her dark eyes sparkling with unshed tears, her chin tipped up in determination glaring back at me.

She let the bag drop to the floor. "He can't do this, Kieron. I can't let him."

"I know, baby. I know." And I can't stand not having her in my arms anymore, this time when I try to hug her close, she lets me. The moment her body crashes into mine, all the tension is gone and she holds on for dear life. "You know you're not alone anymore, right? You can't let him do this, no, *we* can't let him. And we won't." I cup her face softly, bringing her lips to mine. "You and me, we're a team. We're going to be married. Your problems are mine and mine are yours."

"And Luca is one big fucking problem, isn't he? And it's not just me he might hurt."

"Trent?" I call out, hoping the connection was still live.

"Yeah?"

"Let's go sit and talk this through. We can't do anything; protect you at all times from mercenaries or protect the people the Italians are after without a solid plan." I tell her softly, kissing her forehead. "Remember what I said, wifey." Smirking at her and walking over to the couch to straighten out this shit-show that potentially could ruin the best thing I have going for me in my life.

Chapter Twenty-Seven

Talia

I'm not going to lie; I was checked out for most of the conversation the two guys were having. They bounced around ideas and talked about the different people they were going to bring in, I just couldn't focus. My mind was in a fog about anything that wasn't a fantasy where I put a bullet in Luca's brain. My anger had turned me murderous.

"Talia," Trent said, pulling me out of my daydream where I was gouging Luca's eyeballs out with dull spoon.

"Hm?"

"I was saying that you shouldn't worry. Bryan, Kieron and I will take care of this." I couldn't help but give him a pouty smile because he was just so sweet. There wasn't anything for me to say really, so I just nodded.

Of course, I was going to worry.

"Okay you two," Trenton clapped. "I've got a meeting for the Garzino's I have to get to. I need to inform Bryan of the change in plan and Kieron, you'll let the boss know?"

"I am your boss, but yes, I'll conference with Skipper." Kieron said.

"I'm sorry I didn't have good news." Trent said sadly, which was ridiculous in my opinion. I knew what he was risking going undercover. I knew how stressful it seemed to be for him. I was thankful, and it was obvious that Kieron was too.

"It's okay, man. Thanks." Kieron said and signed off.

He closed the computer and the two of us were thrust back into silence and darkness. Kieron squeezed my knee, got up and opened the wooden blinds to let the sunlight and sea air in. "You're not still thinking of trying to leave again, are you?"

I chuckled and shook my head, standing up to join him by the window.

"No, that was a rage-filled fantasy. I wouldn't be able to take on Luca." I sighed. That was the truth and it fucking sucked. I'd never been the bodybuilder type girl or the one always in the gym, but my attitude and confidence was usually enough to get whoever it was to back off. Since everything that went down, I have no confidence. I'm barely healed from the last beating I'd taken, then the explosion, and I wouldn't be able to cause any damage even if I was able to find Luca to try and hurt him.

"We will train together; you'll get stronger and more confident on how to defend yourself. Then, hopefully, if anything slips by my very carefully placed defenses, you can get a few damaging punches in." He smiles down at me. "You're always a badass."

"Train me. We have time here in this isolated protective bubble. I want you to teach me how to take someone your size down and I want to learn how to shoot." I ask, without really asking.

"As you wish, baby."

* * *

"Let's go surfing. Get out on the water, let the waves take away some of this stress." I was making a cup of coffee, Trent's call waking us up way too early, when Kieron wrapped his arms around my middle from behind. After the initial jolt of surprise, I relaxed into his embrace. "I'm dying to get out on my board." He said wistfully.

"Oh yeah?" I take a sip of the scalding liquid, pretending to think about it. When really, surfing with him, getting to see him in *his* happy place, was much too tempting.

"Come on, baby. You said you wanted to learn." He kissed my shoulder, and his voice dropped lower, "Plus I'd love to see you in a bikini."

"That's the real reason, huh? Just want to get me naked."

"Always. I always want to get you naked." He chuckled. "So, what do you say?"

"I don't think I have a swimsuit, but I'll figure something out."

"Yes! I'll go grab my trunks quickly and then go get the boards from the shed. Meet me out front when you're ready." He said excitedly. Watching Kieron bound out of the room, each step he took was lighter than the last. I love seeing him like this and it's like a breath of fresh air in the midst of our crazy life.

I wasn't sure what I'd do for a suit since there was no way I had one in the go-bag, but I'd just wear dark underwear and sports bra and Kieron would just have to deal with it.

Pulling a black sports bra from the bag, I realized that the only underwear I had were boy shorts that showed way too much cheek for my liking, but they would have to do. It was that or full-on thong. Slipping the makeshift bikini on, I pulled on Kieron's shirt that he'd left yesterday for a coverup.

Walking out of the house, I pulled my hair up into a high bun and tried to contain the strands while looking for Kieron.

The view was amazing. The sun rising over the water, the sea gulls cawing overhead, the faint sound of the waves crashing on shore. It was still so early that there weren't many people around. It was perfect. Like we had our own beach.

Kieron was standing closer to the water and I saw him pull his curls into a secure bun on the back of his head. He looked… goddamn, did he look good. His arms raised to fix his hair and the lean muscles all shifted under him, his abs flexed with the movement giving me a view of the hard-earned muscle. His body was always a nice treat for the eyes, but what really got me was the carefree and easy smile he was sporting.

He was gorgeous. And all mine.

"Come on," he called out to me and I ran out onto the beach, ready to learn all I could about the activity that brought my man this much joy.

* * *

After a full, long day of Kieron teaching me to surf; we were in the water for hours, I kept falling down but getting right back up with his encouragement and patience, and on how to throw a decent punch, a powerful kick; my muscles screaming at me, and plenty of ruminating over the early morning terrible phone call and mini-meltdown, I wanted to do nothing but sleep.

I somewhat wondered if that was Kieron's plan all along. Tire me out so that I didn't think of what Luca was planning to do.

God, this was so fucked up. We just got engaged and we couldn't even enjoy it for a full 24 freaking hours before everything blew up.

I dragged myself into the house slowly, legs and arms already sore because, of course, I saw Kieron start to do some bodyweight exercises, I thought I should join in on. After spending the morning surfing, which uses a lot of muscles that I didn't even know I had. I was going to be in so much pain tomorrow.

"You do that every day?" I ask, huffing and puffing as I walked into the living room and plopping out face down on the couch. The best noise ever filled the room as Kieron let out a full-bodied laugh. Damn, he was so light and relaxed. I hadn't seen him like this before and I love it. I wanted to be the one to make him feel like this every day.

"Do you think these biceps and these abs just happen? I do double what we did today, plus weights." He tells me and I suddenly have so much more appreciation for the view I get every time I see him. Because he works really fucking hard.

"That's miserable."

"Eh, I don't mind it anymore. I like the escape and the time to myself." He explains as he sits on the couch, pulling my feet into his lap. "Plus, your reaction every time I take my shirt off really makes it worth it."

"I'll always react this way, handsome, regardless of what you look like because you are you." I say, sitting up and pulling him closer to me by fisting his shirt. "For the rest of our lives. I can't believe your mine."

"Always." He smiles and kisses me sweetly. "Speaking of the rest of our lives…"

I can feel an uncontrollable smile and blush start to cross my face.

"Yes, what did you have in mind?"

"What do you think of getting married tomorrow? At the court house here in town? I would normally send for someone from the Clan but I'm not wanting to draw any attention to us." He explains, pulling me into his chest and maneuvering me over his lap so I'm straddling his thighs. "Don't worry, after things settle down with the Italians, you and I will have our wedding. A big, proper wedding in a church in front of all our families and friends. A big ceremony, a tux and you in a big, gorgeous dress where everyone can see."

I chuckle. "Is that something you want?"

"A wedding?" He asks, confusion coloring his tone.

"Yeah."

"It's not a deal breaker by any means. I just know that weddings are important to girls."

"Not this girl. I don't care about the wedding. I care about the marriage. That is so much more important to me than a big party." I say truthfully. If he wanted a big, white wedding, I'd do it for him, to make him happy because that's all I want; Kieron and I together and happy.

But I don't need the ceremony. Don't want it even.

I just want him.

"So instead, tell me more about our marriage." I lean in and kiss his throat once, twice, three, soft times.

"It'll be one for the history books, baby. The thing of fairy tales." He whispers, sliding his hands up my waist and around my shoulders. "I don't give two shits if we have a wedding. I just want my ring on your finger and my name behind yours."

A shiver runs through me at his words. "Then let's get married tomorrow. Mr. Tavish."

"I can't fucking wait, Mrs. Tavish."

Chapter Twenty-Eight

Kieron

I'm getting married today.

Married.

To Talia. The girl that I thought had gotten away.

Sitting up out of bed and astounded by the sheer luck I had. I knew growing up I would more than likely be forced to marry a suitable match for the Clan, rather than for love. Then all the bullshit I had to do to prove myself to be worthy of the Second-in-Command, all the soul-damning bullshit that I've done along the way… I was certain that no matter what, I would never have the person I wanted, truly wanted, by my side.

But I must have done something right because here she is. And she's all mine.

Talia was cuddled up against my side and reaching out in her sleep for me and my warmth. Her arms were no doubly going to be sore from the training from yesterday, but the view of her long, lithe arms, naked from our late-night festivities slid across the grey sheets, was strangely a turn on.

But anything was a turn on when it came to Talia, I'm finding.

Getting out of bed, I made my way to the kitchen to throw together some food for us. While standing at the coffee machine and waiting for the much-needed caffeine, I start scrolling through my phone to try and find a place where we can go to get an expedited marriage license.

"Why'd you leave?" Talia's arms wrapped around my middle.

"We need food, and I needed caffeine. Someone," I said with a smirk, "kept me up all night."

"Are you complaining?" She nipped my back and I turned around quickly, grabbing her and sitting her on the counter.

"Not in the slightest." I step in-between her legs and drop a kiss to her neck. "I found a place to get married."

"You did? Man, that was fast. You must really want to lock me down, huh?" She pulls the neck of my shirt in to have me closer. I can see just how happy she looks; how light and joyful she is. I love it.

"Absolutely." I smile and kiss her. Talia wraps her arms around my shoulders and locks her ankles around my waist, effectively keeping me in place. This was a kiss that could quickly become something much more fun but we didn't have time for that today.

"Come on, go get changed for our wedding day and I'll make us some breakfast." I say, smacking her ass lightly and stepping back so she can slip off the counter.

"Ugh. Fine." She teases me, cupping my cheek. "I'll be in the shower, feel free to join me."

"Don't tease me." I groan and turn around to face the fridge and pull the ingredients to make us breakfast.

All while willing my boner to go down.

* * *

I made quick work of getting ready and changing clothes myself after bringing some eggs and bacon along with coffee to Talia while she's blow drying her hair. I got ready quickly in the only clothes I had that were more dressed-up in my go bag; a black button down and black jeans. My combat boots would have to do but honestly, it didn't matter what we wore. It mattered that her last name was Tavish by the end of the day.

I watched her get ready as I sat on the bed facing the open bathroom door. I just watched as she moved around the space, putting on powders and creams, concealer and mascara, all while humming softly.

"If you're going to stare, at least talk to me." She says with a snarky smile in the mirror.

"What would you like to talk about?" I lean forward with my elbows on my knees and bite my lip and raise an eyebrow.

"Not about that!" She laughs at me. Seeing her so happy makes me feel invincible, like nothing can touch me.

"Damn. I tried." I lean back on my hands.

"I would like to know what you and Trent decided to do about the Italian situation. I may or may not have checked out a small bit while you two were talking."

"I know, I could tell. It's okay, it's overwhelming." I said, standing up and walking over to the door frame, leaning my shoulder against it. "As of right now, the last message I got from Trent, he was invited to a "fundraising" event that they've organized very last minute. Garzino Senior has invited some very shady parties. Gangs we don't associate with because of their particular 'tastes'. But Trent and Bryan both think that they could be making the first drop of cargo within that party. They're gathering more information."

"You're really making it out to be that you guys in the Irish mafia are better than the rest, but…" She said with a smirk, rolling her eyes slightly.

"I'm not trying to. We are just as terrible, as awful. The shit I've had to do because of orders from the top… We are the things of nightmares, baby. That's what family you're attaching your cart to. The Irish Mafia rules with the iron fist and Kellan isn't one to give second chances. We all know to do what he says or die and that's just something that happens in my life." I don't want to go into detail with her about all the shit I have to do. The murders, the torture, the lying and stealing and manipulating. I don't want to have to explain that I literally had to learn how to extract organs and flay open a man's chest all while he was still alive in order to gain information. Some things you just can't come back from.

"But, like I've said before, there are just some lines we don't cross. Some unspoken rules that we adhere to and demand the rest follow. Human trafficking is one of them."

"So, what is the plan, then? You guys already started a war." She states while fluffing her long hair and twisting to the side to see how it looked from a different angle.

"Yes, we did, but now we need to go from defensive to offensive." I cross my arms. "We are trying to figure out a way to get into the fundraiser without being detected. One of our soldiers has started interrogation on one of theirs. We just need to wait now."

"Interrogation?" She turns and looks at me. "What kind of interrogation? Obviously not the kind that's shown on cop shows."

I chuckle. "No, baby. Definitely not that kind. Our interrogations have more…blood."

"Have you interrogated someone before?"

"Yes." I answer honestly. Even if I don't want to scare her, I won't lie to her.

"And they've been…bloody."

"Yes."

She purses her lips and her eyes look off to the side.

"Does that bother you?" I ask, looking down at my hands.

Talia takes a deep breath and I look at her. Her eyebrows are pulled together, but when she looks into my eyes, it's like a decision was made.

"No. No, it doesn't." With those words, I lean in, taking her face in my hands and kiss her. "Although, it probably should."

"Good." I quickly kiss her again before letting her go to let get finish getting ready. As I'm turning to leave the bathroom, she grabs me by the hand.

"Do you think… it might be easier if a woman got the information from a low-level officer?" She asked, timidly.

"What?"

"What if instead of waiting for someone to beat the information out of them about when and where, what if I was to show up at the event and flirt with some of the lower-level guys?" She offered with a shrug.

"Absolutely not." The words were out of my mouth before I fully understood what she was saying.

"Kieron, think about it." She said strongly, setting the brush she was holding down. "I don't look like I did when I was with Luca. He never took me anywhere with his underlings or whatever, if I do my hair up or wear a wig and go heavy on the makeup, no one would recognize me. I doubt Luca himself would. Plus, Trent and Bryan said that they've recruited a bunch of new people since I've been gone, they wouldn't know what I looked like or who I was to Luca. Not only that," She said, her voice getting higher and more excited as she kept explaining what she'd thinking. Unfortunately, each sentence she spoke caused my blood pressure to spike and my jaw to clench. "It's perfect, no one would suspect *me* infiltrating the Italians."

I shook my head, doing everything I could from screaming out how crazy it was and how I wouldn't ever let her do anything so stupid and reckless. But I needed to take a breath and think it through.

"I don't like it. Not at all." I tell her through clenched teeth, walking out of the room.

"Kieron, wait." She says, but I can't without blowing up.

"Just give me a minute. I need a second." I say as softly as I can. It is painful obvious that I'm controlling myself as each word and breath I take is measured.

"I can help!"

"Not like that, you won't." I snap and her eyes widen slightly. "Please, give me a fucking second to get my head on straight and we can talk."

Talia nods, and I sprinted into the next room. I wasn't a smoker, I cut that habit out of my life a long fucking time ago but I could really use a cigarette right now.

What pissed me off the most was that it was actually a good plan. It's a plan I would suggest if it was anyone other than her. But putting her directly in the way of Luca and all those other fuckers… It would drive me absolutely crazy with worry and anxiety.

I was pacing back and forth, messing with the few rings on my fingers. Could it work? Could she help us and be kept safe at the same time?

I pulled my phone out and messaged Trent. He should be off at this time, able to call me from his burner.

A moment later I got a call from an unknown number and heard his voice as he snapped, "What's going on?"

"She wants to go to the event and get the information out of a low-entry."

"Not a bad idea actually." Trent says quickly.

"Were you fucking listening to me? She wants to go to the event, filled with Italians, filled with other gangs who are known for their treatment of people, go up to one of them and fucking flirt information out of him." I sneer. Was no one getting this was a terrible idea?

"I understand, and I can totally get how this would feel for you. But Kieron, think about this as the Second. You know Skipper would think this was a good idea. A better idea."

"And how do you suggest I keep her safe in the lion's den?" If Trent wasn't my right-hand man and my oldest friend, there's no way I'd be okay with him speaking to me like that. He was talking to me as a friend right now, not as someone who worked for me, and he'd always been able to tell when I needed him in which role. It was one of the things I really respected about him.

"We'll figure it out. Spencer's in the basement right now having his fun." Trent says. "Once we get some information out of him, we can go from there."

"I'm going to be there." There's no way I'm letting her go in by herself. Fuck no. "I will be there with her."

A deep sigh came through the phone. "You know you can't."

"The fuck I can't." I snap. "I'm the Second-in-Command to the Irish Clan. I'll do what I want."

"You know that doing that will only put her in more danger. But we can discuss this later…when we have a plan."

Damn him and his calmness. I needed that fucker to be as determined and angry as me. Even through my anger haze, I realize that he's right. So, instead of yelling at him and ripping him a new one, I took a deep breath and listened.

"Fine."

"We will figure it out. When I hear information from Spencer, I'll get back to you." Trent tries to reassure me.

"Thanks, man." I say and hang up the phone. Running a hand over my face, I take a deep breath and roll my shoulders.

"I'm not intentionally trying to ruin your hard work of protecting me, but I want to help." I turned and saw Talia.

"Wow." She took my breath away. "You look… so beautiful."

She really did. She was wearing a deep red dress that showed off her curves that she was regaining, it was short and flared out around her thighs, but nipped in at her waist, showing off her hourglass shape. Talia walked closer into the room and I was sure my mouth was dropped still. She walked over to me with an intoxicating mixture of nerves and confidence, like she wasn't sure what she should feel but was pulled in just as much as I was.

"This is all I could find in the bag that was appropriate for getting married. Is it okay?" She says with a cheeky, shy smile, looking at me through her dark lashes.

"You look perfect." I whisper.

"Like what you imagined?"

"Better, baby." And it's true. She was a perfect image of the Talia I'd met long ago and the one I'd just found, both versions I'd fallen in love with. Hard.

"Thank you," she says, her eyes locked on mine.

"Go on, baby. Show me." I take her hand and turn her. "Give me a twirl."

And as she turns slowly, I see the black combat boots she paired with her pretty dress, the way the skirt faired as she moved, the long, dark curls bouncing along her back. She's breathtaking.

"Gorgeous." I say and pull her sharply towards me. "But then again, you're always gorgeous." I said softly, placing a kiss to her waiting lips.

"You're not so bad yourself, Tavish." Pulling me back into a kiss. When she released me, I rolled my eyes.

"Just trying to get on your level, baby."

"This is perfect." She said, pulling at my button down. "You look so yummy."

"Yummy?" I said with a smirk.

"Yes, yummy." She reached up on her tippy toes to kiss my neck lightly. My eyes rolled back.

Reluctantly, I pulled away from her lips before things could progress.

"Okay, okay." I move her back, a step out of my arms. "As much as I want this to continue just the way it's going, I want to marry you more."

The look in her eyes told me I said exactly the right thing. Her hands went to my chest and instead of the sexual electricity at her touch, there was a comforting sweetness filled with love.

"Then let's go." She took my hand and pulled us towards the door.

Chapter Twenty-Nine

Talia

We drove in Kieron's beautiful black Mustang into the small beach town. Kieron gave me a small tour as we drove pointing out different places he likes or things he thought was important; small hole-in-the-wall restaurants, the library, the tiny store. Then he pulled up finally to the city hall, a two-story building that fit in perfectly with the quaint little beachside town.

"Here we are, baby. Next step is actually getting married." He said as he put the car in park. There was such a look of anticipation on his face; his eyes bright and he was nervously running his fingers through his hair and over his short beard. He kept looking at me out of the corner of his eye, almost surprised that I was still there.

"Yay." I said with a smile, grabbing his hand and threading our fingers together to show him that I was indeed there; ready and wanting to be his partner.

We make our way into the building, hand-in-hand, and Kieron leaves me for a moment to go fill out the marriage license.

"Need any help?" I come up to the little desk where he is hard at work trying to fill out the different pages, his eyebrows are pulled together in such a cute way. I just want to smooth the crease that formed, but instead, I slide my arm around his and rest my chin against his shoulder.

"Nope. I don't think so." He says quickly, absently kissing my forehead and turning back to the paperwork. "I'm almost done."

"Then?"

"Then I turn it in to that lady over there," He points to the secretary with the end of his pen, "and we go in front of the judge. Say a few small words and that's it. You're all mine. Forever."

"Hmmm." I drag the sound out in joy. "That sounds very nice."

"Done." Kieron signs one of the papers with a flourish and picks up the others. Together we walk over and turn in the paperwork before finding a seat and waiting for our names to be called.

* * *

"Do you take Kieron Aleksander Tavish to be your husband?" The bored looking judge asks me from behind the podium in the dark, all-wooden, courtroom. It was depressing in here, but even that couldn't bring down our moods.

"I do." I say with a huge smile that wouldn't leave my face, squeezing Kieron's hands in mine.

"And do you take," The Judge looked at the paperwork and squinted at it, "Talia Rose Jones, to be your wife?"

"Fuck yes I do." Kieron says and the Judge looks at him in admonishment.

I could care less about that old geezer and his feelings about swearing right now. Kieron's response was so him, and so enthusiastic, I couldn't help but giggle. I didn't even wait until the judge said we were officially husband and wife; I wrapped my hand around the nape of his neck and pulled his mouth to mine.

"I now pronounce you husband and wife. Congratulations." The judge said hurriedly and the clash of his gavel sounded through the room. But the kiss didn't end.

I tried to pull back, but Kieron was faster. His hands wrapped around my waist, pulling my body close to his and deepening the kiss as he lifted me slightly.

"We are very busy today, thank you for coming and congratulations again."

The judge said, his tone sharp and very obviously trying to get rid of us.

Kieron pulled back, putting me back down on my feet but keeping me still in his arms. A large, tattooed hand cupped my cheek, and his dark eyes held mine. The smile on his face was just so soft, so serene and excited that my heart skipped a beat.

"To the beginning of forever." He whispers and kisses me lightly on the lips.

"Sounds amazing."

* * *

After signing another paper, I am officially Talia Tavish and I love it. And from how Kieron's touching me, he loves it just as much.

He won't stop touching me; caressing me, placing sweet kisses here and there. He's touching me like I'm precious, but also like giving me his last name awakened something feral that he was barely able to hang onto his awareness.

"I need to get you home." He says roughly in my ear, slapping my ass lightly as we walk out the doors of the courthouse and pulls me quickly to his car.

"Yes, please." I smile and climb into the passenger seat quickly. When he slides into the front seat I lean over, pushing my front into his side as he starts the car. The rumbling of the engine adding another level of anticipation. "Sir." I whisper in his ear, and drag my teeth over his earlobe.

Kieron groans, his chest rumbling under my hand splayed across his chest. "This is going to be the quickest drive of your life, wife." He shoves the car in reverse, whipping the car out of the parking spot with a squeal.

I smirked, biting my lip before throwing my head back and laughing as he drove way over the speed limit to get us back to our marital bed.

Our hands wouldn't stop roaming all over each other. One of his hands held the steering wheel and gripped it tightly as he drove one-handed.

I didn't know that could be so fucking sexy.

Overall, Kieron was gorgeous to look at, had a heart of gold and was willing to do whatever it took to keep me happy and healthy. And by some luck of fate, I'd locked him down for life. I felt giddy. The hand that wasn't holding the steering wheel was locked around my upper thigh, his thumb sliding over my skin as his fingers gripped into my skin erotically.

I was trailing my fingers up and down the forearm that was holding me. I didn't want to be separated from him in the slightest either.

We drove in charged silence for a while, everything passing by the window quickly – too quickly – before Kieron slowed down, parking the Mustang a few blocks away from the house. Just in case.

He ran around to my side and opened the car door, holding out his hand for me to take.

"Let's get home. We need to seal this marriage deal, wife."

He leaned over and picked me up, bridal style, and made a dash for the house. My laughter ringing through the sea air around us and the sand flying up behind us with each step he took.

Chapter Thirty

Kieron

Fuck, if this was how married life was going to be, I would have proposed the moment I met her.

Our breathing was erratic after we finished, bringing each other to orgasm for another time since we arrived home. It was like the gloves, if we had had any kind on before, were completely pulled off. She was insatiable, a sexual goddess come for me.

I couldn't get enough of her.

I held onto her, holding her close while our skin cools and our breathing regulates, watching her eyes flutter shut. I need water, I need food, so instead of resting I waited for her to fall asleep and I snuck out to get water.

"Don't leave." She whispered as I opened the door as quietly as I could. "Please."

"I'm just getting water, baby. I'll be right back." She moans softly and steals my pillow to hold against her chest. I can't help but smile. I would climb right back in as soon as she said please, but I needed to take care of her. Of both of us.

When I walk into the kitchen, I get the biggest glass of water and drink it quickly before refilling it and sipping it. Thirst temporarily stated, I grabbed my phone and see I have a new message from an unknown number just saying, "Encrypt".

It's Trent or Bryan.

"What's up?" I ask Trent once I get online.

"Couldn't at least put a shirt on and cover up? My delicate sensibilities are offended." Trent crosses his arms over his chest and leans back. I was probably a sight to see, Talia's fingernails had made a trail of pleasure all over my back and her teeth had made marks all over my front. I didn't mind a little pain with my pleasure, and as it turns out, she *really* liked marking me up.

"Oh, don't be a jealous lad. It's not becoming." I smirked.

"Enjoying the married life, I see?"

"So, so much."

"That's good, and I'm very sorry I have to ruin it." Trent ran his fingers through his red hair. "They set a date for the fundraiser."

I suck in air, holding my breath for a moment before letting the breath go. "When?"

"This weekend." He said sadly. He knew what this meant, what was going to happen and how very likely it was that my sweet new wife could be taken from me.

"Fuck." I run a hand through my hair, pulling that the loose strands. My mind is overwhelmed with all this means. The plans that we had now have to be put into motion. Talia now *has* to get better at fighting, at learning how to defend herself for infiltrating this fucking fundraiser like she wants. Like Kellan approved.

And when the Skipper says something is going to happen, it's going to happen.

"I guess I better get make the next few days count then. She's got to learn how to disarm with a knife, block a blow and at least how to fire a gun. We don't have the time to teach her how to full out fist fight anymore." I sigh. She's going to be frustrated at that, annoyed too. A door hinge opens and I know she's up.

"I gotta go. Thanks man, let me know exactly when we need to be there and I'll…take care of the rest."

"Of course." Trent says and signs off.

Her soft footsteps pad into the room and I feel her body fall against mine on the couch.

"You didn't come back." She says with a yawn, obviously still sleepy and pulled from our warm bed before she wanted to be.

"Trent called." I lean my head against hers.

"Oh?"

"It's really time to get to work now." I tell her.

"Okay," My strong girl takes a deep breath and pushes her hair out of her face, taking on the look of a warrior. Determined, settled and ready to go. "What's first?"

* * *

"Again." I say sharply, my arms folded over my chest as I pace back and forth a few steps behind her chair. I decided to start with gun training, seeing as she's already been taught how to throw a halfway decent punch.

I'd showed her how to load and unload a gun, put the safety on and off, and was making her do it over and over to build muscle memory.

Talia presses the button and slips the clip out of the gun, pulling the bullets out quickly with her thumb before sliding them back in as quickly as she could and slamming the clip back into the butt of the gun and sliding the top to bring the bullet into the chamber.

"Done." She said, flicking the safety on and setting the gun down on the table. Rationally, I know she can do this, but she doesn't have the muscle memory that is required in a high-stress situation when her mind is on something else, like figuring out how to get away from someone.

"Okay," I take a deep breath and pick the gun and tuck it in the waistband of my pants. "Now, come take it from me."

Her eyebrow lifts up with a small tick and she bit her lower lip as she looked at me, then looked down to my waistband.

"Not like that." I smirk at her, "Naughty girl." She laughs, but lunges for the gun anyway.

Easily deflectable.

Much too easily.

I grabbed her forearm and used her momentum to push her to the side. Talia tumbled slightly but found her footing before turning around and facing me with all the angry energy of a pissed off chihuahua.

I couldn't help but chuckle.

"Don't piss me off more." She threatens me, and her words make me laugh even more. Covering my mouth and swallowing down the rest of my laughs, I stand tall and put the mask that I use to intimidate others on. My arms fold in front of my chest, my shoulders rise, my eyes narrow and my jaw clenches.

"Jesus, it's like Dr. Jekyll and Mr. Hyde." Talia says, moving closer to me and looking at me like I'm an animal at the zoo. "How the hell do you do that so quickly?"

"Years of practice. Now, try to take it from me." I tell her, gesturing with my fingers in a come-hither motion. She rolls her shoulders, determination filling her face as she thinks this time before just going in like last time.

She walks closer to me and I put my hand out, knowing what she was going for. When one of my hands wrapped around her wrist, the other shot out and pulled the gun. I grabbed the wrist holding the gun, but she flipped the safety off as she pointed the gun at my balls.

I froze.

As would any other guy.

"Creative." I say, approval lacing my tone.

"Maybe just the threat will keep them away from me."

"Maybe. But if that doesn't, you shoot it off. Understood?" I tell her, still holding on tightly to her wrists and pulling her closer.

"Yes, sir." She says with a smile and kisses my lips sweetly.

"I hate this, you know." I whisper against her lips, while I take the gun from her and flick the safety on. "I want you nowhere near these people. If I had it my way, you'd not be involved in the mafia life at any time but now you have to walk right into the center of everything bad? I couldn't even ease you into this life." I shake my head and turn away from her. She's still not healed from everything she'd been through. We don't know how she'll react to seeing her tormentor in person again.

That was what was making me so worried. She shouldn't have to ever be in the same room as that waste of space.

"It's not fair to you." I said softly, cupping her face. I'm sure the agony was clear on my face; I wasn't trying to hide how I feel.

Talia wrapped her arms around my waist and rested her head against my chest.

"I understand you're worried. Scared for me. But I have to do this, Kieron. I have to. There will be people, *people*, sold and put through hell because of me. Because Luca can't get over the blow to his ego and because I'm the cause for this stupid war where lives could be lost. I have to be a part of the solution." She pulled back to look into my eyes. "Besides, I'm a Tavish now. It's my job to help the Clan in any way I can. Right?" She smiled at me and I swear, I fell a little more in love with her.

"That's right, lass." I tell her with a smirk and laying on a thick Irish accent. "You are a Tavish now. The wife of the Second, a survivor and damn strong."

The smile she gives me lights up her face like the sun.

"I am. And that's why I want to be useful." She says, "You know it's a good plan."

I sigh, "I know."

Holding her close, I felt my phone buzz in the pocket of my jeans.

Saturday, 9:30pm EST. Martinique Hotel and Bar. Ballroom C. A Ms. Jessica Destoni is on the guest list. This is for sure a coverup for the 'cargo' drop. We need the location. Do not fuck this up with your possessive caveman jealousy, Tavish.

Another text comes in quickly.

Tavishs.

Another one.

But I mean you specifically, dumbass.

With a chuckle I show Talia the phone and take a deep breath. She looks strong, full of conviction and I know that no matter what, Talia is going to give this fight her all.

And it finally clicks with me, that maybe she needs this.

Chapter Thirty-One

Talia

Saturday came way too quickly.

The few days between when we got the information and the actual drop day were filled with constant defense training, gun training, going over and over the emergency information, knife use, peppered in with information about the different mafias and gangs. Kieron even made me take a few runs on the beach just in case I needed to run away.

As scared as I was about having to actually be face-to-face with these people, I was going to show them how they haven't gotten me down. I'm still here. I'm still fighting.

"Knock, knock!" The front door slams open against the wall and I grab for the gun on the side table in the bedroom, taking a novice aim to the door. "Wait, lass! It's just me!" Cara's sweet, but scared face, peeks around the corner.

"Oh my god, Cara. Thank god it's you." I flick the safety back on and put the gun down.

"Talia?" Kieron comes running into the living room, his hand hovering behind his back where I know his gun is resting in-between the waistband of his pants and his back. "About time, Cara. Some notice would be fucking nice though. Maybe don't slam open doors when we are on lockdown over here."

"My apologies. Really, I wasn't thinking. And it's not like I have any free hands." Cara says, gesturing to the big gown bag and duffel in her arms.

"What is all this?" I ask, walking forward to take the bag out of her arms but Kieron beats me to it.

"Your dress and things to get ready for the fundraiser." Cara says with a smile. "You didn't think you could wear black leggings and one of Kieron's t-shirts to a formal fundraiser put on by the Garzino family, did you?"

"A girl could hope."

"Oh shush, I'm going to doll you up like Cinderella and you'll forget all about this crazy mission these boys are sending you on." She says with a raised eyebrow in Kieron's opinion.

"It's not like I wanted her to do this." Kieron mutters under his breath which earns him a smack in the arm from her.

"And ye got married! Congratulations all around! This is such a great thing, I'm so happy for you both." She says with a big smile and hugging us both.

"It's been a great week." I smiled at Kieron. The smile he gave me warmed my heart; like he was surprised, grateful and happy, all in one.

"It has." He agrees.

Cara claps her hands in excitement and whoops loudly. "I knew this is where you two would end up. Like I told you in the beginning, I've never seen him this smitten with anyone. I'm glad it's you."

Her joy is infectious and I smile brightly back. "I'm glad it's me too."

Pulling me in close, she touches my forehead to hers. "Let's get you ready."

* * *

"Is there going to be any of my skin showing that isn't covered in a powder or foundation?" My ass hurts from sitting on this stupid wooden stool for so long. Cara had me sit down and close my eyes as she did my makeup and hair. When I said I would do it myself, she said not to because Luca might notice if I did my hair like I was used to.

234

A thin-veiled excuse to let her dress me up. I saw right through it but I didn't fight her on it.

My black eye had finally faded to barely noticeable, but Cara, being the sweetheart she is, was very lightly dabbing around it to cover up anything left. Her hands lightly brushed around and over my eyes.

"Do you want people to see *you* or your cover? I'm trying to make you not look like you but still as beautiful as you are naturally." She snapped.

"Ugh," I groaned and shifted. "Fine."

"Besides, I'm done." She said, and I saw what she meant.

She had somehow made me look like a completely different person with all this makeup on. Cara had contoured my face; my cheekbones were different, everything was more angular than my natural look, my eyelids were hooded and darker, my lips overlined and a deep red color. With my dark hair, I truly did look like a different person.

"Wow."

"I know, I had to be dramatic. But I still think you look nice." She said, setting down the mascara wand.

"I look...very different."

"That was the point, lassie." Cara laughs.

My hair had been flat-ironed heavily, the violet strands falling like curtains on either side of my face. With how it looked today, I was pleased I hadn't cut my hair. Because of how it was styled, my hair reached my waist. It was the complete opposite of what I used to do; curling each strand of hair perfectly and then pinning behind each ear to keep the curls out of my face. I'd perfected one formal look and what Cara did was the opposite, and it looked so great. I felt sexy as I watched the light shimmer in the near onyx hair as I moved.

"I'll go get your dress." Cara said with a smile, leaving the bedroom where she had banished Kieron from before we started to get ready.

It was such a different look. I felt like I had zipped on a new skin and was a completely new person.

"Oh," I turned to Kieron's voice in the doorway where he peeked around the door. His dark eyes trailed over my body from top to bottom, taking me in. "Wow"

"That's what I said." I said with a chuckle and put my hair over my shoulder.

"Cara is really talented at this stuff. It doesn't look like you at all. I mean, I can see you. The real you. But a quick glance, no one would know it's you." He reached for my hands and held them tightly. "Thank god."

"I'm going to be okay." I whisper as Kieron stood me and wrapped his arms around my waist, dropping a kiss to my bare shoulder.

"I know."

We stand in silence, simply swaying in each other's arms as the weight of what we are going to do settles in.

* * *

"Can you wear this dress again when you're not covered in makeup? Just you, that dress, me and the bed." Kieron looked in the mirror, looking at me from the driver's seat. Kieron had made sure to wear a black suit with a white button down, and had tucked his long hair into a driver's cap that dipped down just enough to obscure his face.

"It's borrowed from Cara."

"Where do you think Cara got it from, baby?" He winked in the mirror. "That dress is all yours."

Of course, he'd bought it for me. I shake my head and playfully roll my eyes at his teasing tone. "Did you pick it out too?" I asked.

If he did, it made sense. The dress was deep red; a soft, velvet fabric and tight. Tight like a second skin and moved so perfectly with my body. It was short, hitting me a little higher than mid-thigh with a high neck and long sleeves. But the back of the dress… The back of the dress was open and deep. It had a deep V that rested low on my back, showing off a large portion of skin and the dimples just above my ass.

I could see just how much it affected Kieron, his eyes barely leaving my body for a second until we had gotten in the car.

236

"I, uh," Kieron rubbed his neck. "Fuck yes, I picked it out because I thought it would look amazing on you. And I was completely right."

I laughed out loud at being able to distract him and straightened the neckline of my dress out.

"Thank you very much. That's high praise." I smile to him in the mirror.

"In the box next to you, there's a small earpiece. Get it out, turn it on and put it in your ear to make sure we can talk." I do as he asks while he continues to go over the plan.

"Once you're through the entrance, you're going to locate Trenton in the room. You remember the photo I showed you?" I nodded, "Good. You find him, nod to him twice and that is it. Then, your target is name Joseph Franchini. He is a fairly new addition to the Garzino security empire and a brand-new initiate into the Italian mafia. Less than three months if Bryans information is correct." Kieron handed me a photo, obviously taken stealthy from across the street somewhere. A young guy, maybe no older than 20 with dark, over-gelled hair and wearing a loose white cut off t-shirt, stared back at me. He was striking, very angular. Everything about him was sharp; his look, his eyes, his jaw and shoulders. He looked almost frail.

Not someone I would think Luca would hire for *security*.

"Bryan and Trent have it on good authority that Joseph is involved intimately with the cargo moving and drop off tonight. If anyone is going to know where the girls are being kept, it's him. And it's your job to get that information out of him. By..." Kieron stopped, that last sentence trailing off and dying.

"By what?" I ask.

"This is where I would normally say, 'by any means necessary.' If you were anyone else, it's what I would say. But you're not anyone else." He said and the grip he had on the steering wheel tightened.

I like seeing his protective side, it's definitely a turn-on.

"After you get the information, you're to bump into Trent, say "I'm so sorry. It's been a long night. Too much champagne." That's his signal that you got it and are ready to leave. He will escort you out of the ballroom, I'll pick you up outside those doors." He points off to the side.

"Got it." I nod, checking my bag for the fake ID and wad of cash that Kieron had gifted me upon walking out the beach house door. Kieron pulled up to the front door of the hotel and didn't turn to look at her, staring straight ahead with the car still running.

"Check the ear piece works, pretend you're paying me." He ordered, and I whispered check, hearing his affirmative that he could hear me.

I leaned forward and set some bills down in the front seat to fool any of the security watching that he was just a driver.

"Anything goes wrong, you run. Do you understand?" He says right before I open the door.

"Nothing is going to go wrong."

"Talia," His voice was strained and almost desperate. The pulse point in his neck was jumping with his heartbeat and he rolled his shoulders back. I knew he didn't want me doing this, he was very vocal about his opinion after all, but looking at him now, I realize that it wasn't just that he was protective of me. Kieron was scared. He was genuinely scared for my safety and because he couldn't physically be in there with me, he didn't feel as confident.

"I understand." I say, looking down at my bag like I was looking for something. I just needed a few moments to make him feel calmer. "I promise you; I will do everything in my power to walk out of this building and back into your arms."

There was a brief pause, but then I heard him exhale. Sighing out his stress. "I know."

I open the door and step out, ready to take this awful family down in any way I can.

Chapter Thirty-Two

Kieron

Watching her walk away and into the lion's den, without me, was excruciating.

I'm going to fucking explode from adrenaline and rage from not being able to be there with her. Fuck, I'm supposed to put myself in between her and any danger. What the fuck was I thinking letting everyone talk me into this?

The leather of the steering wheel groaned under my hands and my gaze snapped to where my fists were clenching around the wheel tightly.

"Fuck," I whisper and pull out of the parking spot to make my way to the coordinates Bryan had sent earlier to a location where I could see into the 360-degree, glass window, enclosed ballroom at the top of the hotel building.

And yeah, I had to scale the building where he sent me in order to get on the roof but, I hadn't worked out properly in a bit. My fingers and nails were all cut up from climbing on the bricks and drain pipe, I shoved myself over the ledge with my backpack, I waste no time in getting into position to stand guard.

The rooftop is cold as shit and I'm in for a long night. I pull the binoculars out of my bag and get it focused.

It was a terribly filled room, a surveillance nightmare, and it looked stuffy, even from here. All gold decorations and fake, plastic flowers on big foldable, circle tables where people were talking, probably making boring small talk. I'm partly glad I'm not in that room. It looks boring as shit.

I have a Bluetooth earpiece in, and double tap on it, connecting my earpiece to Talia's.

My ear is filled with the cluttering sound of muffled background conversations. Loud enough to force you to raise your voice, but dull enough that you couldn't really hear the individual words that other speak.

"Hey baby," I murmur, and try to search for her in the crowd of people. Her red dress makes it easier to spot her. That gorgeous woman. "You're looking damn fine. Best looking girl in the room, easily."

"Aw, shucks. Thanks, handsome." Her voice comes through muffled, but there.

I do an overlook throughout the room, getting a location on exits, people, finding where Trent was standing by Garzino in, of course, the middle of the fucking room. Surrounded by dozens of people. But this could be a good thing; the more people they were surrounded by, the less likely they would notice Talia.

"Garzino Prick and Trent are in the middle of the room, far from you. Garzino Senior is at the far end of the room. Joseph, is to your right about midway to Trent. He's standing along the wall, not doing a good fucking job at pretending he's actually paying attention." I snarl into the mic. My wife nods her head subtly and moves over to him, picking up a champagne glass on her way.

Of course, Joseph notices her right away. I wasn't kidding when I said she was the most beautiful woman in the room. And obviously, other guys were going to pick up on it. Watching his beady eyes trail over her body, I wanted to gouge them out with my fingers and have him feel every moment of it.

I'd done some background on this guy and he's bad news. It's part of the reason why he's working for the Italians, paying off some very expensive, very damaging and very life-threatening debts. That's not to mention his record of assault. The fact that I had to let him get close to *my* wife made my skin crawl.

"Hey darlin', how are you doing tonight?" His voice filled my ear and my grip

on my binoculars tightened.

"Better than it was a minute ago." Talia said to him, I could see a smile on her face as she trailed a finger down his arm.

Jesus, if I thought him flirting with her was going to be hard it was nothing compared to her actively encouraging him.

"So...what do you do? You're standing around looking all serious and working hard so I'm going to guess you're some kind of security. You're certainly built for it." Talia borderline purred the words as her trailing finger turned into a full hand wrapping around his bicep. And it went straight to his head, you could almost see his ego inflate.

"Who taught you how to flirt?" I murmur into the mic.

Talia's shoulders shake slightly, her smile brightens and I can tell she's holding back a laugh.

"In fact, I am." The fucker smirks; taking in her short skirt and very revealing back.

"Wow," Talia says. *"That's so impressive! You must be important to work security for this big event. That's so great. I've never met anyone with such a serious job before."* I can see her bat her dark eyelashes from here and she's laying it on so thick but this prick is eating it up.

"Oh, yeah? What is it that you do, baby?" Joseph turns to face Talia straight on and he leans one of his shoulders against the wall, crossing his arms to try to making himself look bigger. It is a struggle to not roll my eyes.

"I'm a nanny. I work for one of the families here, watching their little boy run around. I love it so much. They invited me here tonight as a thank you." Talia says wistfully. Her cover story is interesting, but I'm glad she's picking something that's far from the truth. She's planting a cover for if Joseph asks around for Jessica. I'm impressed.

"You know what they say about work. If you find something you love, you'll never work a day in your life." He smirks at her, eyes sparkling as he thinks he actually has a chance to get with her.

Fat fucking chance of that, asshole.

"I'm Jessica." Talia says with a smile, holding out her hand for him to shake. Which, of course, he does and presses a kiss to her knuckles.

"Joseph."

"I know you're working, but could we go sit down and talk? I'd love to hear more about what you do."

"Sure, let's get some drinks as well." He offers and it amazes me how quickly he folds on his job.

I watch on bated breath as they move through the room to get Talia a glass of champagne – she hadn't even sipped out of her first one – and the guy gets a shot of liquor.

Why would Garzino ever trust this guy on security? He was far too relaxed. Was it a trap or was he just an idiot?

As I mull it over, working through the probabilities in my head and the chances of him fucking everything we've planned up, they chat and flirt. All while, I try not to mentally plan his murder in too much detail at the lewd and possessive advances he's making.

"They put you in charge of that? Wow." Talia's voice pulls me out of my murderous planning. Surprisingly, she hadn't had to prod more than just ask him about his job and rain him with compliments for him to open up like a book.

"Hell yeah, they did. I'm the best. I actually just got this brand-new gig; it starts later tonight. That's why I'm on security right now, I'm on transport later."

Perfect. "We need to know where." I nudge her.

"Transport? How is that security?" Talia asks.

"I'm securing the cargo from the transport. We are waiting for the delivery of goods, then I'll be the lead security guy transporting it to the drop-off." Again, cue the eyeroll from me. I'm so fucking done listening to this fucker talk, but we are so close to getting the information we need.

"Really? Oh my god." Talia sounded like she cared but there was an edge to her tone that I could tell was sarcastic. *"And that's happening tonight? Soon, if you're waiting for it. What are you transporting? Nothing too scary, I hope."*

The fucker laughs. He actually laughs at the 'cargo'. Like he was moving nothing but teddy bears and cotton candy. Not real people.

Not to mention, he's definitely not high up in the security hierarchy and he's totally trying to bullshit his way into her pants.

"No, darlin'. Nothing bad at all, don't you worry your sexy ass about it. I've got it all handled."

"What if you get hurt?" Talia asks, her tone fake worried and high.

"I won't. Not at all. The cargo won't be getting out of the semi-truck. It's completely sealed so there's no risk of anything happening." And as he's explaining, he reaches up and cups her face in attempt to comfort her and get his grimy, nasty hands on her body.

"You better get where the truck is going to be soon or I'm going to rip his hand clean off." I say into the mic through clenched teeth.

"I guess it's nice then, you can just relax." She says and puts emphasis on the last two words, directing them towards me.

"Another drink?" Joseph asks, having downed his but Talia still had a full glass. Even I could hear his words slurring.

"Yes, please."

He gets up and clumsily orders more drinks for them. As I'm watching Talia sit there through the lens, it's plain as day to me that she's starting to freak out.

"Baby, you're doing great. Really." I tell her. "I know this is crazy and you're walking a fine line, but I'm here and I've got you.' I watch her smile softly, take a deep breath and push her hair behind her shoulders.

"Thank you," She whispers just before putting on the big, fake Jessica smile. I see Joseph walk up and clumsily hand her another glass of champagne.

"So, I was thinking, we should go find someplace quieter to talk." He says and slides closer to her.

"Over my dead fucking body." I snarl. Probably not the best thing for her concentration.

"Do you have that kind of time? I don't want to be rushed...and I don't think you want me to be either." She says, low and seductive.

Chapter Thirty-Three

Talia

I'm fairly sure that Kieron is about ready to shoot Joseph from wherever he is. I have no idea where he is but if the growls coming across the earpiece are any indication, he's quickly losing patience with the boy in front of me. I can't blame him either, having to act this way and touch this guy is revolting and very triggering.

I can practically feel Kieron's anger vibrating through the little earpiece at the suggestion I made. He'd have to get over it though, especially when I find out where this fucking drop was.

Joseph bit his lip and looked me over again from head to toe, pausing and practically salivating at my chest and thighs. I felt dirty and gross, but kept my face dark and sultry like I welcomed his gaze.

He wasn't a bad looking guy, not my typical type but not unattractive. He was wearing a suit and was well-groomed but there was no way I was attracted to him.

He wasn't Kieron.

Joseph looked at his watch and made a decision. "I have twenty minutes before I need to be at the location. Luckily, it's just around the corner." He steps closer to me, wrapping his arms around my waist. It's so obvious he's hammered as hell, I doubt he could get it up if he tried, but that wasn't going to deter him from trying apparently.

"I need to know what corner." Kieron's deep voice says in my ear. He's trying

to conceal his anger in his voice but I can still hear it. His possessiveness coming through and I can't lie, I really like hearing it.

"Let's go closer to where you need to be and then we can have more time. How does that sound, handsome?" I say, lowering my voice and putting my hand on his chest.

I had to pull out some serious fake confidence in order to pull this off. I'd never had to be so obviously flirty and I feel so ridiculous doing it, but I can see that it's working.

"That sounds perfect." One of his eyebrows lift and he grabs my hand, leading me out of the ballroom.

He's pulling me quickly and my heart beats faster and faster the closer we get to the door. I see Trent's eyes tracking my movements beside Luca, who is talking to a blonde-haired woman in the shortest dress I've ever seen in my life, and he looks over to me quickly. My whole-body tenses under his eye, and it feels like the room stills

"Baby, keep walking. I'm getting someone to follow you now." Kieron says in my ear, breaking me out of the staring contest with my past tormentor.

The whole room sped back up and I felt stronger knowing Kieron was watching me.

So, I kept walking.

* * *

The night air was refreshing, but right now, it felt choking.

In the ballroom, it was fully lit. There were a bunch of other people around. I had Irish backup in the room. There were levels of safety. Out here in the dark, it was just up to me.

Well, me and whoever Kieron said he had following me.

"Where are we going?" I ask Joseph, his hand tightly holding mine as he looks at his watch on his other wrist.

"Just up here." He says, rushing even quicker.

"Where are you?"

"On Sparrow and 101st?" I ask, my voice wobbly as he pulls me hard enough that I stumble slightly in my heels.

"I'm three minutes from there. Hold on." Kieron says roughly and I can hear him on the phone with someone else relying the information.

Joseph cocked his head at me with a surprised expression on his face. "Yes," he says quietly.

We reach the corner of the intersection and Joseph stops, pushing me slightly into the dark alley. The impact of the brick wall making me grunt from the force.

"You're so fucking hot." Joseph slurs, his hand going to my ass and his other to my boob. He's kneading both like dough and it hurts like hell.

It takes everything in me to not knee him in the balls and punch him in the throat like Kieron taught me.

"Thank you," My voice cracks and I pray that he thinks it's because I'm turned on.

"That fucker." Kieron snarls as Joseph's lips hit my throat. It feels all wrong, but I can't leave. I can't move. My whole-body tenses and I feel like I'm back with Luca. Just stuck, letting him use my body because the alternative is worse.

This man is drunk as hell, I could just push him away. Maybe he'd forget me and just fuck up the transfer all on his own. But I can't move.

"Baby, yes." He moans, which is cringing because I'm barely touching him. His hands are, however, are touching me everywhere. My ass, my chest, and then one hand snaked up the front of my dress.

And that was it. I couldn't take it anymore.

I went to shove him off me but was met with empty air.

Appearing like a tall, tattooed knight-in-shining-armor in all black and leather, Kieron was standing over Joseph. Kieron had gotten to him and pulled him from my body laying him out so hard his head hit the concrete.

"What the fuck?" Joseph yells as he scrambles to get up.

"Don't you touch her." Kieron said, putting his body in front of mine like a wall of muscle and protection.

"I wasn't doing anything she didn't want. Fuck, man." Joseph tried to stand his ground, but you could see in his eyes as he looked at Kieron that there was no way he was going to be able to take him. I prayed that he was drunk enough that he didn't notice it was the Second of the Irish Mafia was threatening him and protecting me. If he did, it would be just a small leap to get that Jessica Destoni is really Talia Jones and there is a mole somewhere in there with the Garzinos.

"Piss off!" Kieron hollers, pushing Joseph back roughly.

"Oh, that's how it is, huh? You beg for it and then don't give it up? What a bitch." Joseph spits in my direction and I flinch. "Fuck you! Fuck you both!" He shoves Kieron back, pushing him into me and that's the last straw for Kieron.

He lunges forward, grabbing Joseph by the shirt and punches him once in the stomach and uppercuts him in the jaw, throwing his head back. Joseph goes down and Kieron stands over him menacingly.

"You sad sack of shit. Pathetic." And he punches the drunk man in the face, knocking him out.

I knew what tonight was going to entail for me, what I was going to have to do and face, but that didn't mean that I wasn't going to have a reaction. Being touched like that, after surviving what I had, was too much. I felt my hands shaking as I watch Kieron make sure that Josephs not getting up before he turns to me.

I felt dirty still, feeling the wrong set of hands on me and touching me places I didn't want them to, but watching Kieron knock him out felt pretty damn good.

"You okay?" Kieron cradled my face, looking for his answer.

"I will be. I just want a shower and to go home." I answer truthfully.

"We're almost done. I wasn't expecting him to actually take you here."

"Me neither."

"I have a group inbound to tag the truck and make sure the innocent get home safe." Kieron says, looking at his phone and placing a call.

"We're here, where's the squad?" His business tone is clipped, straight to the point and undeniably sexy to me.

"Hurry up. There's no time to waste, it should be arriving in two minutes according to our intel." He orders and cancels the call. "We need to get to a secure position, if anyone sees me…"

If anyone sees him and recognizes him, everything is toast. "Let's go."

Kieron and I hustle down the dark alley as he surveys were to go, we need to be able to see what happens.

I need to be able to see that I did something right. That I was able to save someone from this awful fate.

"Up we go." Kieron says, pulling a fire escape ladder down as far as it will go and picking me up. I grab ahold of the bars and start to climb, assuming we're heading to the roof. The highest point of the building where we'll be able to see everything.

Shit, it's hard to climb up four-story tall building in heels quickly.

Needless to say, when I finally push myself over the top, I'm breathing so hard it's fairly embarrassing.

"Are you going to be okay?" Kieron asks, reaching out his hand to me and helping me stand.

"Fuck high heels." I gasp out and he laughs quietly. We make our way to the edge overlooking the intersection, crouching down to make sure we aren't seen.

"There they are." He says, pointing into an alley, and I watch as a group of Irishmen arrive but blend seamlessly into the darkness. If I hadn't been specifically looking, I'm sure that I would've brushed off their movements as tricks of the light or just shadows. They moved like trained miliary; their footsteps silent and their movements minimal.

The pressurized sound of a semi-truck slowing down filled the otherwise silent street and my heart beat faster.

"Here we go." Kieron said, then spoke into his earpiece. "Visual on the semi-truck."

I watched in fascination and anticipation at what would happen next. The semi pulled onto the side of the road, the whole block empty because of the late house of the night, and parallel parked. The driver jumped out of the cab, slamming the door shut, when all the Irishmen descended on the truck like avenging angels.

All at once, two people took out the driver, two slashed tires to prevent anyone from taking the truck, four worked at picking the lock on the back and two stood guard, watching and making sure everything was okay. In a matter of seconds.

I started to breathe easy, thinking we'd done it, but I should've known better.

A group of guys attacked from the darkness. All the Irish that weren't focused on breaking into the truck to get the people out of the back were engaging in battle. There were brass knuckles, baseball bats, and full-on fist fights, and I looked to Kieron. The distress was rage was clear on his face.

He was watching, completely enraptured in the battle, his fingers gripping the cement edge. Kieron didn't like staying out of the fight, he wasn't one to let his soldiers go into battle while he just sat back and let them fight for him.

The thuds and grunts from the street filled the air, the men below not making any extra chatter. The men that were working on opening the truck got it open just as one of the fighters took down the last attacker.

The street was littered with unconscious, probably dead, Italians.

"It's finished." Kieron said, letting go of a deep breath he'd been holding. "I just got the official confirmation." He points to his earpiece and we turn back to the street. Dozens of women and men poured out of the back of the truck in tears and screaming, they were holding onto their saviors and each other.

"What happens now?" I ask Kieron, stepping into his arms to combat the cold night air and hopefully give him some comfort.

"Now, we go home." He says, kissing the top of my head.

Chapter Thirty-Four

Talia

It had been a couple days since we'd bested the Italians plans for human trafficking in Boston and the whole time it was eerily quiet. Everyone thought so.

It was like waiting on pins and needles for the other shoe to drop.

Kellan asked for a debrief the night everything went down and luckily, the earpiece that Kieron made me wear also recorded everything.

"It's a good habit to get into, baby. Recording all conversations with your enemies or people you may need to take down. Not only will you be able to turn the audio clips into the police if they need to be taken into jail and held, but also if you need blackmail on some people higher up the food chain." He'd said.

After a quick stop to headquarters to tell Kellan everything in person and to pick up more clothes, Kieron and I decided we wanted to go back to the beach house. We'd already proved it was secure and I felt more comfortable there than in the apartment, if I'm honest. The beach house felt like it had the potential to be *our* house.

Luckily, Kellan was okay with us taking a bit of time off to recoup after everything that had gone down. I was really concerned and worried about how they were going to handle making sure all the victims were safe and protected, but Kellan assured me he had it handled. Who was I to question the Irish mob boss?

It was day two into our little bit of time off, most of the time we had spent wrapped up in each other. I'd had a bit of an episode after everything that had happened with Joseph and such. Not to mention seeing Luca so closely again. But after spending the first night with Kieron wrapped around me like a protective octopus, whispering calming words into my ear, I felt much more stable.

Waking up this morning, my eyes puffy from crying through the night, I look up at Kieron's sleeping face. His strong, dark features relaxed with sleep, his hair undone and mused from sleep. He is so handsome. So caring. So loving.

His eyes open slowly, blinking away the sleep from his eyes as his gaze settles on me.

"How long have you been up?" He says huskily, his voice still deep with sleep.

"Not long." I smile and roll onto his chest, resting my chin over his heart. "Thank you, for last night."

"Anytime, baby."

We'd fallen asleep holding wrapped around each other, after he had spent hours rocking me gently while I was having a panic attack.

I leaned up and kissed him softly, just reveling in the domesticity and love filling the moment. And like always, the chemistry between us builds and takes over after a few kisses. Our tongues fight for dominance and I don't give up this time, forcing him to let me run the show. I hear him moan and feel him submit, and climb over his hips, straddling him.

"Talia, are you sure?" I can feel how much he wants me, I know how much I want to, but what gives me pause is the conflicted look in his eyes.

I can't blame him. I just spent the last day and a half crying in his arms because I was so affected by a man's unwelcome touch on me.

But I welcome his touch on me every moment. Every kind and any kind of touch. I trust him, wholly and completely.

The fact that he's pausing and worried about me, makes me trust him even more.

"So sure." I say breathlessly and kiss him deeper rolling my hips against his at the same time. I don't want him to worry at all about *if* I want this, I want him to *know* I do.

Kieron sits up, wrapping his arm around my waist to keep us close together. It's perfect. It's sweet.

"You're so fucking beautiful." He says, pushing my hair back behind my ears with both hands. "I'd do anything for you, baby." He vows.

"I know." I smile at him, bringing our mouths back together for a searing kiss. I lift my hips up and grind down onto him, pushing my heat against his thickening hardness. As dominant as I was feeling before, it was nothing compared to when I open my eyes and see Kieron's eyes roll back in his head in pleasure.

I went feral after seeing that.

My hands went to the bottom of his shirt and pulled it up as far as I could. We separated for a millisecond to rip it off his head before our mouths crashed back together. Kieron shirtless was a magnificent sight but feeling his skin against mine is even better. His hands grab at my tank top, pulling the straps down my shoulders to expose my tits. The cool air hit my chest, causing my nipples to pebble before they're both covered by his hands.

Tipping my head back, I groan at the feel of his hands as his lips drop to my neck. His teeth graze my skin right by the pulse point and I shiver.

"Kieron," I moan, threading my fingers through his long hair and pull slightly.

He hisses, but when I look at him for any pain, he had such a look of lust that I smile bigger.

"You like that." I whisper against his lips and he nodded.

"So do you." He smirked, sliding a hand up against the back of my neck, slipping his own fingers through the hair at the back of my head and pulling slightly. It stung, but in a good way. In a leading way.

I pull his hair and it pulls his head back as I grind against him. We grind against each other harder like we are two teenagers afraid that we were going to be caught making out.

"Take your pants off. Now." I growl, sitting up and scootching down his body, dragging his pants off as much as I can. He quickly agrees, moving to rid himself of the pants like they personally offended him, throwing them across the room.

"Your turn." He says, his voice somehow deeper.

I stood up, keeping eye contact with Kieron the whole time, and pulled the tank off, letting it slip through my fingers. Under his heady gaze, I felt sexy. Powerful. Confident.

He's silent, but the look in his eyes says everything.

I hook my thumbs in the waistband of my pants and slip them down my legs along with my panties. When I stand back up, I'm completely naked.

In any other situation, I'd be self-conscious. I'd be trying to cover up and shrink in on myself, but with Kieron and all we've been through…

I stood straight and tall, letting him look as much as he wanted. My dark hair fell around my face like curtains, making it so all I saw was him.

"Come here." He orders, his voice low and his eyes sharp and full of want.

I follow directions and quickly moved to his side, crawling on top of his thighs. I'm so sure that he could feel how turned on I was with my wetness dripping down my thighs.

"Now, climb on." He ordered, sending a shiver down my spine.

"I thought I was in control here."

"Did you?" He smirks at me, holding my thighs and thrusting up so his hardness grinds against my naked pussy. Heat and tingles spread through my body and everything zeroed in to where we were touching. Nothing mattered except for his skin on mine, his heart beating against mine, his tongue licking me, his hands in my hair.

Before he could tease me anymore, I sat down on him, bringing us together roughly with a sigh of relief. Kieron moaned, holding me with one arm tightly around my waist and the other hand grabbing my shoulder to hold me down onto him. It feels amazing, and the way he is holding me just made the intimacy between us explode. We were still fighting for dominance but it just made our movements more electric.

"Fucking perfect." He muttered, turning his face into my neck. I stayed still for a minute, really soaking in the moment while I kissed whatever spot on him I could reach.

Being on top was an odd sensation for me. It'd been so long since I could take control in sex in this way. I lifted up and sat back down, experimenting with movements to see how they felt for me and how Kieron responded to them. When I rolled my hips forward, my clit brushed against his pubic bone and I nearly melted.

His hands spread the expanse of my thighs before gripping the meat of my ass. But instead of taking over the rhythm like I thought he was going to, he simply held my hips in his hands, encouraging me to keep going, helping me keep the speed.

I sat straight up, pushing my hands through my hair while I rolled my hips again and again. Kieron thrust up while I grinded down, as I finally found a rhythm that made my eyes roll back and made Kieron hiss.

I moved quicker, my orgasm within reach and approaching fast. My breathing was more like panting as my body rolled against Kieron's. His eyes were open and focused on where our bodies were joined together. He looks up into my eyes and I can tell he's as close as I am.

"Goddamn it. Fuck," He groans as he starts to meet me thrust for thrust and I keep rolling against him, his dirty words and noises fueling my fire. "You feel so good. I'm never going to get enough of you." He leans up and captures my lips, kissing me hard and deep.

"Me neither," I whisper into his open mouth. We both move in sync towards our peaks and Kieron refuses to go first. He grits his teeth and moves a hand to my clit to push me over first.

It hits me like a freight train and I cry out, gripping his hair between my fingers and crush his head to my chest. His lips frantically attack my chest, sucking at my nipples and biting down to enhance the overwhelming feeling going through my body.

"That's it, fuck, that's it." He groans and thrusts incredibly fast up into me before he roars my name and I feel his release flood into me.

I collapse on top of him, and his arms wrapped lovingly around my back.

"I love you," he whispered, sighing contentedly with his face in my hair.

"I love you too." I smiled as I rested my head against his chest.

It was the perfect way to truly begin the rest of our lives together.

Chapter Thirty-Five

Kieron

"Hello?" I answer my phone that won't fucking stop ringing, waking me up from a nap with Talia in my arms. These fuckers have the worst timing. She startled, moving instinctively closer to me. I loved that she did that, always subconsciously looking to me for comfort and protection.

I've always wanted this. And I'm beyond happy that I finally have it.

"Kieron, you're needed at headquarters. Now." My father's voice wakes me up pretty quickly.

"What's happened?"

"We have some new information about the Garzino's and you're needed here." He says.

"Understood."

"You're expected in ninety minutes." And he hung up. It was frustrating, this life. Always having to follow orders, no questions asked but now that I was the Second, I expected a bit more communication. I'd earned it after all.

"What did he want?" Talia asks, her voice sleepy and struggling to wake up.

Both of us had finally fucking relaxed and fallen asleep in the middle of the day. Napping isn't a thing that I ever do, always working, always on guard, but together, we just fell asleep.

It was a bit astounding really. I hadn't fallen asleep that easily since I could remember. And I know that Talia's always had a rough time sleeping ever since the abuse started with Luca.

"How'd you know who it was?" I turned over and pulled her in closer and kissed her neck.

"I mean, you're tone of voice changes a lot when you talk to your dad, especially when it's about official Clan business." She yawned.

"My dad said I need to get to Headquarters. I'm assuming shit has hit the fan with the Garzinos. I've got to get ready." I say, hugging her in closer before getting out of the bed and pulling on a fresh t-shirt. "You should come with me."

"But I don't wanna," she whined, flipping over in to look me in the eye. "Can't I just stay here?"

"Are you sure?" It's a long drive and I'm sure she wouldn't be able to join the meeting, but I still wasn't totally comfortable with leaving her all alone. Especially when I would be so far away.

"This is our house, our *safe* house. I'll be fine. You don't think you'll be overnight, will you?" She sits up, bringing the thin knit blanket with her. She just looks so fucking cute; hair tangled with sleep, makeup free, wearing one of my shirts that's swimming on her, and her eyes puffy from sleep.

I lean over and kiss her lips softly. "No, baby. I'll make sure I won't stay overnight."

"Then I'll be good here. I'll stay in bed and binge something, then cook us some dinner and be in bed waiting for you when you get home."

"Wearing nothing I hope." I bite my lower lip and smirk.

"You'll have to wait and see. Husband." She teases me back and pulls the collar of my shirt to bring me in closer for another kiss.

We're getting carried away so I pull back suddenly, shaking my head to clear the arousal threatening to take over.

"I have to go now otherwise I'll need to take a cold shower."

"You won't need a cold shower, I'll take care of you." She says and I have to bite back another groan.

"I really do have to go." I say, kissing her one more time lightly.

"Be safe, be home soon." She says with a smile and lays back down, pulling the blanket up under her chin. A caveman sense of pride washes over me at seeing my woman wrapped up in *my* bed.

"As soon as I can. Wife." I smile. She sits up and smiles back at me, a megawatt smile that lights up her whole face before I have to force myself to leave the room.

* * *

"He called you in too, huh?" I said, slamming my car door shut and see both Trent and Bryan doing the same.

"Yeah, we just got the call." Bryan said.

That set off warning bells. Not only did my father call me in after giving me a few sanctioned days off, but he also called in two deep undercover agents after we just had the first battle with the Italians.

"This feels wrong." Trent said ominously.

"Let's go see what he wants," I say, making my way to the elevator up to Kellan's office.

"The call won't go through." Bryan said, holding his phone to his ear.

"What the fuck is going on?" I snap.

Out of the corner of my eye I see a shadow lunge for Trent and I push him away, landing a solid blow to the masked figure. Figures dressed in all black with ski masks on surround the three of us and attack.

Trent, Bryan and I form a circle, keeping our backs together as we take on at least three guys each. We give as good as we get and I'm pleased when I see the unconscious or dead bodies littering the floor. My knuckles were screaming, but I welcomed the pain.

Whoever formed this attack clearly wasn't counting on the three of us being such good fighters because hit after hit, man after man, I could see in their eyes the shock and surprise that the three of us were still standing.

Trent already was bruising; his pale skin showing every mark on his face he received and his eyebrow and lip were both split, bleeding profusely.

Bryan was fairing a bit better as he was much better at blocking than Trent was, but he was clearly favoring his right side, covering his ribs as he fought. He had a cut at his hairline and half his face was covered in blood. Head wounds always bled the most.

I was sure I looked just as bad. My right eye was already swelling shut and one of the fuckers had gotten a decent blow in on my collarbone so each punch was especially painful.

Body after body fell before it was just one masked man remaining.

"Go check on Skipper. Call in the squad and have them sweep for others. I'll take care of him." I order and Bryan runs off with a nod.

"Now," I say with a snarl, turning all my anger and rage to the one lone guy. "Who the fuck do you work for?"

He couldn't possibly be the man in charge, I could see the fear in his eyes as he tried and failed to hide it. He didn't say anything, but put his hands up in a fighting stance.

"I'd answer him if I was you. He's not exactly known for his patience towards assholes who attack him." Trent said, crossing his arms. "Then again, neither am I."

The guy stayed quiet, just waiting.

"Fine." I snapped and threw out the first punch messily, giving the guy enough time to deflect if and return with a punch of his own. When he did, I grabbed his hand, twisted and pulled him into a choke hold while trapping his other hand behind his back and Trent pulled the mask off.

"Joseph." Trent said roughly. "You weaselly little fucker."

My heart seems to simultaneously stop and eat even harder in my chest.

He has a cheeky fucking grin on his face, like the cat that got the cream, and it sets me on edge. His skin was clear of bruising so he must have just hidden while the rest of his team did the dirty work.

Like a coward.

"What do you want?" I snap, my hand going to his throat. He didn't even flinch, didn't move to protect himself whatsoever.

I felt my hackles raise, and my eyes narrow.

He wasn't here to hurt us or take us back to the Garzinos…he was there to send a message.

One that I'd fucked up.

"Nothing more than to see the look on your face when you figure it out." He says with a cocky grin. "Figure out you've left her all alone. Figure out that it was me who you wasted these precious seconds on. Call it payback for knocking me out."

The elevator opened and Bryan ran out, "Skipper didn't contact us." He said breathlessly and a few other guys followed him out. They were checking their guns, waiting on orders from me.

I turn to Joseph slowly, all the pieces clicking into place. "You slimy motherfucker."

"I wouldn't waste time on insults if I was you. I might be running back to Talia before someone else finds her." He smirks, like he has absolutely nothing to lose.

Dread fills my body. I've played right into their trap and somehow, they've discovered the safehouse. I walk quickly over to Cillian, glad he's here to back me up, and wordlessly he hands me his loaded gun. Without another word, I take it and shoot Joseph square between the eyes without further question.

His body drops to the floor before the blood splatters fall.

I've killed before, killed in cold blood, without mercy or any question. I've killed good people and truly despicable people, but I've always had some reaction to it as soon as I pull the trigger. With Joseph, I felt nothing but relief. And I couldn't even dwell on it for an extra minute.

"Get the unconscious back to the Italian's door. Leave a fucking message that we are not to be messed with. Dispose of the fucking waste. Bryan, Trent and Cillian, you're with me." I bark orders and run to my car, hoping I can get to Talia in time.

I hear them hustle to keep up with me as I rip the driver door open. "Hurry the fuck up!" I roar, smacking the hood with my palm.

The three guys break into a sprint and slid into the car in record time. I barely let the doors close before I peeled out of the garage, burning the rubber of my tires before driving as fast as I possibly can. I had to make up time because I sure as hell wasn't going to drive the hour and a half at a normal, legal pace.

"Holy fuck, man." Trent says from the passenger seat.

"Did you not hear what he said?" I yell. Emotions are high and I can't for one minute have one of my three closest people suggesting I slow down. I will 100% lose my shit.

"You'll not be able to help her if you're fucking roadkill, Kieron." Cillian said from the back seat.

"Every goddamn moment I'm driving, means another moment she's in his fucking hands."

"I know man, I get it. But you're going to kill us driving 110 miles per hour, not to mention if we get pulled over and have to take time to deal with all that bullshit." Bryan pipes in.

"Then we'd fucking call Kellan!" My voice is boomed in the small cab and I'm aware that our phones are being monitored and tapped by the Italians but I was done with their rational excuses to get me to slow down.

They all shut up, thank fuck, and I focused on driving, letting the buildings and other cars fly by.

I just hope I was fast enough to keep my promise to my wife.

Chapter Thirty-Six

Talia

Standing at the stove, I stir my mac and cheese. I know, I know, dinner of champions but I was hungry and Kieron wouldn't be back until later and I had plans to make actual food.

Chicken was thawing in the sink and I had the stuff to make chicken pot pie from scratch, Kieron will love it.

Today had been so nice and resetting for me. I fell back asleep after he'd left, watched a bunch of trashy TV and now, here I am. I was actually relaxed, safe and comfortable by myself, and in this house with my husband.

Jesus, *my husband*. I have a freaking husband. And he was the man I'd wanted for years but not able to be with. It was like a fairy tale. A smile crosses my face and my eyes tear up because it really is like a fairy tale. It's a dream that I never thought I'd ever get and one I'd given up.

I'm so thankful that we found each other again.

The door to the kitchen closes with a slam and I jump, screaming in fright. When my senses came back and I realized there wasn't anyone in the room with me, I went to open the door again but stopped.

How did the door close on its own? I was by myself and I had all the windows closed. Warning bells went off in my head and I was once again thankful that Kieron showed me where he kept the hidden guns. I was also thankful that he kept one in every room of the house. Of course, at the time, I thought he was being paranoid. But now I know better.

I grabbed the small handgun he had hidden under the ledge of the cabinets and as quietly as possible, I checked the magazine, flicked off the safety and waited for what was to come.

The sound from the TV show came through from the other room and the regular creeks and groans of the house and the sea that I've come to recognize. Then there was a slow scuffle that was not normal. It sounded like Quasimodo was in the other room trying not to make a sound.

I look around and curse when I realize I left my phone by the couch.

I'm kind of fuck out of options to try and contact Kieron; there is no phone in here, no computer, no way to get out of the house either. There's a small window above the sink but I learned before that it squeaks loudly when opened.

I'm going to have to fight.

The footsteps get closer and closer to the kitchen door. The closer they get, I back up slowly towards the knife block by the stove. Then the steps stop.

My heart feels like it's about ready to burst from my chest. I tried to remember all the lessons that Kieron taught me; how to throw a punch, how to block, how to evade and what to do in a tight spot, but my mind was just swamped with fear and adrenaline.

"Come out, come out, wherever you are, darling."

It was Luca. His accent dripped heavily with each word, his tone was just like it got before when he was going to let loose on me and I was going to hurt. Everywhere.

My feet felt like they were rooted into the floor. I knew what was coming next. I knew how his fists would feel against my body. I knew what his body would feel like as it violated mine. I knew the angry and horrible words he would spew at me.

And I also knew I couldn't go through it again. Not when I'd finally healed some.

Tap, tap, tap. Luca was knocking on the door with something metal.

"I know you're in there." He said in a sing-song way.

I kept quiet, pointing the small gun towards the door.

Bam! The door burst open, splintering down the middle as he kicked the door in. I screamed and closed my eyes instinctively, losing the second that I would've had the jump on him. I fired a few shots off blindly, but I could already tell I'd lost.

Luca advances on me and we grapple for the gun. Having him this close to me is torture, making me physically sick and like I want to peel my skin off but I use all my might to try and keep a grip on the one small piece that might mean my salvation. I headbutt him in the middle of the face, hopefully hard enough to break his nose. The gun is knocked from my fingers as Luca swats at me, trying to grab my hands.

"Fucking bitch!" He screams and releases me for just a second to cradle his nose. My head hurts like a motherfucker but it got me free enough that I could dart forward. I scramble out of his grip and scramble to find the gun that dropped. "You'll pay for that." He snarls, blood dripping from his nose, running into his mouth and staining his teeth red.

"Get away from me." I say, trying to put confidence and have some kind of threat behind my words. I feel around behind me for something, anything to defend myself but keep coming up empty.

"After all I've done for you?" He says and steps closer, tossing his own gun to the side. I watch it like a hawk, seeing it fall under the cabinet. He balls a fist and swings at me, and my fight-or-flight response kicks in. I feel the end of the punch, having dodged most of it and my cheek explodes with heat and pain but I'm out of his reach again. I fall back on my ass from the force of getting away.

"After all I helped you with? After everything I provided and gave to you?" His voice got louder with each word, his face getting more and more red, the vein in his neck pulsing. A full-force punch rained down on the side of my head. My vision started to darken.

"After all I did for you, you go off and whore yourself out to the enemy."

He stalked towards me; his eyes trained on my every movement. I crawled backward, refusing to let my fear paralyze me. It was obvious that Luca wasn't planning on making my pain quick. He wanted to feel each and every injury he inflicted on me but I had no idea if he would stop or if this was the time I would die by his hand.

My back hits the cabinets on the floor, there's nowhere else to escape to...

"Do you know how embarrassing it was to explain this all to my father?" His fist hit my face in the same spot and I cried out in pain.

"Do you realize how good you had it?" He hits me on the other cheek and my head flips to the side.

"Of course not, you stupid bitch." Luca goes to hit me again, but I block it by bringing my forearms up to absorb the blow.

I see Luca's eyes widen in surprise.

"The brutes been teaching you something other than cock sucking, huh?" He sneers and kicks me in the stomach, making me gasp for breath. I double-over, my forearms hit the ground as I try to cover as much of my torso with the floor.

I just need an opening. I need to wait until I can turn the tables on him. What had Kieron told me?

A kick to my ribs. I felt like I had all the air in my lungs pushed outward and I couldn't breathe in.

Focus, Talia. What did Kieron say about getting out when trapped?

"If you can, block every blow you can. Let them get tired and then when they falter, you attack with the biggest, strongest and truest punch you have. One well placed punch could win you the fight."

I could already see, through my swollen eyelid, that he was slowing down. Luca's adrenaline had been running so high and his hits had a shit-ton of force behind them so I know he wasn't holding back. He was already coming down and getting tired.

"Pathetic." He said with a chuckle. Before I could fully sit up, Luca had grabbed my hair and lifted me to look at him. "What the fuck did you do to your hair? I told you to keep it blonde because you look like a fucking clown with it like this, just like back then. I thought I trained you better than that."

The searing pain from my scalp brought tears to my eyes, more so than the other injuries, but this was my moment. My hands were holding his forearm, trying to hold myself up so he wasn't ripping out my hair, so I used my legs. I gathered all my strength and picked him between his legs as hard as I can. Immediately, the grip on my hair lessened and I backed up.

I mentally went over what Kieron taught me on how to throw a powerful punch. Making sure that my thumb wasn't in my fist, I planted my foot and punched him straight in the nose.

He didn't move, but the shock knocked his head back and I got giddy at how red his cheek got. Even if I didn't draw blood from the punch, he'd have a hell of a bruise.

"You think you're tough? You're nothing. Nothing." He growled in my face. Luca looked like a rapid animal; his blood-stained teeth bared at me, spittle stuck around the corners of his mouth, his eyes were narrowed at me in anger and I could see him shaking.

He asked me if he thought I was tough and I realized that; yes, because I was. I'd just lost sight of it.

I threw another punch, aiming for his ribs this time. "Leave." I snap, venom laced the word tightly.

"Who the fuck do you think you are to tell me what to do? What would your dear sister think of you now? As soon as I'm done breaking you in every way possible here, I'm going to make sure she ends up in prison, cursing your name every moment of every day." Luca wipes the blood from his nose and tries to punch me again. I can see it coming from a mile away though and block the blow to my chin with my forearms again.

My vision tinges with red and I go on the offensive.

I am done taking hits from him.

I am done listening to him spew nastiness and awfulness that absorbs into my conscious.

I am done letting Luca control my life.

"You won't touch her. I'll make sure of that." I let the anger fuel my strength and I start attacking him. I know that the fight wasn't pretty, but I was keeping Luca so busy blocking that he couldn't strike out.

"I'm going to kill you, you fucking asshole!" I scream, Luca takes a step back to get out of range, but I follow. "You've stolen so much from me and I'm going to make *you* pay!"

The blood dripping from his nose and his eye made me smile. As I falter in steps, I knew it was going to give him the upper hand. I'd lost my footing and a punch didn't land, giving Luca the chance to get my hand and pull me into him by a bruising grip on my forearm.

"You stupid bitch." He laughs manically. "My turn."

I kick and fight as best I can, but he has a tight hold on me. He wraps my arms tightly around my back and pushes me to the floor, pinning me down with his weight. Luca straddled my hips and I know just the kind of trouble I was in. I was in serious, serious trouble.

If I couldn't fight with fists, then I would need to fight with words. Buy myself some time. He smacks me, hard and sharp with an open fist and I felt my head swing to the side.

"What do you want with me, Luca? Really?" I cry. "I can't be worth all this! Just forget about me and let me go!" Tears were streaming down my face, but not in sadness, in anger and frustration. I'm so done with this, so done with this life and pain the surrounded him. I want to go back to the bubble I'd made with Kieron.

I honestly thought he'd be overjoyed with me being gone. But it was all about possession and control with Luca. Always had been and the fact that I couldn't be controlled, even through force anymore, was like a slap to the face and a major blow to his ego.

"Just let me go," I sneer.

"Shut up, you bitch. Stop crying, you know how I feel about the crying." He snapped, hitting me across the other cheek.

I grit my teeth, refusing to give him anymore tears or begging, and slowly turned my face back to look at him. I have to figure out a way to get out, a way to get free of him, once and for all.

The look in his eyes was unhinged, dark and murderous. He was actually going to kill me and the look on his face said he would enjoy it.

"Before you die," He says, and I'm almost happy he's going to monologue since it gives me more time to find an escape plan. Kieron was a couple hours away and dealing with his dad so I couldn't count on him saving me this time. "You should know that I have plans for your sister."

"Don't touch her!" I scream, my hands clenched into fists behind my back.

"You aren't getting it. You'll be dead, your debt will transfer to her. What, did you think that the disposal and coverup of the murder she committed had been free? For either of us? You called me and I had to pay the team. I believe you still have a couple hundred thousand left to work off. And if you aren't going to be working for me, either in my bed or for my group, then you're of no use to me. But we *will* be paid. That means once your used up corpse hits the ground, your sister will pay. Although, I think her payment will be being…passed around my crew." He's leaned down and saying these horrible words with such excitement and glee.

I couldn't let him leave this house.

I lunge up as much as I can and hit him in the nose with my face again, the ache in my head worth it when I heard the crack and feel his blood splatter onto my face joining my own. Luca leans back to cradle his twice broken nose and it gives me just enough space to pull my arms free. Before he can recover, I buck up and throw him off of me grappling for space. I go to kick him to gain more space, but he holds onto my ankle. His grip is tight and bruising, pulling me to him. I sit up and punch him in the throat. Luca lets go and grabs his throat with both hands, gasping for breath.

The hits to the head were starting to mess with me. I didn't have much time before I passed out, the darkness was creeping in and not leaving.

I waste no time at all, and dive for the guns, grabbing both and flicking the safety of mine. I point both guns at Luca and look him dead in the eye.

Time stands still as Luca realizes I've bested him. The deadly look on his face transformed into amusement.

"Oh wow. I'll admit your fighting is better," he says with a fake laugh, wiping the blood from under his nose "but I know you well enough to know that you won't pull that trigger. You can't, you're too soft. Too weak. Too pathetic."

For a moment, I believed him. I was weak, I was soft, I was pathetic and I wouldn't be able to pull the trigger. For a moment, I hesitated. But then he started to laugh again, laugh like a deranged person and a chill went down my spine. Maybe he'd finally snapped.

"I'm not scared of you; some fucking stupid whore who knows nothing and is good for nothing."

"I'm so glad to be rid of you." I say softly, my decision made and my hands steady.

"Oh amore, you'll never be rid of me." He says with a wild, evil smile, his teeth stained red with blood.

"I will. I'll be free." I say strongly and pull the trigger.

Chapter Thirty-Seven

Kieron

*B*ang!

My heart beats faster and I push my legs harder, running inside the house. Bryan and Trent run around each side of the house to the back door and Cillian stayed by my side, running inside the front door with me.

I pull my gun out, fully prepared to kill that son of a bitch and any other fucker I find in that room.

There's a heavy clatter of something being dropped in the kitchen. I push through the house, Cillian right on my heels. What I see brings me to a stop before darting over to where Talia knelt, her face blank and completely zoned out right in front of a dead body. My heart breaks and I fall to my knees to hold her.

She looks like she'd taken a hell of a beating; her cheek split open and bleeding, her lip swollen and open, her eyes already turning blue with bruising. There was blood all over her. I tried to keep my anger in check, tried to breathe through my desire to kill a dead man again.

"Talia, baby." I held onto her hands, uncaring of the blood staining them. She still hadn't moved, hadn't looked at me or said anything. Her eyes wouldn't leave the hole in Garzino's chest.

Cillian had stayed quiet, but Trent gasped softly when they arrived and took in Talia's injuries.

"Did she do that?" I heard Bryan murmur, but I didn't take my attention off Talia. She was going through shock. I played with the plain wedding band on her left hand, fingering it softly. The gentle motion pulled her attention to her hands.

"I did it." She whispers, her voice soft enough that only I can hear.

"Go clean everything up, get started on the body and dispose of the guns. Hurry." I order the guys, turning away from Talia for a split second.

"I did it. Again." She breaks and looks to me. "What have I done?"

"You did what you had to do. It was you or him." I tell her. She should never have been in this situation; I should have been able to protect her from this. But, I'm so proud that she was able to defend herself.

"There's blood." She whispers.

"It's okay, baby. We'll take care of it." I promise and her eyes flash to mine in alarm.

"No! No! Not again!" She screams and leaps out of my arms.

"Talia, it's okay. Nothing is going to happen to you. I promise." I can't help but be hurt by her reaction, at her pulling away from me. I couldn't dwell on it right now. Not with how she looked like she was breaking.

"He said…He said…" She hiccupped and it dawned on me. Talia had relied on Luca to cover up the murder of her sister's boyfriend and then he started beating and raping her. He must have said something similar if my words caused this reaction.

"Talia, Talia, look at me." I pull her hands between us and cup her cheek, softly making her meet my eye. "I promise you, on my life, that I will never raise a hand to you in anger. I will do everything I can to not harm you with my words. I will always, and I mean always, keep you safe. That's what I'm doing now, I'm keeping you safe by cleaning this all up. You did this in self-defense and no one will challenge that. No one will know what happened outside of us and Kellan."

Talia nods slowly, my words sinking in as she's pulled out of the panic haze. I see the light return to her eyes and she focuses on me.

"You promise? Nothing will change?" She asks, her bloodied fingers gripping the lapels of my jacket.

"With everything I have, with everything I am, I promise. Nothing will change with us." I kiss her forehead, and feel the tension leave her body as she fell into mine. I catch her, holding her waist and supporting her weight. "I've got you, baby. I've got you."

* * *

After I'd cleaned her up, all the while she stayed quiet and staring at me blankly, I laid Talia down on the bed, tucked one of the blankets around her and left the door cracked open so I could hear her when she woke up.

"How's she doing?" Trent looks over my shoulder towards the cracked door. I knew he had a soft spot for her, and the way he was looking told me he felt somewhat responsible. Which he shouldn't, her safety is my responsibility. One I'd failed.

"She's as good as she can be." I run my fingers through my tangled hair and shake my head. I don't know how I'm going to help her through this. Help her heal.

"She's strong. She'll get through it." He slaps me on the shoulder. "Unfortunately, she's had to do this before. Right?"

I nodded, understanding that for us both, the need for compartmentalization for repeat killings is just part of our daily life. But not for her. Talia had only ever killed for defensive reasons be it for herself or her family and now, when she wakes up, she's going to have to deal with what she's done. Even if none of us would spare an extra breath on the Garzino prick's death, I know she will.

"That won't matter." I say quietly.

"I know." He nods. "Cillian disposed of the body and Bryan is working on wiping down everything in there. Everything should be fine. The only thing you need to worry about right now is making sure she's okay. And later, we will worry about the Italians."

"Thank you." I grab his hand and pull him in for a hug, slapping him on the shoulder. "It is safe to say that your cover has been blown with them so welcome back to the Clan fully, brother."

Trent laughs and his smile is so bright and stress-free. It's been very obvious how hard it's been on him to do this and I'm so glad he's out. He doesn't have to be the man in his cover story anymore. "Glad to be back."

Cillian came in wearing just his white under tank tucked into his black jeans and covered in dirt.

"It's done." He said, his chest heaving as he tried to catch his breath. "How's she doing?"

I hadn't realized how each of my close friends had been won over by Talia, but it warmed my heart that they cared for her in their own way.

"She's coping. She has pretty bad bruising on her ribs, maybe a broken one or two, her knuckles are bruised to shit, split lip, two black eyes, a deep cut on her forehead, probably a concussion, but the worst one is her emotional wounds. You know?"

Cillian nodded, we all understood. Even though killing was easy for us now, it didn't mean that it had always been.

"She'll get through it." He said softly and put his hand on my shoulder. "We'll all help."

"Who knows?" I say and shrug my shoulders. "Maybe she will wake up and be fine." I chuckle weakly, then swallow the lump quickly forming in my throat, knowing that wouldn't be the case.

Bryan walked in, also having stripped down to his undershirt, and pulled the yellow rubber gloves off his hands. "It's clean in there. I left the trash bag with everything in there, ready to burn."

"Thank you."

"Yeah, of course." He shrugs and pulls his t-shirt out of his back pocket and slips it on over his head. "Now, it's way too late for us to head back to Boston. Are you good if we crash here?"

"Of course, man. The couch pulls out, and I have a mat I've used for camping in the storage unit out back." I may not know how I'm going to handle things when Talia wakes up or what's going to happen when the Italians find out about Garzino, but I do know how to take charge.

"Trent, go get the mat out back. Bryan, I have extra sheets and blankets in the closet by the guest bathroom. Cillian, go shower man. You're getting dirt everywhere. I'll start making some food." I give everyone their jobs and march off to the very clean, very bleached kitchen. Every single surface is sparkling clean and the smell of chemicals is so strong I want to open a window. On the stove is the pot of what looks to be completely blackened macaroni and cheese.

I just can't believe I let this happen. I brace myself against the counter with my hands and my head hangs as I try to slow my heartrate. He was in our house.

He was. In. Our. House.

He could've done anything to her; all the things that she's terrified of, a repeat of all the torture she's endured. And I wasn't here to protect her.

The light glints off my thin silver wedding band and I clench my fist. If that fucker wasn't dead, I would've killed him myself. Beat him bloody and when he was begging for death, beat him some more. Sliced him up with a dull knife and watch him bleed out slowly. A quick death wasn't what he deserved.

My breathing quickened and I *needed* to calm the fuck down. Punching the counter once, hard enough to make my knuckles sting, I turned to the fridge to try and make something for my friends who'd just spent hours doing dirty work for me. I could pretend that they were just here because I'm their Second, but I knew it was really because they're my friends. They proved that when they stayed not because I ordered them to, but they just jumped in and did what needed to be done for me so that I could take care of my girl.

"Find anything edible?" I turn and see Trent leaning against the door.

"What?" I look back in the fridge and my heart breaks all over again at the grouping of ingredients on the top shelf that Talia must have put together for the dinner she said she wanted to make. She'd put everything into a little basket and I can just imagine her putting it together, excited to cook something for us to enjoy together, like the freshly married couple we are.

"Food, Kieron. Did you find anything we could eat because I'm starving."

"Yeah, yeah, I did." I pull out sandwich stuff, throwing the bags of lunchmeat and cheese on the counter.

"It's going to be okay. She's going to be okay." He reminds me, walking over to the bread box and pulling the loaf out. "She's not in the hospital and she stood up for herself. She shot the fucker. Maybe it will be cathartic."

"That's not it, man."

He pulled a couple knifes out of the drawer and set them down gently. "You couldn't have known."

"He was here. In our house. The one place she's told me she felt safe." I slam the bottle of mustard down on the counter harder than needed. "And he took that away from her."

"You can make it safe feeling for her again."

"Yeah." I say, unconvinced. Trent and I work in silence, making enough sandwiches to feed the four of us and then some because we can eat a lot. Taking the plate piled high into the living room, I see Cillian and Bryan standing around the made-up bed with their arms crossed, talking quietly.

I set the plate down, grabbing the top sandwich and sitting down on the chair beside the couch silently. Each of the guys follow suit, and they seem to just respect my need to be quiet. My eyes flicker towards the bedroom door and I see a shadow move quickly.

My heart drops to my stomach. *Not again.*

I drop my sandwich, jump up over the table, pulling my gun from my waistband, ready to murder the motherfucker trying to hurt her.

I push the door open and it hits the wall with a loud bang. I swing my gun around the room, eyes searching for the intruder, but there's no one there. Seeing there is no threat, I calmed down just a bit. Talia was standing topless at the dresser, pulling a fresh shirt from the drawer, which she wrapped around her chest tightly and screamed when I barged in.

"I'm sorry, I'm sorry." I flick the safety on, tucking the gun back out of sight, and pull her into my arms. "I thought there was someone in here."

"Just me." She says hoarsely, hugging me back. "Gave me a goddamn heart attack."

"I'm sorry. I just…I thought there was someone else here." I end lamely. I hadn't even thought that she could be awake, just fearful that someone else was coming for her and I acted.

"I woke up and felt like there was still…" She says, looking down at her shirt and her hands.

"I know." I breathed her in, kissing the top of her head.

"Is he," she gulps, "is the body still out there?" I could see the fear and guilt in her eyes, her body tensing as she thought Garzino was out there.

"No. No, baby. Cillian got rid of it. Bryan cleaned up everything, so there's nothing out there. Just our house and friends." I hoped that it brought her a little bit of comfort. It was all I could do for her right now.

She looked up at me in alarm, alarm that I didn't understand.

"I should've been the one to clean up. I…I did this." She said, sobs in her voice that made my instincts go into high gear.

"Baby, no. We took care of this for you, no strings attached. Nothing will change, just like we said. There is absolutely no reason why you had to have done that."

"But I did it!" She cried, "It's on me! I killed him." Her head cocked to the side and her eyes darkened.

"I killed him. Oh fuck, I killed him." She started repeating over and over. Hysteria in her voice and tragedy in her eyes.

I grabbed her shoulders, making her look right at me. I needed to put a stop to this spiral.

"You did it to protect yourself. He wouldn't have stopped and you know it." I said carefully.

"I…why does this keep happening to me?" She whispered, her head falling into her hands. Wrapping her in my arms, I could feel her shoulders and chest shake with silent sobs.

"It's not you, baby." I rested my chin on the top of her head. "It was him, him and that other abusive motherfucker who wouldn't stop beating on your sister."

"My sister," her eyes flash in fear "is she okay?"

"We haven't gotten any updates from the guys watching her, so I'm sure she's fine. We can call her, if you want."

Her body slumps against mine, all her energy and the tension in her body gone with that knowledge. I wrap my arm around her waist, letting me take some of her weight and giving her some of my strength.

"Come on baby, let's get you something to eat. I'll have one of the guys call on your sister and then you need to sleep more." I pull her through the bedroom door out into the living room where the guys are sitting awkwardly, pretending like I hadn't just tore through the living room like a bat out of hell.

"Hi." Talia says quietly.

"Hey, lassie." Cillian says with an easy smile, wiping his hands from the sandwich.

Trent smiles at her softly, where Bryan stands up and stops in front of her, holding his hands out for her to take them.

She looked at him and slowly placed her hands in his.

"I'm so sorry." He says. She nods and gives him a tight smile. She may be reeling from everything that happened, but I can see how much it means to her to have them there with us. It meant a lot to me, too.

"Did you guys save any of those for us?" I said after a moment, and tried to put a smile on my face, pulling Talia with me to sit on my lap.

"Had to fight these two, but yeah, we have one or two for you guys." Trent joked, nudging Cillian with his shoulder.

"I'm hungry! Leave me alone." Cillian says and I hear a small chuckle from Talia. It makes me smile brighter and gives me hope for our future.

Chapter Thirty-Eight

Talia

Here I sit, a week or so after Luca… died, back in Kellan's office. His armchairs in front of his desk didn't feel as comfortable as they had been the last time I was here.

Kieron is standing behind me with his hands in his pocket like some kind of guard instead of my husband.

I give him a pointed look and move my head toward the empty seat next to me, indicating for him to sit down and stop pacing, but he is a stubborn ass and refused.

"You don't have to look so nervous, Kieron. Everything is handled." Kellan said, plopping down in his leather desk chair, unbuttoning his suit jacket, and smiling – not unkindly – at his son.

"Everything?" Kieron asks, raising an eyebrow and leaning over my chair.

"Everything. So, you can stop fronting like that, trying to intimidate me."

"Garzino Senior?" Kieron said, his voice tight and he moved his hand to my shoulder.

We'd both been nervous about how the Italians would retaliate when they found out that Luca was dead. Kieron did everything in his power to make sure that there was no link back to us, and Cillian had…definitely disposed of the body and any evidence. We were just waiting to hear if there was any retaliation. Any indication that they knew we'd done something…

Kieron was more worried than I was, seeing as he knew the ins and outs of this life, and they must have known something seeing as Joseph had attacked them in the garage. We just didn't know if that was a sanctioned attack or if Luca had over played his hand.

The only way to see how that situation would play out was to wait and see.

"It's been reported that Garzino has returned to Italy. Sicily. Probably to lick his wounds and regroup. With the amount of business he's lost in the last three weeks, there's no way that he could continue on. Uncharacteristically, he is doing a smart business move and not getting caught up in appearances and reputations. I wouldn't have expected that." Kellan said, picking up a file, looking it over and placing it to the side.

"Has there been any word on Trent and Bryan's cover being blown?" I ask. I'm still so worried about them being targeted, especially because of how close of friends we've all become.

"No news yet. I've pulled them from their missions, their covers have mysteriously left Boston, and we will deal with the fallout when something comes of it. Trenton, I thought would be good to put on your sister's protection detail seeing as he's been a part of this whole thing from the beginning. What do you think?" Kellan asked.

The smile on my face grew. "I think that's a great idea. It would definitely make me feel better to have someone so close to Kieron and I watching over my baby sister."

"Good, good. He's already agreed, he will take over for the other guard tomorrow morning." He told me, eyeing my ring finger. I look down at my new sparkling, massive engagement ring that really was much too big for my taste, but Kieron swore was just for show and he got me another one for everyday use. I protested and tried to return the big one, much preferring the smaller one that fit my style and personality more, but Kieron just rolled his eyes, telling me that it was the first of very many expensive things I could expect. That it was time I was treated like the goddess I am. That I'm the Second's wife and I deserved nice things.

And when those lines didn't work, he literally made it impossible for me to return it by ripping up the receipt and not telling me where he got it from so I couldn't even take it back. I'd taken to wearing it only when we were at headquarters.

"Trent and Bryan will be safe though, right? From Luca's dad?" I ask.

"Of course." Kellan says, shrugging his shoulders and acting like it was no big deal that some of his men could be in danger. Although, I guess, as Skipper, his men were in danger at all times.

"We're trained spies and warriors, baby. Don't worry." Kieron whispered in my ear.

"What happens now?" I put my hand over Kieron's on my shoulder, looking up at him but asking the room.

"Now, Mrs. Tavish," Kellan says with a knowing smile, "you can move on. Do whatever you'd like. Maybe something to do with airplanes?"

"I can do that?"

"Of course, you can. We aren't going to keep you locked inside or force you to give up your dreams. I want to give them to you." Kieron kneels by my chair with my hands in his, his expression is open and honest.

"Could I…Could I go see my family?" I ask in a small voice, worried that that might be the line for him, it might be impossible because of safety reasons.

But I never should've doubted him, not even for a moment.

"Baby, you can do whatever you want to do. Go visit your family, bring them here, hell, let's all go on a trip together. Whatever you want, I'm down with. I'd love to meet your family, if you want me to." Kieron said, kissing my knuckles.

We hear a cough and look over to Kellan who is looking off to the side, then looks to us. "I would also be honored to meet your family. I'd like to know my in-laws, and the people who raised such a strong woman."

My eyes well with tears and I beg them not to fall. "Thank you," I say pointedly to Kellan and then look to my husband, cupping his cheek and gazing into his dark eyes.

"Thank you so much."

Epilogue

Kieron

Six Months Later...

"Auggie, how are you?" I hold my arms out to welcome a hug from Talia's little sister. Trent and Auggie came to visit us at the beach house for the week. Talia and I had organized it so she was able to take time off from her new, albeit entry job, working as an assistant to an aircraft engineer.

I'd offered to talk to one of the company's, whichever one she wanted, and get her an engineering job, no grunt work or dues paid required. But, as per usual, when I try to use our name and resources to help her out, she refused.

I didn't tell her, but it filled me with pride that she didn't want me to step in. I know she could do it and I wanted her to be able to prove *to herself* that she could. She still worries and has problems understanding how worthy and amazing she is, so the fact that she is willing and pushed hard to work for her dream… I hope it means she's starting to feel like she believes how amazing she is.

Shortly after everything went down with Luca, Talia and I reached out to her family. I got to meet her precious baby sister who Talia sacrificed so much for. I could see the first moment I met her, that Auggie would no doubt have done the same for Talia had she known. Her parents were kind and respectful to me and my dad, but there was a wall of tension between us. I didn't take it too personally.

They had just lost their daughter for years because of a man and then she reappears married to another. And it's not like we can tell them exactly what all went down or what my real job is.

I've been slowly chipping away at them though, hoping to win them over. Now that Talia has them in her life, I don't want her to ever feel like she has to choose again.

Auggie, however, is a different story. Talia had apparently told her little sister all about how we met and her feelings about me way back when, and so Auggie was ecstatic how everything had turned out. I did get the sibling speech of 'hurt her and I'll hurt you' and I did my best not to chuckle through it. Talia was short but her sister was even shorter, she embraced the blonde hair and had big blue eyes to round out the sweet image. The image, though, was just that. She was like a freaking rottweiler when fighting, but your best friend when she wanted to be.

I wanted to stay on her friend side.

"How was the drive?" I asked them, holding my hand out to shake Trent's hand.

"Long. And this one," Auggie jabbed her thumb towards Trent, "only listens to the worst music ever."

"Oh shush, you were singing along too." Trent rolled his eyes. I had to do a double take at Trent, but I swear I saw some sparks flying.

I raise an eyebrow at him and the hint of a smile on his face vanishes. I laugh, unable to keep it contained at the panic on his face.

I don't have a problem with him liking my sister-in-law, but we will have to wait and see how Talia feels about it… and she will fight tooth-and-nail for her sister, as he well knows.

"What else did you expect me to do for four hours?" She rolls her eyes, trying just a little too hard to deny liking the drive. "Where's my sister?" She asks me excitedly.

The girls hadn't seen each other in two weeks and the way they craved being with each other just showed how anxious they were to make up for lost time. It was clear to me when I watch them interact that Auggie felt indebted to Talia. She might not know the extent of it just yet, as Talia had told me she didn't want to talk to anyone about what she'd gone through with Luca, but Auggie knew Talia had saved her somehow.

"She's just getting your room ready." I say, standing aside so they could come in. In the six, almost seven, months since that night, we've added some rooms to the beach house. Added a whole floor actually. Expanded the kitchen. Made a panic room in the basement. It's been a process, but well worth it.

"Talia!" Auggie yells, dropping her bag at the door and running up the stairs.

"Auggie!" Talia yells back and I hear them start chatting and laughing as they start teasing and joking as they do. My heart warms with how happy Talia sounds.

"Goddamn, you look like someone so far in love you don't even know what to do with yourself." Trent says with a laugh.

And I join in the laughter because when I think about my life just a short eight months ago, I was a shell of the man I am now. I didn't let myself feel anything; I fucked whoever I wanted, drank my worries away and worked all hours of the day, never feeling anything but numb and angry. Then I found Talia again, it was like I could breathe and it's stayed that way throughout.

Our relationship, while far from fairytale perfect, was exactly what we both wanted it to be. We work through our shit together, letting each other hold onto the emotional and mental load of all we've gone through – together and apart.

I look at her and see my future.

"I am. I so am."

Author's Note

What a freakin' journey.

I started Kieron and Talia's story years ago when their college meeting wouldn't leave my head. They both went through multiple sessions with me; telling me who they really were and what they wanted throughout this time and I am so happy with where we ended up. With where *they* ended up.

I have a bunch of people to thank people who encouraged me and helped me make this book a reality.

My husband; thank you so much, babe, for listening to me talk through my plot points, giving me advice, pushing me to keep going, and most importantly, taking the babies so I could *actually* write. Love you, handsome!

To my family who has supported me throughout it all. They've laughed right along with me as I tried to figure out how to bring this story to life, and they've pushed me to keep going and pursue this passion of mine.

Leia Faiga (@leia_faiga); an author herself (go check her books out, you won't regret it!) who helped me with everything from blurb work, to letting me vent, to consoling me when shit hit the fan in this indie world of publishing. Thanks, girl, I appreciate you so much!

My cover designer, Maja (check out @_m_design3 on Instagram for her work), who knew exactly what direction I wanted to go and made this bomb-ass cover that made everyone drool. Thank you, thank you, thank you!

To all the readers, it is so amazing to me that people read my stories and I appreciate each and every one of you!

Check out other works by Alina Martyn

<u>**The Heliander Chronicles**</u>

Secretly Born

Living In Secret

Secrets End (Coming Fall 2023)